The Landmark Library
No. 4
THE LEFT LEG

The Landmark Library

THE LEFT LEG

Theodore Francis

T. F. Powys

CHATTO & WINDUS

LONDON

Published by
Chatto & Windus Ltd.
London
*
Clarke, Irwin & Co. Ltd.
Toronto

First published 1923
This edition first published 1968
© *The Executors of Mrs. Violet Powys 1923*

SBN 7011 1298 0

Printed in Great Britain
by William Lewis (Printers) Limited
Cardiff

CONTENTS

THE LEFT LEG

TO
SYLVIA TOWNSEND
WARNER

THERE I met an old man
  Who would not say his prayers;
I took him by the left leg,
And threw him down the stairs.

CHAPTER I

THERE was an idea in Madder that if Mr. Jar ever came to the village again something would happen.

According to rightful history, old Jar, or Uncle Jar as he was sometimes called, really belonged to Madder. He was certainly related to Farmer Mew, and was even said to be a kind of second cousin to Mrs. Patch.

There were some—Mr. Billy's wife amongst others—who went so far as to say that Minnie Cuddy was Mr. Jar's natural daughter. Mrs. Billy used to tell her friends that one evening when the wind blew open the shop door, she had heard Mrs. Cuddy, who was passing in the road, say " dear old Jar." " She could not," remarked Mrs. Billy, " have meant her dead husband." Though whether the remark was meant in mere affection or real relationship, Mrs. Billy did not know.

Anyhow, there was no doubting the fact that old Mr. Jar used to live in a rough wooden hut, close beside what was always known as " Jar's stone," under the shelter of the Madder hills. It was he too who, coming one day down from the hills, and meeting Shepherd Squibb, had given the name " God's Madder " to the village, in order to distinguish the Madder of our story from the Great and Little Madder that are at the other side of the county.

Mr. Jar s hut of wood under the hills was a wonder in itself. The hut expressed, tottering though it was, the will to live. By the proper laws of gravity it should have fallen fifty years ago.

Perhaps John Soper's belief in a hammer alone kept the hut standing. For John Soper, the Madder carpenter, often said that a good nail, driven firmly into stout wood, would hold together the boards even to the time of the hammerer's great-grandchildren ; the carpenter, we will suppose, having driven in the nail as a young man. Yet when Mr. Soper chanced to walk by old Jar's hut, he would slowly shake his head, look up at the sky and pass on. This was the way that John Soper would call out " Miracle ! "

James Gillet, who farmed in Madder as well as Mr. Mew, was also said to be bound to old Jar by the ties of relationship, the reason being that when Mary, James Gillet's daughter, was a little babe, Mr. Jar had given her a necklace of pink beads. The child, who had no other way of making a proper return for the present, was wont to call the giver thereof in her baby way " Our Father." It so happened one day, when Mary was playing on a bank of flowers and Mrs. Patch was watching in the hopes that a nettle would sting the child, that Mr. Jar came by, and Mary, whose hair was mixed with white clover, laughed and called him " Our Father." With this news in her head, Mrs. Patch went off and told Mother Button that old Jar must be something to the girl—a stepfather, perhaps.

Mother Button had a son named Tom who was mad, and Mad Button used to say that Uncle Jar kept tame stars in his hut. Tom Button would have it that he once saw a large star fall from the heavens and enter the hut window, where it shone as bright-burning light. Tom waited in the lane and watched the sky, wondering how it came about that this one had dropped, while all the others remained still fixed. He did not wait long, however, before his attention was caught again by old Jar, who came out of his hut door with a burning light in his hand that he threw back into the sky.

When Mr. Jar left Madder the people still thought about him. They remembered his tall, spare and commanding figure, his ragged clothes, and above all his great beard. They remembered that good luck had always come to those to whom old Jar was related, and that even to those who gave him a meal good fortune would be sure to follow.

It was a sad day for Madder when the hut under the hill was discovered to be empty. Mr. Jar had gone, and God's Madder was left to its own desires.

Of course, every one said that Mr. Jar was more than an ordinary human man, and that they were sure he would return one day and do something wonderful, though whether good or bad no one could say. "When Uncle Jar comes," naughty Nellie Squibb would call out to mad Tom Button, "you will be whipped." And when Mrs. Patch hit Jackie Squibb on the head with her bony fist only because the child was playing in the mud and looked dirty, Jackie called out through his tears, "I'll tell Father Jar when 'e do come."

But although Mr. Jar's return was talked of by

the well, and at Mrs. Billy's, and beside Mrs. Minnie Cuddy's white gate, and although the longer he stayed away the more accurately he was remembered—which happens sometimes to honest folks—still, he did not return, and Jar's stone stood solitary beside the empty hut, and Madder life went on in ways that I will tell you of.

These ways of God's Madder are most closely connected with the behaviour of two men, James Gillet and Farmer Mew.

Farmer Mew's habit of life was to clutch all. To him living was a matter of continual getting, or rather of obtaining power over anything that he desired, so that it might, in the end, become completely his own.

James Gillet did quite otherwise. Possessions fled from him because his affections were gone elsewhere. His treasure was in a different place than Farmer Mew's. He found it in prayer, and he sought in the ecstasy of prayer for the meaning of life.

The village of Madder lay within a ring of little hills. These hills were watchful on fine nights when the stars shone. In the day they slept. Beside the Madder green and along the two narrow lanes, cottage chimneys peeped at the sky out of their thatch, while the three more modern houses looked boldly out into the fields; the modern houses being like strong, vulgar men, while the thatched cottages were like little old women who cried in wet weather.

As to Madder Church, its pride knew no bounds; it believed that nothing had ever lived beyond the fifteenth century, because it was built in those times. It was fairly easy, with a little blinking, for the church to hold this belief, because from its tower only Madder was visible, the rest of the world being shut off by the hills.

Every little bird in Madder thought that there was no place like its own nest ; so did the hills ; so did Mrs. Patch, for her name was Ann.

Ann Patch's cottage was built under a high bank. It was her constant fear that naughty children would roll down the bank, break through her wire-netting at the bottom and steal the eggs her black hens laid. One Madder family she dreaded most, the Squibbs. Whenever Ann Patch went to Church or to Mr. Billy's shop, she would turn and look distrustfully at the bank as though she suspected it of being too friendly with the children.

One Sunday, when the poppies were out in Mr. Mew's corn, Mrs. Patch took up her Bible and blew away a speck of dust that had fallen upon it. It was the first Sunday in June, and she was dressed in shiny black ready for Church. After locking her door and placing the key under a large stone, Mrs. Patch proceeded to pass down her garden-path. Near to her gate she trampled upon a beetle, meaning to do it, and then looked crossly back at the bank as though the beetle had come from there.

When she reached the church she was no better pleased than she had been when looking at the bank, for outside in the churchyard there were all the younger members of the Squibb family busily engaged in their usual game of rolling, while inside the church the newest and youngest of the Squibbs was being christened, and thereby hindering the proper afternoon service

from commencing. Mrs. Patch could see, through
the open door, the Rev. George Summerbee taking
the child in his arms and saying in as grave a voice as
he could manage, for the little Squibb kicked, " Jane
Eva, I baptize——"

Ann Patch sniffed disdainfully. She hated all
young children, and the Squibbs most of all. She
thought that old women who lived in cottages
that they swept and mopped themselves every day of
their lives were the only people who had any right
whatsoever to live in the world.

Mrs. Patch was poor, but as she was rich in tidiness
she valued herself the more for her poverty. She
had a very small pension given to her by a distant
relation ; some even hinted at Mr. Jar, while the ruder
ones said " the parish." She also sold mushrooms,
when in season, to Mrs. Summerbee.

The person in Madder village, setting aside the
children, that Mrs. Patch most hoped would die
soon, and be buried and rotted, was Minnie Cuddy.
Not that she minded Mrs. Cuddy having a little
money. " She didn't care about that," she said ;
" but it's always the men with Mrs. Cuddy, always
the men and they white hens."

Ann Patch herself kept hens, but black ones, so there
really was no reason for her to speak of them, though
it is well known in the country that there is always
rivalry, almost amounting to hatred, between the
owners of white and black hens that live in the same
village.

Beside the children and Minnie Cuddy Mrs. Patch
hated beetles. Whenever she saw a beetle, however

small, she would set her short, fat foot upon it and crush it pleasantly.   She was always saying to herself that she was a good woman and feared nobody in the world, not even Uncle Jar, " who was no uncle to her as she knew of."

Mrs. Patch liked the churchyard path, because now and again she would have the luck to catch a beetle crawling upon the flat gravestones near by. She would go to Church very early for this reason, and look sharply about with her little green eyes.

She was in luck this Sunday : she knocked a beetle off John Barton's gravestone, and stamped firmly upon it with the heel of her Sunday shoe.   She had just finished with the beetle when Mr. Billy of the shop came quietly up to her with his large prayer book in his hand.   It was common knowledge that Mr. Billy would as soon leave sweets upon the counter as his prayer book in Madder Church.   When quite near, Mr. Billy remarked timidly " That there were a great deal too many of them," and added " That the elm trees looked green," which indeed was true.

Very soon, to Mr. Billy's great relief, they were joined by Andrew Corbin, the local horse doctor, who lived in one of the brick houses in Madder.   Mr. Corbin remarked "That the flies were about," meaning perhaps the Squibb family, but said no more, because Mrs. Cuddy was coming up the church path, followed at a little distance by John Soper, the carpenter.

Mrs. Cuddy had once been married to a captain of a tramp steamer who liked rum, and who had died " hoping," so it was said upon his tombstone. What the captain hoped for was not explained.

Mrs. Cuddy lived at "Love Cottage," a name chosen by the captain, and kept, as we have said before, white hens.

Before John Soper had quite made up his mind whether to catch up Minnie Cuddy—he knew his wife to be safe at home cooking the dinner—or to continue silently admiring her back as he had been doing all the way up the Madder lane, Mrs. Joan Squibb, a gaunt woman with a long neck, appeared at the church door, carrying the newly christened baby.

Her appearance at once caused Frankie Squibb to roll down Mr. Tuffin's high, grassy grave-mound, and for naughty Nellie to sit in an indelicate manner upon the top of the stone of John Riggs, dairyman, who died in 1874.

Seeing that the church at least had emptied itself of the Squibbs, Mrs. Patch, with a look at Nellie as though she could kill her, which was not what Nellie wanted, entered the church, followed by the others who were waiting.

CHAPTER II

DROWSY summer hung heavy in Madder Church; Mrs. Patch's shadow was upon the damp-stained wall, with her head somewhat larger than reality. She had espied a beetle crawling down the aisle, and wondered whether it would take her pew. She moved her left foot a little in readiness.

Mr. Summerbee preached about Jacob; he explained that Jacob was a pastoral character who kept hens and ducks, and who, no doubt, grew cabbages.

In the middle of the sermon a voice was heard calling excitedly in the churchyard. As is the habit of folk in a church, no one paid the least attention to the person outside who continued shouting. God's house in Madder was filled with thoughts that could not be interrupted. Minnie Cuddy was thinking of her white hens, and John Soper was thinking about Minnie Cuddy.

There was the beetle that wandered vaguely near to Mrs. Patch's pew. No call from outside could prevent Mrs. Patch from hoping to crush it. Also there was a smell of holiness in the air that deadened sounds from without, and raised hopes in a little heap of dust near to the tower door that it might be saved.

At last Mr. Summerbee caught the word " garden " in the shouting. Looking through the window that was next to the pulpit, the Rector of Madder saw Mad Button standing upon a tombstone and waving excitedly. Seeing Mr. Summerbee look his way, Tom called out more loudly than ever that Mr. Mew's cows were in the Rectory garden.

Now Mr. Summerbee thought a great deal about his garden and about the seed that he planted. Whenever the first sign of a potato or pea plant appeared above ground, the good man would at once hasten into the kitchen to tell Mrs. Summerbee, and the pair would come out lovingly into the garden and peer down at the new leaf with a surprised tenderness in their eyes.

Seeing poor Tom standing upon a tombstone and

shouting out about the spring cabbages could only have one effect, and that was to bring the matter of Jacob to a hasty end.

They had been planted with such care, the seeds first and the plants later. The seeds he had grown in the frame, and had taken Mrs. Summerbee out in a snowstorm to see the first sign of them. And now Farmer Mew's forty dairy cows were in his garden.

Mr. Summerbee said the blessing in the pulpit and hurried into the vestry ; the last hymn was not sung.

Going out into the lane in the hope of getting some help, Mr. Summerbee saw Will Squibb, who worked for Farmer Mew, and politely requested the man to drive the cows out from his garden. This was as good as inviting the whole Squibb family to do it. And when the cows were driven out, the Squibbs were all still there, in the garden.

"Suppose," thought the poor priest, "that the younger Squibbs should begin to roll, why the few plants that the cows have left will be done for. After the locusts the flies, after the cows the Squibbs."

Eli Squibb, the father, had come to help too, and was carefully shutting the garden-gate with all his family inside.

"Gate be shut now," he remarked gravely, "an' farmer's cows be drove out."

"And your children," said Mr. Summerbee, "call them out too ! "

"There be so many," replied Mr. Squibb, "that I do only mind the name of the baby." Presently, however, Mr. Squibb was hit with an idea and called

B

out with a loud voice, " Dinner be ready." His
family ran off at once.

" How did the cows get into my garden ? " Mr.
Summerbee asked Eli Squibb as he was moving off.

" Farmer Mew did let them in his woon self,"
replied the man.

When the Squibbs were gone Mr. Summerbee
stood for a moment looking sadly over his gate at the
ruined cabbages. He did not remain troubled for
long, he was a man who forgave easily ; besides, he did
not believe that Farmer Mew could have let the cows
in on purpose. They had got into the garden and
they were now driven out, so there he let the matter
end. Mr. Summerbee forgave easily. A person
who is happy is nearly always forgiving.

Whenever tales came to Mr. Summerbee about
the merry doings of Minnie Cuddy with the men,
he would merely walk down his garden-path and look
at the flowers.

Only now and again Mr. Summerbee would
venture a little advice to Mad Button when he found
the innocent either running after the girls or else
teaching them about the affairs of nature. Mr. Summerbee knew that the only person in the world that
Mad Button feared was old Jar. He feared Mr. Jar
because of his long beard, and because he could take a
star up in his hand without being burnt.

" Tom Button," Mr. Summerbee used to say with
a smile, " you shouldn't tell the girls about such
things ; suppose Father Jar were to come. And you
mustn't run after naughty Nellie, because if you do,
perhaps Mr. Jar might catch you as he did the star

and throw you up into the sky, and then let you fall down again on your head."

After Mr. Summerbee had given Tom Button this little lecture, Tom would mope about in the village lanes for a day or two, either looking at the sky or else at the hills, or else sitting mournfully beside Jar's stone.

But however repentant he felt about his doings, one day or other he was sure to come across naughty Nellie rolling down a bank, or else swinging on the top of a gate. The sight of Nellie in these situations would be sure to cure Tom of his fears, and he would run after her again as often as ever. When Mr. Summerbee saw Tom as a sinner again, he would smile as a good man should, and go and attend to his kitchen-garden.

CHAPTER III

MAD BUTTON always looked out for the first star to come in the evening. When he saw it, he would call out " Uncle Jar," and clap his hands. He believed that the first evening star was the very one that Mr. Jar had lit his house with and then thrown back into the sky. He never liked to linger at twilight near to Jar's stone, because he feared that the star might fall out again ; he preferred to watch for it in the churchyard.

After he had shouted out the news about Mr. Mew's cows, Mad Button quietly went home to his tea. Finishing his bread and treacle, he went out into the lanes to look for Nellie. He could see nothing of her. As it was growing near the time for Mr. Jar's star to come out, he wandered towards the churchyard. Once safely there he leant upon John Riggs's stone and watched the sky.

There was still daylight above, coloured with the glow of summer, and Uncle Jar's star was as yet hidden. Mad Button walked amongst the graves. Between the roots of an old elm tree he came upon a man kneeling upon the grass, praying. Mad Button knew the man well; it was James Gillett.

As I have said, there were two important farmers in Madder—James Gillet and Farmer Mew. James Gillet had lost all his interest in the soil, because he had found a more terrible idea—God.

Though a quiet, sober man, James Gillet had commenced a startling journey.

Once sitting in a field where he had been hoeing mangel, he had felt another hand holding his. He had been asleep, and the hand that he held was his own. But this did not alter the belief that he had had when asleep, that the hand was not his. "Whose was it, then?—God's." Gillet had heard a voice in his sleep calling "James, James."

After that day, though he worked upon his farm, his heart was elsewhere. Every day he thought he drew nearer to God. Sometimes he prayed in the church and sometimes in the fields. The farm began to do badly.

One morning, shortly before the accident to Mr. Summerbee's cabbages, James Gillet found all Mr. Mew's cows in his hayfield. The cows had been let in there for some days and there was no grass left.

James Gillet's own cows would have to go hungry, but he never murmured or said a word to Mr. Mew.

Mrs. Gillet was dead, and Mary, his only daughter, made the butter and milked the cows.

After the vision James Gillet went to plough as before, but he never drove a straight furrow again.

The people of Madder saw that James Gillet prayed and they wondered. Every one wondered what he meant by it, and Mad Tom wondered more than all.

Looking up he had seen Mr. Jar's star in the sky, and had clapped his hands. Mad Button expected James Gillet to look up too, but he never did ; he only went on praying.

Mad Button watched him in a frightened way.

" What be doing ? " he said at last, unable to remain quiet any longer. " Who be 'ee talking to ? "

James Gillet looked up then, but instead of answering Mad Button, he only looked into the sky.

" Yes, yes," called out Tom excitedly, following his gaze. " There, there, there it be, wold Jar's star a-shining." But as he watched the upturned face of James Gillet, Tom Button became more than ever frightened.

" Be thee a-talking to Father Jar ? " he whispered into James Gillet's ear. " For if thee be I best be a-going."

Thinking this course to be the safest, after one or two doubtful looks at the sky, and leaving James Gillet still praying, Mad Button walked on tip-toe out into the lane. By the side of the lane upon the bank the grass had been pressed, as though some one had been rolling down. Looking at the pressed grass

Tom saw a little black garter. Putting the garter thoughtfully into his trouser pocket, Mad Button went down the lane singing.

As soon as he was gone James Gillet rose from his knees, and after wandering a little amongst the graves took the path to his house.

Under the trees in the lane there was black darkness and Gillet nearly walked into the form of a girl who was running towards the church. The girl was Mary Gillet, who had run out to meet her father. She took his arm and clung closely to him as though she was frightened. They walked on together.

" Father, do you think Mr. Mew is a good man ? " Mary asked, trembling.

James Gillet did not answer. Mary held more closely to him ; she rubbed his shoulder with her cheek to attract his attention.

" Father," she said, " I wish Mr. Jar would come to live here again." The name Jar recalled Gillet to the earth.

" Oh, it's you, Mary," he said, and held her more kindly.

There were footsteps in the lane, and the figure of a man taking long strides passed by them.

" That wasn't Tom Button," said Mary.

When they reached the farm, Mary began to busy herself about the supper ; she moved her father's chair to the table. When all was ready she ran upstairs to tidy her hair. She looked round her room timidly as though she fancied some one might be there.

After brushing her hair, and smiling at herself while she did so, she went over to the window and

looked out into the still summer night. Outside
in the road she heard the heavy footsteps of a man
who seemed to be striding up and down.

CHAPTER IV

E VERY one in Madder knew that Mr. Jar had
set Farmer Mew up in business. But no one
expected Mr. Mew to succeed as well as he had
done.

He now nearly possessed the whole village. By
degrees, by little and little, he had clutched near all
there was to be had. It was said in Madder that
if Mr. Mew looked at anything, whether sheep,
oxen, house or land, he could charm the thing to
be his.

"Farmer do swallow all," Mother Button said.

One day Farmer Mew saw Mary Gillet in her
garden. Only the day before he had seen a hundred
young ewes at market and had bought them.

Farmer Mew was unmarried.

If he saw a blackbird on a hedge and wished for
it he would get his gun, and very soon the bird would
be in his hand.

He now wanted Mary.

Mr. Mew was tall, he had a broad back, and a hand
that clutched. His eyes were grey and his look dark
and gloomy. Mad Button would run away when
he saw Mr. Mew in the lane.

Soon after the farmer saw Mary Gillet in that way,
things began to happen in Madder.

The Gillet farm went from bad to worse. After

Mr. Mew's cows had eaten the hay worse things befell. All the Madder flocks of sheep that belonged to Mr. Mew were one night driven into Mr. Gillet's young corn. James Gillet hardly noticed the damage, his thoughts were all with God.

One day Mother Button espied Farmer Mew leaning over the barton gate and looking at the Gillet homestead. Every one said that James Gillet would soon be utterly ruined, which was true enough. James took no notice of his affairs; he merely prayed. Mr. Mew's flocks and herds had eaten up his corn and hay, but he ate of God, and so did not care.

As a boy Mr. Mew had got together things for himself. When he was five years old he collected stones, in the Madder lanes, that were flat and heavy, and piled them up upon the green. Once a little girl was found tightly bound to a tree; she could only say, when let go, that she was "Willie Mew's."

All he possessed were to him more than merely his; they became himself.

He would covet a cow and buy it, and the cow would chew the Madder grass and yield milk for the master. No beast of the field had ever been known to deny Mr. Mew. No mere greed led him on. His will was more than that. He drew all things, the grass, fields, houses, sweet cows and women, into himself.

William Mew was the giant of Madder. And he intended one day to be carved, a monstrous shape, upon the chalk hills.

CHAPTER V

THE chalk hills guarded the wide fields of God's Madder. The fields belonged to Mr. Mew. The farmer had taken up his neighbour's landmarks. Even Squibb had once owned land that now belonged to Farmer Mew.

Since James Gillet's farm had been purchased by him—James's debts eating up all the purchase money —there was only one cottage left that was not Mr. Mew's. Mrs. Cuddy owed the very existence of her white hens to him.

Farmer Mew's sheep covered the hills, his cows fed in the low meadows, and the Squibbs tended them.

Eli Squibb was the shepherd, George the dairyman, Tom Squibb the ploughman, and so on, for even naughty Nellie sometimes scared the rooks away from Mr. Mew's corn. Nearly all Madder worked for Farmer Mew, and those who had nothing better to do would watch the Squibbs rolling.

John Soper sometimes said to his wife, "Those girls will roll themselves into trouble one day, my dear. Farmer Mew will eat them all before Christmas."

"But what about yourself?" Mrs. Soper would answer. "I don't believe that Mrs. Cuddy has a summer-house to be repaired every summer day."

"Oh yes, she has," John Soper would say, "and they fowl-houses are always needing a nail driven in"—Mr. Soper carefully took out a little chip of wood that had got into his plane. "Besides," he remarked, " Mrs. Cuddy wants it all to look smart before Mr. Jar comes back to Madder."

" Oh, don't Mr. Jar me," replied Mrs. Soper. " No one can be as fat and round as Mrs. Cuddy is and live chaste."

" Well, isn't there Mrs. Summerbee ? "

" Oh, she—she makes him wonder," said Mrs. Soper. " She likes to pick summer beans."

CHAPTER VI

IT was evening, the Madder hills had been shocked: they had overheard Mercy Corbin tell Mrs. Billy, John Soper's wife standing by and agreeing, that old Jar was a ragged travelling tinker, who hammered old pots and pans for a living, and was just nothing to anybody.

" A great, dirty beggar," said Mrs. Soper.

In order to forget the unbelief of these women the hills remembered Tom Button.

After Mrs. Manners had let the children out of school, Tom had followed naughty Nellie down the lane. He had run after naughty Nellie holding something in his hand.

All the children were afraid of Mad Button. They would run this way and that when they saw him coming, but the big girls would run slower than the others, so that they were sometimes caught.

It was said that Mad Button had a fearful secret hidden somewhere, and every girl in Madder wanted to know what it was.

Naughty Nellie said she knew, but the others did not believe her. One day she promised to tell Flossie if Flossie gave her a packet of bull's-eyes. So, during playtime, Flossie and Nellie went and hid behind some bushes and then came out laughing.

The day was sunny, and the little boys, all elbows and legs, were playing horses.

Flossie and Nellie walked by them proudly and tossed their heads.

There was always Susan Summerbee for the Madder hills to talk of. She lived as a pretty lady should—in a garden. To her all Madder was but one name, "George Summerbee." Susan's one fear in life was that Mr. Summerbee should have money left him and go and live in hotels. She believed that rich people lived more than half their lives in hotels. She had herself gone to an hotel in Weyminster when they were first married. Mr. Summerbee and she stayed for one day.

Susan would always remember that dreadful day. She was haunted by the idea that in the kitchen the cooks used dirty knives. Just before dinner she had peeped over the railings and looked down some greasy steps that led to the kitchens. This was within a few yards of the palm trees and deck chairs where the deans in gaiters sat and read the papers. Mrs. Summerbee thought she saw a dirty knife, and was sure that she smelt bad fish. She would not stay in that house one moment longer, but insisted on their leaving at once for Madder, where they slept together upon a mattress covered with overcoats, because the proper furniture had not yet arrived.

Mr. George Summerbee walked out sometimes in order to get the pleasure of walking home again. During these walks he was wont to wonder why he had no children.

Mrs. Summerbee would be always cooking pleasant dinners, or else making apple jelly for tea. She would wear a charming apron in the mornings and be always so soft and pretty. She would turn up her sleeves sometimes and show her white arms.

Beside the apple jelly, Susan Summerbee could make good custards, and if any small matter put her out, she would go to her cookery book and find a recipe for fish-cakes or some other dish, and so would be happy again. She liked sweet peas upon the table, fresh air coming into the window, and a clear fire and a hot oven in the kitchen.

Susan Summerbee believed her husband to be the best of men, and her garden the best of gardens.

Whenever Mr. Summerbee seemed to be wondering, she would promise him that it would happen as he wished one day, while secretly in her heart she hoped that old Jar would return to Madder and eat bread in the Rectory kitchen. Whenever she thought of this happening, she would grow serious.

Mr. Summerbee was out walking ; he had left his wife picking sweet peas. He thought the Madder lanes were more delightful than ever. He saw Madder as a proper place for himself and Susan Summerbee to live in. The thought of her made him wonder. Though he had learnt by experience that each day soon turned to bedtime.

In the middle of one field there was a lonely barn
of Mr. Mew's. Two people were entering the
dark doorway of the barn. One of these was Farmer
Mew, who was holding Nancy Squibb by the wrist.
He appeared to be pulling the girl after him. As they
went into the darkness the girl gave a frightened
cry. A large owl flew out of the door, and Mr.
Summerbee fancied that the owl had frightened the
girl. He remembered the sweet peas. Were the
flowers faded in the Church ? He thought he would
go and see.

Mr. Summerbee always entered Madder Church
very gently, walking upon his toes and peeping
inquisitively about him, as though he expected to
come upon old Father Jar fast asleep in Mr. Mew's
pew.

Madder Church was a pleasant place for thoughtful
men. And Mr. Summerbee after looking to his
flowers would often sit down in one of the altar
chairs from whence he could admire the colour of
his roses and lilies. Entering Madder Church this
time with his usual care, he saw James Gillet
kneeling beside the altar.

As Mr. Summerbee entered James Gillet's prayer
was finished. Turning round towards the nave he
slowly raised both his hands as though to bless all
mankind. For a while Mr. Summerbee could not
remember where he had seen that sort of expression
upon a man's face. But soon he recollected. Once
he had met Mr. Mew, who stood upon a little hill
that overlooked his flocks and herds. Farmer Mew's
face had shone in the same way.

CHAPTER VII

ANN PATCH was in luck. From her bedroom window one morning she saw some shining white dots in Mr. Mew's field. These white dots she knew to be tiny mushrooms.

During the day her luck still held, for coming from the shop, she crushed two beetles and met Harry Billy playing in the lane.

Harry in a merry mood threw a little twig at Mrs. Patch. A second after he wished he hadn't, for she caught him and made his legs smart for it.

When she reached home Ann Patch threw a few broken bottles upon the most tempting part of the bank above her cottage ; some slipped down to the bottom but a few stayed. "Anyhow, they bits of glass will tickle the Squibbs," she said pleasantly.

That night Ann Patch had an ill dream : she dreamt that she was a large black-beetle crawling across a road, and that a heavy foot was coming down upon her. She dreamt that she saw Uncle Jar's beard in the sky, so she supposed the foot to be his. She awoke in a sweat of terror, and went to the window to see if Madder was still there.

Opening the window she saw all Madder asleep with the full moon high above. In the white mist of the low meadows there were dark spots ; these were Farmer Mew's cows. Looking down into the garden that was overhung by the bank, Mrs. Patch saw something that made her shiver. This was the shadow of a man.

The following day she went into her garden to pick gooseberries,

As she picked, happening to look into the sky, she saw a large bird. This was a heron who, flopping his wide wings, slowly passed over the village. Its wings too made a shadow in the garden. Mrs. Patch had begun to notice things—shadows.

CHAPTER VIII

BY the side of the white gate at Love Cottage three men were standing. It was quite by chance, they each said, that they happened to pass that way. But seeing Minnie Cuddy by her gate, they had naturally stopped to have a word with her. They were talking about the ways of God's Madder.

John Soper had one hand upon the gate, in the other he held a foot-rule. Looking upwards John Soper saw a white cloud in the sky. The cloud looked like a white hen. Minnie Cuddy saw it too and blushed. Mrs. Cuddy had been leaning against the gate, but now she moved back a little. The pressure of the gate had interested her, but she could not lean in that way before three men with a white hen in the sky.

Mr. Billy moved a little too ; he saw a vision. He looked up, and behold, Minnie Cuddy had become one of the little Madder hills, green and thyme-covered. She lay soft and gentle, with large grass-covered limbs and yellow-flowered bosoms. There was so much of her that a flock of sheep could nestle in her lap. Her daisied limbs were there to be embraced by all men.

With a vision of this kind in his head, Mr. Billy

hoped that his wife would have no excuse that evening to leave the shop. He had tried to clean the windows that afternoon, but knew that Mrs. Billy would have to go over them after him. He had fallen off the steps with the duster in his hand into the flower knot, and his wife had remarked—rather rudely he thought—" Minnie Cuddy bain't changed to a pink, be she ? "

" Even the gate is warm," said Mrs. Cuddy, leaning upon it again.

Andrew Corbin looked at Minnie Cuddy too, though not in the visionary manner of Mr. Billy. He saw her as the lady of Love Cottage ; he knew what a horse was, and here was something different from a horse—a lady. Mr. Corbin was a grave man, but he too hoped.

" Farmer Mew owns the whole village now," Mr. Corbin said.

" All except Ann Patch's cottage," remarked Mr. Billy.

John Soper was watching Mrs. Cuddy. " The gate bain't so very warm," he said harmlessly.

Minnie Cuddy was looking into the fields. Down a grassy lane that led through the fields there were three men leading a bull ; the bull was being taken to the field one side of which was Mrs. Patch's cottage.

The evening was one of shadows, dark clouds moved mournfully, a dull, coloured cloud shadowed the bull. The bull moved heavily, a mass of red in the lane, but its horns were white. Naughty Nellie had climbed upon a gate to see the beast go by. When it came near she slipped down into the nettles, screamed, and ran away. Mad Button, who was waiting in a ditch near by in order to catch Nellie, began to howl like a dog.

The bull, foaming at the mouth, pulled at the rope ; Eli Squibb beat it heavily. The bull pulled the three men into the field where the mushrooms grew. The men let it go. The beast roamed about the field bellowing, and tossed the grass into the air, pawing with its feet. The cloud hung over it, so that the whole of the field and even Mrs. Patch's cottage was covered in summer darkness.

Presently a man came and leaned over the gate that Nelly had climbed. This man was Farmer Mew.

Mad Button saw him from the ditch, and left off howling like a dog, and instead began to call out for Father Jar.

Love Cottage was still in the light, the gnats were happy in the garden, and a blackbird sang on the top of the ash-tree.

" Ann Patch won't sell her cottage to Mr. Mew," remarked Andrew Corbin.

" She do like mushroom time," said Mr. Billy.

John Soper was thinking of other matters. " I've left my screws in the new fowl house at the back of your garden, Mrs. Cuddy," he said reflectively. " With your leave I will fetch them."

Minnie Cuddy opened the white gate. " The hens are all gone to roost," she said blushingly, " but I know you won't frighten them."

" Oh no," answered John Soper, " I won't frighten them."

John Soper walked with a businesslike tread in the direction of the fowl houses, Minnie Cuddy followed more slowly.

c

Andrew Corbin and Mr. Billy turned away and began to walk down the lane. Madder was a pleasant field, the lane fair to walk in. There was always something to be done in Madder, always something to talk of. Even Mark Button, Tom's father, could tell stories while he lived, stories of things he saw while he leaned over the gates.

Mark Button had indeed seen all that could be seen of human life. For God's Madder, when it has a mind to be truthful, can tell the whole story. What the whole story was Mark Button told no one but his son, who went mad. What of that? There was no Minnie Cuddy in those days, and Mrs. Soper said there was no Uncle Jar either. Mark Button believed in angels and snowdrops, and he had once asked the snowdrops a question. "Do they buried folk talk down under grass?" he asked the snowdrops in the churchyard. "No," replied the snowdrops, "but what is much more important, they listen."

"Minnie Cuddy be a kind one," said Andrew Corbin, thoughtfully expressing his inward state.

"So she be," spoke up Mr. Billy promptly, "but all same I do like to see Mrs. Summerbee picking strawberries."

CHAPTER IX

ONE day Farmer Mew unlocked his safe and taking out a sum of money, put it into a bag. For some days past he had watched the Squibbs working in a thoughtful manner. He had stood so near to Eli Squibb that the old man had grown nervous and asked his master to move back a little farther. He had watched Will Squibb milking, with so close and attentive a look, that Will began to think that there was something the matter with the back of his head, and rubbed it very hard when he was alone again. All one day the farmer walked up and down where George Squibb was ploughing in a field where the sheep had eaten the mustard. George thought his master was admiring the clever way he drew his furrows, and curled the lock of hair upon his forehead more jauntily the next day, which was Sunday.

Mr. Mew even looked at Naughty Nellie, who was pretending to scare the sparrows from the wheat. In reality she had run into the fields hoping that Mad Button would follow her, for however much she learnt about things, she always fancied that there was something else more exciting still left behind. The farmer watched her clapping her hands at the birds; she went on clapping until her hands were quite sore, and then she waved her handkerchief. At last Mr. Mew left her.

Holding the bag in his hand, Farmer Mew went towards the Squibbs' cottage. Mr. Squibb was not surprised at seeing him there. He had waited by the garden gate more than once and watched through the open door the family at dinner. He had even watched the baby rolling, which refinement of attention had brought tears of pride into Mrs. Squibb's eyes. But this time Farmer Mew opened the garden gate, walked along the little garden path that was almost paved with potato peel and other matters, and knocked at the door.

Mrs. Joan Squibb at once began to dust the dresser. Even though the place was all in a riot of dirt and babies, Joan used to fancy that if only she could get the dresser dusted all would be well. Even with the cat on the table eating the last of the bacon she would dust the dresser. Even with Mr. Summerbee knocking, the kettle boiling over, and baby Jane playing with George Squibb's open razor, she would dust the dresser.

As a rule she was moderately successful at her dusting, but this time with her master at the door she broke two plates, which was not to be wondered at, considering how her hands shook.

It was evidently something of importance that Mr. Mew had come to tell them, because he wished to have all the family brought in to hear it.

All the Squibbs soon assembled to hear what it was that the master had to say.

Mr. Mew stood in the middle holding his bag of money. He began to speak, carefully choosing his words so they might understand him. The Squibbs lolled everywhere with their mouths open. The elder girls blushed and tittered. Nellie looked at her sisters with scorn and began to scratch her legs, pulling up her clothes in order to see exactly where the spots were.

The baby rolled.

Mr. Mew said gravely : "You have always worked well for me."

Eli Squibb moved his head from side to side in order to show that he knew the master always spoke the truth.

" Only this is not enough," continued Farmer Mew. " This does not satisfy me ; I must have more than this ; I want to buy you ; I intend you to be not my servants but mine—my own."

Joan Squibb slowly moved her duster up and down the dresser ; she avoided the plates. She knew what buying anything meant because she had bought the dresser. Joan reasoned wisely, " If anyone buys a thing, they pay money for it." Joan Squibb owed Mrs. Billy at the shop £3 15s. 6d., and Mr. Billy had said that, though he would still supply the family with bread if they paid ready money for it, that they should neither have jam nor tinned salmon until the £3 15s. 6d. was paid.

Eli Squibb scratched his head—the idea of selling himself for money pleased him. He became a proud man and called the baby by its name.

" I own near all Madder now," Mr. Mew cried excitedly, holding up his hands.

" Yes," said George Squibb, " 'tis only wold Mother Patch that won't sell she's cottage to 'ee."

Farmer Mew's brows lowered ; he looked fiercely at George Squibb as though he could have struck him.

" What be thee talking for ? " said Eli, looking at his son. " Bain't I your father, and bain't I worth money, same as thik prize ram that all they rich farmers were talking of last fall ? Don't 'ee say nothing more to offend farmer. Don't 'ee cry out Mother Patch to 'im no more."

Farmer Mew opened his bag and gave to each adult member of the family a sum of money. When he had done so he said : " You are now mine—mine. You belong to me as my flocks and my herds belong to me, as the fields of Madder belong. I have bought you with money ; you are mine."

Joan Squibb had hardly listened to the Master's words. She was thinking that the next day there would be no potato peeling because there would be tinned salmon and jam for dinner, and that instead of cooking, she would go out and talk by the well. She had missed so much news lately and Mrs. Soper always liked to see the baby.

Eli Squibb fancied himself standing in the middle of the Stonebridge market and being admired as a thing of value, as the prize ram had been. The elder Squibb girls giggled. Farmer Mew had already given one of them money. The other was envious and wanted Farmer Mew to take notice of her too ; she thought he would now that he had paid so much.

When Farmer Mew turned to go, the face of Mad Button appeared at the window.

" Wold Jar bain't bought yet," he said, and vanished.

*　　　　*　　　　*

Farmer Mew passed a restless night. All night long he saw the figure of Mary Gillet. Sometimes she would be driving up the cows, that were now all his. Sometimes she would be stooping and collecting sticks for her father's fire. She became almost as bad as Mrs. Patch, who withheld her cottage from his hands. Both eluded him—the old woman and the young.

As he tossed upon his pillow Farmer Mew imagined

himself possessing Mary by force. All night long he thought of different plans. And at length he decided upon one. He knew that Mary Gillet walked upon the hills in the evening, and thought he would wait till then. She was already his servant and worked for him; the other must follow.

The next morning Farmer Mew restlessly paced the house. He spent the day in walking from room to room keeping a watch from the windows. As the hours passed by he grew more and more restless.

He began to move the furniture to and fro to counteract the nervous silence of expectation that tortured his heart.

He roamed here and there as though he were a wild beast in pain and snapped his teeth as if he bit the air. He stood before the windows with clenched fists and then he would turn and walk again.

When evening came he stood still with his eyes fixed upon the hills. After standing thus for an hour he went out.

*   *   *

Mary Gillet liked the Madder hills; she would walk to them sometimes in the evenings and gather sticks. She walked there now. Her housework was over and she had seen her father walk off towards the Madder Church.

Mary went by Jar's stone. She remembered him very well. Looking round suddenly, she saw an owl pounce upon a little bird in the hedge near by. The owl carried the bird away in its claws. Mary was frightened and fancied she heard Mr. Jar's voice telling her to go home. But still she went on up the hills. She began to pick up sticks and soon forgot her fears.

But again she thought she heard old Jar's voice calling to her, but she could not tell what he was saying.

She smiled to herself for thinking that anyone was near. She would have liked to have met Uncle Jar, of course. She had loved the old man so much when she was a child, and now she wanted to tell him all about her father and about the way Farmer Mew pestered her with his gloomy looks. She wanted to tell him, too, how kind Minnie Cuddy had always been to her.

Mary carried a basket for her sticks because she did not want to soil her white frock. She had not worn this frock since the bishop came to Madder. She thought about that day ; Fanny Squibb had been confirmed too. The people had joked about Fanny, because after she had been confirmed Mad Button caught her in the fields. Mary had seen Fanny running between the shocks of wheat. A September wind was blowing and Fanny's brown hair had blown in the wind as she ran. When Fanny reached the other end of the field, as far as possible from the village, she hid behind a shock of wheat and Tom would have run past her only she laughed as he went by.

Mary gathered her sticks ; her thoughts became odd and fearful. In every gorse bush she passed something seemed to stir, and she thought she saw a hairy horned head peep over a stone wall. Putting down her basket, Mary looked for a while at Madder village.

Madder seemed a place of peace and contentment. Nothing could look more harmless. Something in white stooped in the Rectory garden. " This must be Mrs. Summerbee picking strawberries."

Mary smiled to herself. All the village spoke of plenty, peace and quiet labour. The cottage shadows were slowly lengthening.

Mary Gillet sighed gratefully. She loved God's Madder.

On her return she saw some ripe blackberries that grew on the hedge near to Jar's stone. She reached up to pick them. In doing so her white frock was caught by a bramble. Mary did not wish the thorns to tear her frock, so she began cautiously to liberate herself.

As she was doing so a man sprang out from behind Jar's stone and seized her. Mary was utterly terror-stricken, she could not scream.

The man carried her to Jar's stone.

Mary had fainted.

In the Madder Rectory garden a spot of white, that was Susan Summerbee, still stooped and picked strawberries.

Farmer Mew lifted Mary upon Jar's stone and knelt beside her. He felt her with his hands as though she were a young heifer that he had bought in the market.

This feeling gave Mary her consciousness again ; she wept and begged, she even struggled. Farmer Mew examined his new property again, this time more carefully. When she tried to raise herself, he hit her with his fist so that she might remain in her place. The man was quite at his ease; he carefully made ready his new purchase. He had, in order to gain full ownership, to possess this one as a man possesses a woman.

Mary helped him herself.

She again became unconscious.

CHAPTER X

WHILE Mary was lying upon Jar's stone, James Gillet was praying in the Madder churchyard.

In the churchyard hedge there grew a large elm. The knotted roots of this tree protruded out of the bank and formed ugly heads, long twisted arms and wide misshapen legs. There was a niche between these roots where James Gillet was wont to kneel. In the tree above there was a rude head formed by nature in the bark of the tree. This head slightly resembled Mr. Jar the tinker.

James Gillet paid no attention to the head; he looked for the life everlasting. The great tree grew up to the heavens while its roots drank of the sweet clay mixed with the bones of men. James Gillet believed he did the same; he believed that he changed his human clay into life everlasting. God was the substance; God's Madder but a passing dream. A vast peace surrounded the tree and the place where Gillet knelt. The love of God overcame the man and he wept.

A spiritual wonder descended upon him ; he heard the clods of the valley singing praises, and the blades of grass chanting music. James Gillet had taken God as in a net. Worship had led the way and the great bird now lay in his heart caged.

Sometimes things happen like this in country places. A man wanders in the fields ; he is called " one of no occupation." His barns are rotted, his fields sold, and his home is in ruins. Has he gone out to trap the conies ? No ; he is after bigger game than that —he is after God. He lies in the field waiting. He is out to catch God. . . .

* * *

All that day Tom Button had been very much worried.

His worry began at breakfast-time. When Mother Button gave him his bread and treacle, she said :

" Thee be sane enough for running after they girls, bain't 'ee wise enough to do a bit of work for thee's bread ? "

Tom was unsettled by these words ; there was something about them that he did not like. His mother had never addressed him in this manner before. Tom respected his mother and he respected Mr. Jar ; these two he believed to be very wise But now that his mother began to talk about his working, he began to doubt her wisdom. Mr. Jar, he felt sure, would never have spoken to him in that foolish way. He wanted to ask some one why his mother had spoken so oddly to him. All day he loitered about in the lanes, for Tom was thoughtful.

He stood for some hours in one place in the lanes where the children used to slide and roll upon the grass.

Naughty Nellie saw Tom standing there and she came to slide too.

Nellie was in disgrace because she had torn her underclothes, having caught her leg in a bramble-bush as she rolled down some bank or other.

" Thee be all in pieces," Mrs. Squibb said angrily when she saw the rent. " An' I bain't going to sew no more ; thee best go naked." Nellie ran away. Directly she saw Tom Button she decided to slide down the grass. The state of her clothes was her mother's affair and she intended to slide just as usual. After about an hour spent in this way the rent was made worse.

Mad Button had watched Nellie sliding. Growing tired, Nellie looked at Tom ; she had expected him to run after her, but he had remained all the time merely looking.

Naughty Nellie ran down the lane ; she thought Tom would follow. She crept back near to him again, looking flushed and annoyed.

She said something nasty and spat at him and ran away as fast as she could go ; when she reached her home she was nearly crying.

Tom Button had been thinking of Mr. Jar. Even naughty Nellie with her torn clothes had not interested him then. He wanted to ask Mr. Jar a question. Perhaps Jar's stone would answer ! He thought he would go to the stone.

When Mad Button came near to Jar's stone he

saw Farmer Mew crouching behind it as though he waited for some one to come. Tom Button hid himself in the ditch near by. . . .

Later in the evening, when all was quiet and no one about, Tom crept out of his hiding-place. He climbed on to Jar's stone; there were torn pieces of a girl's clothing scattered about. These pieces covered the stone like the feathers of a thrush that a hawk has killed.

Tom thought he would go into the churchyard and look for Jar's star. He ran down the lane, fearing that Mr. Mew might have seen him and be running after him.

Reaching the churchyard, Tom looked up into the sky; the star was there.

"What be doing?" asked Tom. "Thee bain't working, be 'ee?"

Jar's star did not reply.

"'Tisn't for we to work, be it?" Tom asked again in a plaintive tone.

After waiting a little while listening, Tom Button heard a distinct answer in his own heart, that said "No." He nodded in a familiar way to the star.

"Wold Jar do talk," he said, and began to wander about the churchyard.

Seeing James Gillet kneeling between the elm roots, Tom went up to him and said:

"Work be bad, work be. 'Tisn't I or wold Jar that do work; 'tis Farmer Mew."

Mad Button walked slowly away.

James Gillet had not heard him, because his thoughts were burning in God's fire.

CHAPTER XI

ANN Patch cautiously opened her gate. Mr. Mew's bull was feeding quietly in a far corner. The field was white with mushrooms. So far Mrs. Patch had been afraid to pick any because of the bull. But now she had become used to its being there. The bull had seen her in the garden and taken no notice. She had thrown a stone at it once and the beast had walked away quietly.

Mrs. Patch was in good spirits : one of the little Squibbs had cut her leg in sliding down the bank. The child had slid into one of Mrs. Patch's broken bottles. She had had good fortune too with the beetles. For one afternoon, in raising the large stone—she had not done so for some while—in order to put the key under, she found a nest of beetles. She stamped upon them with pleasure ; she had never killed so many at one time before.

Mrs. Patch felt hungry ; she had only eaten bread and an apple for her breakfast. For a large basketful of mushrooms, Mrs Summerbee would give her enough money to buy half a pound of butter. Mrs. Patch was poorer than usual that week because her black hens had not laid any eggs.

Once outside her gate and in Mr. Mew's field Mrs. Patch looked thoughtfully around. Nothing could be seen to alarm her. All Madder was but making its usual noises. In the village schoolroom the children were singing a hymn. John Soper was sawing a plank in his workshop, and beside a distant hedge Mrs. Billy, clad in a veil, was hiving a swarm

of bees, while Mr. Billy made music with a tin tray
near by.

There had been rain of late, and the grass in the
fields shone in the sunlight. The mushrooms shone
too, white and tempting.

Only a great elm tree at the end of the field stood
moody and distrustful. Its heart was eaten out by
worms and it feared that the next winter's storms would
prove its downfall. The elm tree shook its leaves
sadly in the summer wind.

Ann Patch carried her largest basket into the field
and began to pick the mushrooms. The farther she
went into the field, the finer ones she gathered. In
her excitement of picking the mushrooms she forgot
the bull. Ann moved stoopingly from mushroom to
mushroom, cutting the stalks with a knife, so that
they might lie clean in the basket.

As she picked she still heard Mr. Billy beating the tin in order to quiet the bees. When Mr.
Billy ceased beating, Mr. Soper's saw still went
on.

Presently both noises ceased.

Ann Patch was in a hurry to fill her basket : she
thought that if the Squibbs spied her they would
come into the field and gather the mushrooms before
she filled her basket.

In her search for the largest Ann Patch had moved
into the middle of the field. The bull raised his
head and watched her. Presently he sniffed at the
grass. With lowered head he approached Mrs. Patch.
The day being chilly after the night's rain, she
had put on her red shawl. She hurriedly cut the

mushrooms in case the Squibbs might come. She had her back to the bull. . . .

The day passed, the school-children ran out from the school with their usual calls and shouting. All the little Squibbs ran home. Mrs. Squibb was hanging clothes upon the line; she crossly told the children to run out into the lanes to play. The little Squibbs climbed the bank above Ann Patch's cottage.

On the bank they saw Farmer Mew.

They turned and fled.

Farmer Mew held up his hands to the sky. He was glad at heart. The two possessions that he had wished for so long were now his. To obtain Mrs. Patch's cottage now would be easy.

Mr. Mew pointed with his hand to a patch of red in the field, that was still being tossed and trampled upon by the bull. He called out exultingly. The bull's white horns were red.

Mr. Mew walked round by the way of the village towards his house.

Passing the shop, he saw Mr. Billy standing in the garden, trying to pull his trousers off and beating his own leg because a bee had stung him.

Mrs. Billy was setting up the new hive for bees at the end of the garden.

John Soper had finished sawing; he was standing at his own gate and looking in the direction of Love Cottage. Mrs. Soper came up behind him and John said that he had seen a small cloud in the sky and fancied that it would rain again the next day. They both said "Good afternoon" to Mr. Mew.

When the farmer reached his home all was exactly

as a farmhouse usually is. In the yard there was the usual sound of the pigs being fed. Tom Squibb was wetting his hay knife in the rick-yard. He was going to cut some old hay for the sick horse. A hen cackled loudly and flapped its wings upon a straw stack where she had made her nest, hoping to rear her chickens without molestation from man. After cackling the hen looked timidly round as though she wished she had not spoken. Tom Squibb saw the nest and wondered whether Farmer Mew knew where it was.

Mr. Mew went into the room that he used for his writing, in the corner of which was a large iron safe. He sat at his table that faced the open window. Through the window nearly all Madder was visible.

To the right hand, in the field near to Mrs. Patch's cottage, there was a tiny spot of red. And under the elm tree in the corner of the same field Mr. Mew's bull was pawing the ground and tossing up the earth with its horns.

To the left hand, in the Rectory garden, two people were standing near to one another upon a green lawn. These were Mr. Summerbee and his wife; they were watching the sun sinking behind the Madder hills.

CHAPTER XII

AFTER Ann Patch's funeral Mr. Summerbee walked slowly, as a meek clergyman should, home to his tea.

He knew that the strawberry jam was made and

D

would be by that time cold and ready to be eaten.

The idea of eating new strawberry jam made him wonder again about a certain subject. Susan Summerbee was always so lively when the jam was boiling; she liked to see it bubble in the pot when she stirred it with the wooden spoon. Mr. Summerbee thought of the cool dairy butter and the home-made crusty bread that he would eat with the strawberry jam. She had tied it down that very morning, dipping a little round of paper into a saucer of brandy, and then putting a clean white sheet over that. How clean and neat the pots had looked with a sunbeam upon them from the window ! Ah, the summer sun !

Tea-time would pass of course, but later there would be supper. Somehow or other a funeral always made Mr. Summerbee hungry. It might have been the air in the churchyard or the long lesson. He did not know which. At supper he expected there would be cold lamb and salad, junket and gooseberry wine with blue cheese. The gooseberry wine was better than any that Mrs. Primrose had ever made.

Between tea and supper Mr. Summerbee thought he would take a little walk. But the summer hours, however long, soon brought bedtime to Madder.

To Mr. Summerbee Madder was only a pretty plate that held Susan. Madder was the plate and Susan the strawberry. Other figures decorated the plate too. There was poor praying Gillet. Farmer Mew, who gained field after field and house after house. Painted bulls that killed defenceless old women, for whose burial Mr. Summerbee had the fee in his pocket.

There was Mrs. Cuddy. At a distance she could almost look like Mrs. Summerbee. Susan was pink and white and lovely, rounded, though firm and playful. Mrs. Cuddy was larger, of course, but still a pretty woman, though rather too kind to the men perhaps. But she helped in Madder; she was a good mass of colour to meet in the lanes; she always brought his Susan to his mind with a sort of double wondering. Mr. Summerbee liked the way she leaned against gates too, talking to anyone that she met.

He sighed as he entered the Rectory gate.

Oh! it was a pleasant thing to walk under those Madder elms with the summer flowers and the blades of grass to look upon. The apron would be changed into a white frock for the evening, and later of course that in its turn would be taken off. It was all so pleasant at Madder, that Mr. Summerbee could find nothing wrong or out of place. He had his calm and peaceful work to do.

There was the preaching and reading in the Church, the words in the prayer book that leant their aid to the happy utterance of his life. There was his garden. If the weeds became too tiresome, Mr. Summerbee would call in Tom Button, who was for some reason or other willing to work in the Rectory garden for an hour or two, and give him some money for weeding the plot that had outgrown his rule.

The hints of a terrible moving force that raged in Madder he regarded not.

Mr. Mew looked dark and gloomy sometimes, and tales were whispered. But was he not churchwarden and therefore a good man ! And who indeed could believe any evil of the place when the summer scents were in the Madder lanes ?

Mr. Summerbee wished in his mild way that James Gillet had worked a little harder and kept things together for his daughter's sake. But that could not be helped. Mr. Gillet was a most holy man ; he was always praying.

Of course it was sad that poor Mrs. Patch had been gored to death. But things like that must happen sometimes. He would speak about the changes of life in his next sermon and the nearness of death to us all. He too would grow old and die. Die, that was very natural, but it would not be yet, he hoped.

Sometimes God makes His dwelling-place in the heart of a man. When He settles Himself there, there is generally trouble. The man usually ceases to prosper in a worldly way ; his friends often desert him. God cuts all ropes that bind the man to his former ways, and the man often runs naked into the wilderness where strange voices sound. Those voices are the echoes of God's voice speaking inside the man. Against the wall of the world they become distorted and sometimes insane. They drive the man to do strange things. He takes all the world perhaps instead of God. Sometimes they bid him destroy himself ; this he does. God is a queer fellow.

James Gillet liked a new grave. He knelt beside the heap of dirt underneath which Ann Patch lay. James Gillet took some soil in his hands. In the soil there was a little red worm.

No vestige of his former possessions belonged to Mr. Gillet. His daughter and he now lived in Mrs. Patch's cottage that belonged to Mr. Mew.

Instead of choosing the red worm from Mrs. Patch's grave for a dwelling-place, God had chosen a man. The Almighty has odd fancies sometimes.

Grave mould was not plain mould to Gillet now. He saw all Madder afire with the Spirit. Life and death, the creatures, even ants under a stone all burning. The queer presence within had opened his eyes. He saw every blade of grass, every leaf, every movement of the wind, every little red worm, as possessed of God. God shone in the light of the glow-worm that crawled upon the dry slopes of the little hills. He danced lively in the shining eyes of the lizard. He moved with the maggots in the dew-wet carcass of a rabbit, that had died of fright—fright of Him. His fancy reached men. He was the coloured outer ring of Mad Button's mind. He tickled naughty Nellie till she blamed the fleas. The slow tread of Eli Squibb going home to dinner, the footed sound was His. The soft longings of Mrs. Cuddy—— ?

No ; we must not let Him stray so far ; His own Church might read Him a lesson.

By prayer James Gillet had drawn near to the wonder. Death became it. Corruption dressed it fine in the places of silence.

"What and who am I ? " This question was asked by the clay that was once an old woman who picked mushrooms and was gored by a bull.

James Gillet bent his head lower and listened.

"What am I?" the soil asked.
"Be the answer what it will, 'tis God's."

CHAPTER XIII

THE fields of God's Madder lay heavy with damp. The south wind had brought a thin rain that deepened the red of the poppies. Two of the elder daughters of Joan Squibb were helping Mary Gillet to make the butter at Mew's Farm. The Squibbs were talkative and excited. They were talking of Mrs. Patch's funeral.

"They flowers were splendid," said Maggie Squibb. "They nearly covered Mother Patch's coffin."

"Yes, the cross of sweet peas came from the Rectory; Mrs. Summerbee made it."

"The carnations came from Mrs. Billy."

"Mrs. Cuddy sent the white pinks."

"There were no bought flowers."

"What a shame, and our white daisies must have been lost. I never saw them anywhere."

"Perhaps Nellie threw them into the grave."

"More like to have thrown them at Mad Button."

The Squibbs were excited about another matter too. They had moved into the Gillet farmhouse as managers for their master. The Gillets in their turn had gone to Mrs. Patch's under the bank.

Maggie Squibb began to joke about the master. "He be a fine one," she said. "Why he takes a girl without even saying please."

"Oh, you do know," said Fanny slyly.

"You used to run behind trees with silly Tom."

"But I never follow 'e into churchyard same as Nell do."

"Oh, Nell be growing a bad one."

Fanny laughed.

Mary Gillet turned away, and this movement of hers annoyed Maggie.

"'Tis nice to be a lady," she said, mimicking Mary's movement.

"An' 'tis nice to 'ave a father that be so prayerful."

"Wold Jar's stone be a nice bed for courting couple, for mad Tom do talk."

The Squibbs laughed.

A moment later Farmer Mew was standing in the dairy watching the girls. He watched them as though they were beasts in his pastures.

After he had looked at them for a while, he went to Maggie and held her by the arm. Maggie grumbled and grew pale, but allowed herself to be led out of the room. The farmer's heavy steps were heard ascending the stairs ; by the slow way that he climbed he appeared to be carrying something in his arms that struggled.

Mary Gillet went on patting the butter. Fanny Squibb blew into the churn for fun. Her master would not come down for a moment or two she supposed.

Mary hardly noticed when Maggie Squibb came into the room again. She was only aware that the girl had returned and was tidying her hair and putting her clothes to rights.

Fanny Squibb had stopped blowing into the churn and had gone to her sister, and they were soon laughing together.

"Silly Tom do know a lot," said Fanny.

Maggie laughed.

Mary Gillet finished patting the butter. She went to the dairy window and looked out.

A dark cloud of mist hung over Madder. Under the cloud there walked Farmer Mew.

CHAPTER XIV

MRS. MINNIE CUDDY threw out handfuls of golden maize to her hens.

She liked to think that all the world enjoyed a good breakfast.

She went indoors again and plumed herself before the looking-glass. Beside the looking-glass was Captain Cuddy's memorial card. Mrs. Cuddy kissed the card with real affection.

Mrs. Cuddy gently stroked her womanly body. She knew she was round and ripe like an orange, and sweet to the taste. There was gold in her hair like the gold that she threw to the hens.

To Minnie Cuddy's eyes the village of Madder was a kind, friendly thing rather like herself. She thought of the fields of Madder as being gentle young women, not too young of course for bearing, but who felt and enjoyed the pressure of drill and roller and the wheels of the reaping machine. To yield their soft bodies to men, that was what the kind fields did, just as a pretty woman did it too.

Minnie Cuddy admired the church tower that stood proudly amongst the Madder trees. She admired the tall trees too, and the rounded hills that were so gentle and womanly.

She liked to watch strong healthy men walking, and little girls with firm plump legs and boys who ran about calling.

Somehow or other Minnie Cuddy could never abide old women. She would sometimes hear old women whispering about her as they leaned over the well, their grey heads looking dismal and untidy.

Mrs. Cuddy knew that they whispered harmfully, with no love for men in their hearts. They looked dried and bleached and empty, like rabbit skins hung out too long in the sun.

Mrs. Cuddy decided that she would never grow into one of them. When she was old she would be otherwise. She could still love the men and perhaps some Christmas-time a man might kiss her in the dark.

There would be no whispering over wells for her. She would rather look over the dairy meadow gate when the cows were feeding. Poor Mrs. Patch! But she would never watch a lonely bull. Besides, if she wished she could always take a walk through the flocks of sheep in June or September. Sheep are quiet and peace-loving.

Mrs. Cuddy tidied herself and got ready to go out. She threw her white hens some more golden maize, and, opening the gate, went out into the lane. She walked in the village for a little, hoping to find some company to talk to, but, seeing no one, she thought she would go to the Madder hills.

Minnie Cuddy had not been unnoticed, for Madder windows have eyes.

Andrew Corbin thought the moment a proper one, after Minnie had gone by, to start out, so he gravely told his wife, " to see how Mr. Mew's sick horse was a-doing." Mr. Corbin softly closed his garden gate and went out into the road.

Mr. Billy had seen the shadow of a skirt pass by his window. In his efforts to see more, the good shopkeeper upset a large bag of sugar upon the floor. This sugar had been put up ready for Mrs. Summerbee.

Mr. Billy called his wife, who was in the middle of washing up the breakfast things. He said that a large dog had jumped over the counter and upset the bag. Mrs. Billy took no notice of what he said, but began to scoop up the sugar. While she was doing so Mr. Billy peeped out and saw which way Mrs. Cuddy was going.

The imagination of Mr. Billy had wings ; in his mind's eye he saw a distant chalk pit under the hills, perhaps Minnie Cuddy was going there.

Looking round the shop for an excuse, Mr. Billy saw his wife's canary. The canary was eyeing Mr. Billy in a pert manner.

" There is a weed called groundsel," thought Mr. Billy, " that might grow under the little hills as well as anywhere else in the county."

Mr. Billy said in a quiet voice that he intended to go out a moment and find a little groundsel for Toppy.

When Minnie Cuddy passed his shop, John Soper was sawing at a piece of wood that was intended to become a cross for Mrs. Patch's grave. James Gillet had ordered the cross.

From the place where John Soper worked he could

see the road. "He did not wish," when he saw her, "that the lady who kept the white fowls should go abroad so lonely." Honest John could finish the cross the next day; Mrs. Patch, he supposed, would not mind that little delay. There were other matters that could not wait so quietly. John Soper left the plank and followed the lady, taking a short cut across the fields in case Mrs. Soper might be about.

When Minnie Cuddy reached Mr. Jar's hut the rain came on. Mr. Jar's hut was built upon bricks; in the corners between the bricks and the ground there was space enough for children to crawl in under. To crawl in under Jar's hut was a favourite pastime for naughty Nellie.

The door of the hut was open, and Minnie Cuddy stepped in, shutting the door after her. She was alone for a little time and heard the raindrops pattering upon the roof. She also fancied she heard a rat under the boards. She peeped through a hole in the floor, but could see nothing.

Presently there was a soft knock at Mr. Jar's hut door. This was Mr. Soper who, by taking the short cut, had got in front of his friends.

Minnie Cuddy opened the door; she explained that she had gone in to shelter. John Soper said that he had come to mend a hole in the floor. He had only that morning remembered that Mr. Jar had asked him to.

John Soper peeped out for a moment and saw Andrew Corbin and Mr. Billy coming near. He shut the door and cautiously bolted it. Andrew Corbin and Mr. Billy remained for an hour waiting in the rain.

After waiting so long they saw with surprise Mad Tom Button crawl out from under Mr. Jar's hut. Tom, very dirty but smiling, held a garter in his hand. He laughingly said that the garter had fallen through the floor.

Andrew Corbin looked at Mr. Billy.

Mr. Billy remembered that there was roast rabbit for dinner; he believed that roast rabbits are sometimes stuffed with sage and onions like a duck. He fancied he saw the teeth of the rabbit shining out of a browned and basted head.

Mr. Corbin too had a thought to lead him home. Being a careful man, he only smoked one cigarette after each meal. But it so happened that Mrs. Corbin liked cigarettes too, though, being a married lady, she never indulged in public. But suppose her husband did not happen to be in at dinner-time? She would then take perhaps three out of the tin that he kept in the middle dresser drawer.

Andrew saw her taking them now.

Mr. Billy and Andrew Corbin began to go home. On their way they discussed the merits of oatmeal and the price of cotton cake and horse corn.

Andrew Corbin said that the rain would do good to the fields, but Mr. Billy shook himself and remarked that he thought they had nearly had enough of it.

Near to his own gate Mr. Billy picked a little groundsel.

*　　　*　　　*

Tom Button collected garters.

He had more than one specimen of Naughty Nellie's, though not in very good repair, and so he did not prize them very highly. He liked Minnie Cuddy's much better. But Tom was ambitious and he wanted Mrs. Summerbee's.

People go to church for different reasons—some for one thing, some for another. Tom went to church because he wanted Mrs. Summerbee's garter.

Mrs. Summerbee sat in the Rectory pew. Mad Button had taken to sitting beside her. Susan Summerbee was the last person to tell any poor man—and a mad one at that—to sit farther down in a church. Her husband had said that all were equal there, and she believed it.

And so Mad Tom sat next to Mrs. Summerbee.

One Sunday Mad Button caught three bees, put them into an empty match-box and carried them to church. During the service Tom dropped his match-box near to Mrs. Summerbee's foot. It fell under her skirts and Tom was a moment or two in finding it again.

Susan Summerbee blushed.

Presently she gave a little scream and walked hurriedly out of the church. She had been stung by two bees. Mrs. Summerbee went to the elm tree where James Gillet was wont to pray and searched for the bees. After searching for a while she returned to the church and attended piously to the remainder of the service.

In the evening Mad Button came to the churchyard to ask Jar's stone a question. He wished to know in what part of the churchyard Susan Summerbee had searched in her clothes for the creatures that had stung her. He knew Susan wore garters. This was how he knew.

He was once weeding near to the house when Mrs. Summerbee was standing on some high steps cutting roses with a pair of scissors. Tom had peeped.

Jar's star was exactly above the tall elm tree.

This was the answer Tom got. He went at once to look under the trees and there he found it.

Mad Tom wished to tell some one of his good luck. He looked around at the stones.

He remembered Mrs. Patch ; there was only earth upon her grave and no grass. No doubt she would listen. Tom sat upon Mrs. Patch's grave with his knees wide apart. He bent his head between his knees until he nearly touched the earth, and told Mrs. Patch about Mrs. Summerbee's garter.

CHAPTER XV

THE small matters in Madder brought happiness ; the great matters caused trouble and sorrow.

Mr. Mew had taken into his arms all that he had desired. Mary Gillet was his as a possession ; the Squibbs, the farms, the sheep, the oxen, the horses were his.

Mr. Mew saw all Madder as his own.

But one day Mr. Thomas Pye drove into the village. Mr. Pye came into Madder in a large motor-car.

Mr. Pye was the one person Farmer Mew envied in the world. Whenever Mr. Mew drove to market he tried to shut his eyes as he passed Thomas Pye's farms,

Mr. Pye lived in a mansion; he had many more sheep than Mr. Mew; he had oxen and she-asses. The she-asses, Mr. Mew had always understood, were all the women and pretty girls of the neighbourhood. Hardly one of these had Mr. Pye let alone, so folk said.

Mr. Thomas Pye was very rich and generous, and the women liked him. Farmer Parley used to boast at market that Mr. Pye had taken his wife to London.

Whenever Mr. Mew walked upon the Madder hills to look at his sheep, he never dared to look over the surrounding country that was the other side of the hills. For in that beyond world Mr. Pye reigned, and over there were the tops of Mr. Pye's trees and his great barns.

Mr. Mew welcomed Thomas Pye coldly, when he came into Madder in his large motor-car.

He took Mr. Pye into the yard where the fierce bull was kept. Mr. Pye showed no fear of the bull and so the creature took no notice of him.

Next Farmer Mew took him to see the rams. Mr. Pye admired them, but said that he had many better. He asked Mr. Mew how many ewes he had. Farmer Mew told him. Mr. Pye smiled because he had three times as many.

At last Thomas Pye started his motor-car and drove away.

As he was going through Madder he met Maggie Squibb in the road. He invited the girl to go to the top of the hill with him and held out to her a one-pound note.

Maggie Squibb was just getting into the car when

she turned and saw Farmer Mew watching her. She stepped back into the road again.

Thomas Pye cursed her, and drove on.

CHAPTER XVI

FARMER MEW walked in his fields. He was filled full of the glory that comes from having possessions. He had followed the law that gives the most direct pleasure to man.

He had taken from Mary Gillet all that a girl has to give and her destruction was a possible consequence of his act.

Of the Squibb women he was not so certain, but as they were his sworn bondswomen their case was different.

Farmer Mew walked in his fields. He lay down upon the grass ; the blades of grass were his and he liked to feel them.

The meadow in which the farmer lay was full of yellow hawkweed.

While he lay there Naughty Nellie climbed over the gate without noticing her master and began to pick the hawkweed.

Farmer Mew watched her.

To the child the flowers were something to be possessed. Mr. Mew knew that he owned the field, but did the flowers belong to him. They could hardly be his any more than they were Nellie's, before they were picked. Field flowers, Mr. Mew fancied, were the sort of property that belonged to the one who went into the field and got them,

As soon as Nellie was gone, Mr. Mew began to pick the hawkweed. He gathered them till his arms were full, and yet the field was still yellow with the flowers.

Seeing that he had so little chance of possessing all the flowers, he cast the ones he had already gathered into the grass again. He had taken these few, but what did they count amongst so many ? Mr. Mew trampled upon the flowers that he had gathered.

Leaving the field he went and sat down upon a bank by the roadside.

Little Frankie Squibb came by catching butterflies. Farmer Mew told the child to bring him those that he had caught. Frankie came up crying, and opening his hand, he showed three broken soiled wings and a crushed body. Mr. Mew threw these upon the ground. Frankie ran off crying more than ever.

Farmer Mew hit at the flying butterflies with his stick ; he wanted to hurt them as he had hurt Mary Gillet.

In the distance he heard Frankie calling for help from some one, because his butterflies had been taken from him. Frankie was calling out for Mr. Jar.

Farmer Mew wished to remove Jar's stone. In his childhood he had collected little stones and now he wanted Mr. Jar's large one.

"It would be proper to have it," he thought, "by his own door."

The stone was already his in a legal way. But this sort of ownership did not now content Farmer Mew.

He wanted to possess the stone in the same sort

E

of way as he had possessed Mary Gillet. He wanted
to be able to hurt the stone, to hammer it at will,
to break the round ponderous surface, to make the
rough thing feel that he was master.

About noontide one day Farmer Mew stood upon
Jar's stone, whence he beckoned Tom Squibb to
come to him. Tom was cutting thistles. Mr.
Mew sent Tom for his strongest cart, for poles and
levers, for thick planks and for other help.

Eli Squibb when he arrived with the wagon scratched
his head and looked doubtful about the wisdom of the
deed.

"Suppose," he said, "wold Jar were to come to
village again and find his stone a-gone."

Farmer Mew would not listen ; his only fear was
that the stone might defeat him.

His heart beat quick as Tom Squibb forced a heavy
oak beam under the stone. The muscles of Tom's
arms showed like tight ropes as he strained at the beam.
Mew watched, trembling with his fear lest the stone
should not move. Eli Squibb placed another beam
under the stone and pressed upon it. The old man's
face grew red as he worked. Farmer Mew looked
approvingly at him. He shouted out words of encouragement. He called them weaklings. He stamped
with anger because the stone would not move. He
placed a beam himself under the stone and pulled
fiercely.

At last the stone moved, and Farmer Mew, letting
go his beam, stepped back to see his triumph.

The great stone tottered and rolled over.

Mr. Mew looked at the place whence the stone

had rolled. He had won. The stone was heaved into the wagon. Farmer Mew stood by, his desire satisfied.

He had the stone carried into his garden.

When night came and the Madder hills were dimly visible, Farmer Mew took a hammer from his wood-shed and went out to the stone.

At first he stroked the stone and even spoke to it as though it could hear what he said.

He then broke off bits with the hammer, as though to test whether the thing were really his or not. Some-how neither the one manner nor the other of treating the stone satisfied him. Though the stone appeared to be his, neither his love nor hate made any impression upon it. Jar's stone remained silent.

CHAPTER XVII

THE topmost leaves of the Madder elms were touched with gold. And Mr. Summerbee, seeing the day was fair, took his afternoon walk.

Mrs. Summerbee was making apple jelly. She had picked up the apples that had fallen under the trees. The best of these she had peeled and sliced, the remainder she gave to Mad Button for his pig.

Mr. Summerbee strolled through Farmer Mew's dairy meads. He carefully avoided the bull. In the water meadows he came upon James Gillet, who was cleaning out a ditch. Gillet was dragging the weeds out and laying them carefully by the side. Mr. Summerbee stopped and watched him for a moment. In the next lot of weed that James Gillet dragged up

there was an eel.   Mr. Summerbee said the eel might
be nice for breakfast.   James Gillet let it go into
the water again.

George Summerbee continued his walk. He climbed
half-way up one of the little hills and then he sat down
to rest.   He looked kindly at the Madder fields that
lay before him.   The fields were resting after the
exciting growth of the summer.   September gave
them a sleepy appearance.   Mr. Mew's corn from
the hills had all been taken in.

Already there were people picking apples in the
little Madder orchards.

From far-away Love Cottage there came distinctly
to Mr. Summerbee's ears the sound of a hammer.

John Soper was there making a new fowl house
for the white hens.   Some one was resting upon the
bank watching John Soper at work.

This was Minnie Cuddy. Though it was all
so far off, Mr. Summerbee could see quite distinctly
what was happening.   Very soon Mr. Soper moved
to where Minnie Cuddy was resting.   And where
there had been two people there appeared now to be
only one.

Mr. Summerbee looked away from Love Cottage ;
he was beginning to wonder.   He was glad the afternoon was come, the evening would soon be there and
then the night could not be far off, and bedtime.

Mr. Summerbee looked towards the Madder
meadows.   There was a girl out there fetching in
Mr. Mew's cows.   The girl walked slowly.   She was
Mary Gillet.   Mr. Summerbee remembered something.   Whenever Mad Button saw the clergyman

he would come close up to him and shout in his ears something about Mary. Mr. Summerbee took very little notice of Tom, because at the Rectory there was apple jelly being made.

When Mrs. Patch was killed by the bull there was strawberry jam for tea. And now, when things were being said about Mary, there was something nice to eat too.

Mr. Summerbee began to stroll homewards.

CHAPTER XVIII

IT was night. Farmer Mew could not sleep. He rose from his bed, dressed and went out.

Outside the door he thought that Jar's stone looked at him. He went up to the stone and touched it. The stone was very cold. Mr. Mew stood beside the stone and looked up at the hills.

An owl flew overhead and hooted and then lit upon Jar's stone. A sheep coughed from the meadows.

Mr. Mew went slowly out of his garden and began to walk in Madder lanes. He took the way to the hills. Reaching the top of the hills, he stood upon a mound that had once been the grave of a king, and looked towards Mr. Pye's farms. The full moon shone upon Thomas Pye's barns and upon his great trees. Shown clearly under the moon, what he saw, gave to Mr. Mew more than ever before the idea of great possessions. His own farms were small and barren to what he saw below him. Yea, they even dwindled to a mere nothingness in his remembrance.

Under the moon Mr. Pye's rich lands and round

ricks of corn slept as precious goods are wont to sleep, carefully guarded. The very shadows that the moon cast spoke of safety. Here were possessions indeed that a rich man might envy.

In their greatness Farmer Mew was become small. He felt himself to be a beggar before so much that was not his own. A mighty wish and desire rose in his heart; he longed to enter in and possess this good land.

In the far distance a fox barked. The wild beast's voice echoed in Mr. Mew. In thought he followed the doings of this creature of the night. To the fox those silent barns would be dangerous. It would enter stealthily into the whiteness between those guarded shadows.

Farmer Mew found himself crouching as a fox before the door of a well-shut fowl-roost.

He would slink away and cross the wide rick-yard before the dogs were awake. Would he espy a strange chick, forgotten by the hen-wife and perched outside? He would tear it down and fly silently under the rick shadows.

Farmer Mew trembled.

Was there nothing that he could take for his own out of all this guarded security?

He was ravenous; he was like a man who had gone many days without food.

Was there no door left open, no field gate unlatched, so that he could go in and take somewhat of the riches that lay so heavy under the moon?

The fox barked again.

Close under the hills and near to where Mr. Mew

was standing, a large flock of Thomas Pye's sheep
were folded. A lane led down the hills and passed
the fold.

" It would be easy," thought Mr. Mew, " to let
the sheep into the lane."

Farmer Mew descended the hill. He thought
the moon looked at him inquiringly as Jar's stone had
done when he left his house. Going into the fold,
he awakened the flock and let them out into the lane.
The sheep had risen sleepily, stretching themselves
and looking at Mr. Mew as though they wondered
why he had awakened them.

An owl flying out from one of the great barns
hooted. The night bird was telling Mr. Pye that
his sheep were being stolen.

The sheep moved slowly and entered the lane bleating. Very soon they raised a dust that covered Mr.
Mew as he followed in their wake.

Farmer Mew was glad at heart ; the well-known
smell of the woolly creatures pleased him. The
movement of their many feet in the lane made a sound
like the rumble of distant thunder. This sound was
wonderful music to Mr. Mew ; he listened to it with
an immense joy in his heart.

The sheep touched one another as they went along,
and their backs appeared to Mew to be like a thick
woven mat of wool. He felt them all, as if they
were actually in his hands, or as though he were the
fox that held the prey sure.

Mr. Mew laughed. His thoughts thundered with
the sound of the moving feet. His thoughts drank
of the dust and the hot soft scent and fed upon the

droppings of the flock. He had spoiled the great barns and was driving off the prey to his own lands.

The sheep moved slowly, holding up their heads now and again as though they wondered where they were going. One sheep appeared to distrust this new shepherd and ran back past him as though she wished to return to the fold. But seeing the others did not come too, this one followed behind bleating.

Upon the top of the Madder hills the sheep stopped. They sniffed the night air as though uncertain about the way to take. Every black head was raised, and, as though with one accord, every sheep looked at Mr. Mew. They looked at him as with one head, and with that frightened attention that a flock of sheep gives to one who is not their true shepherd.

Suddenly the sheep seemed to smell the sweet grass of the Madder fields. They went down the grassy side of the hill in a long, narrow line, like a slow-moving white stream.

From the mound upon which he had stood before, Mr. Mew watched them. He stretched out his hands in triumph to the heavens.

One lame sheep had dropped behind. This one halted for a moment and looked round timidly at Mr. Mew, who was again walking behind. Farmer Mew went to the sheep and caught it. Taking it up by its hind legs, he threw it over his shoulder.

After he had let the others into one of his fields, Mr. Mew carried the lame sheep home to the farm. Reaching his house, he tied its four legs together with a rope and laid it upon Jar's stone. Fetching a knife he cut the creature's throat. The ewe struggled at first, but it soon lay still. The blood from its throat ran down Jar's stone.

Leaving the sheep's carcass upon the stone, Mr. Mew went to bed and slept peacefully; the sight of the blood had pleased him.

As the next day was Sunday, Farmer Mew dressed himself in his best clothes.

Mr. Mew was the people's churchwarden. He came to church sometimes.

While he was in church Mr. Pye's shepherd came to claim his master's sheep. He counted them through the gate and there was one missing. Mr. Thomas Pye had sent a message to Farmer Mew thanking him for folding his sheep when they strayed in the night.

In church, Farmer Mew sat in front of Minnie Cuddy; more than once during the service he turned and looked at her. Minnie Cuddy was looking at her prayer-book. Minnie liked men to be nice and modest in their looking. When she knelt down she glanced at John Soper, who sat afar off. Mr. Mew looked at her more persistently than ever. He now wished to possess Minnie Cuddy.

CHAPTER XIX

FOR two months nothing happened in Madder. Farmer Mew had done no more than look at Minnie Cuddy in church. He had been busy threshing his corn. He would stand by the sacks as they filled with the wheat or barley, and bury his hands in the cool corn. He also walked much amongst the sheep, still thinking that the sheep he had driven from Mr. Pye's flocks were amongst them.

Mr. Billy awoke one morning glad to be alive. He awoke to the idea of good trade, cold ham and Minnie Cuddy. Mr. Billy believed in happiness.

He was very fond of his wife; he regarded her as one of the blessings of his life. She managed the shop while Mr. Billy would converse with his customers about all things that existed under the sun. Nothing came up in Madder affairs that did not interest Mr. Billy. He could wonder with the best about the size of the large pumpkin that Mrs. Button grew. He would talk about the view from the church tower, and about the best way to reach the Cape of Good Hope.

On the day when Jar's stone was removed, Mad Button had met Mr. Billy in the lane. Tom was very much frightened and he told Mr. Billy all about it. Mr. Billy patted Tom kindly on the arm and said he was sure Mr. Jar would not hurt the village on account of it. Tom was not so sure. He expected to see Jar's stone begin to roll about and crash into the cottages.

Mr. Billy directed Tom's attention to Naughty Nellie, who was passing at the time. Tom did not regard her, but went sadly home, telling every one he passed that it was not he who had offended Mr. Jar.

After eating a very good breakfast, Mr. Billy remembered that he had to take half a bushel of maize to Love Cottage. His wife had her objections as to his going there, but as it was business she permitted it.

Mr. Billy went round to his wood-shed and took out his green wheelbarrow. This he wheeled round to his front door as proudly as though it were a nobleman's carriage. Carefully placing the bag of maize in the wheelbarrow, Mr. Billy set off.

Mr. Billy was a wonderful lover; he was so sensitive. He was very much afraid of Mrs. Cuddy. In his own shop or in the road he could address her without nervousness, but now that he was really going to her house he began to tremble. "Suppose she were to ask him in, suppose she were to ask him to sit beside her upon the sofa?" Mr. Billy almost wished that he had asked Tom Button to carry the maize.

He remembered that Minnie Cuddy had more than once offered to show a visitor right over her house. He felt that he could never set foot upon the stairs without fainting right off.

Mr. Billy trembled so at all the possibilities incident to Love Cottage that he went on his way in zigzag fashion, the wheelbarrow nearly turning over into the ditch.

Reaching Mrs. Cuddy's at last, Mr. Billy carried the corn round to the back door. He prayed for the courage of John Soper.

Minnie Cuddy opened the door; she blushed when she saw Mr. Billy.

Mr. Billy stammered out that he had brought the corn.

Minnie Cuddy invited him to come in. Mr. Billy was more frightened than ever. It was one thing to want to go into Love Cottage, and quite another thing to be there.

Mr. Billy rubbed his right foot so hard upon the scraper that the heel of his shoe came off. At last he turned nervously away from the scraper and followed Mrs. Cuddy into the front room.

Sitting upon the very edge of one of Mrs. Cuddy's chairs, with his hat in one hand and his stick in the other, was Andrew Corbin.

Though Andrew was in Love Cottage, he certainly did not appear happy there. He had told his wife that morning that he was going to see Mr. Mew's lame cow. Instead he had gone to Mrs. Cuddy's. Directly he entered her house he was filled with an odd fear. Suppose Minnie Cuddy offered to kiss him? When seated in her room he only dared to talk to the carpet. He began to think of John Soper as being a hero of the first water, a kind of Lord Nelson or General Gordon. Andrew Corbin had talked to Minnie Cuddy's carpet for exactly ten minutes when Mr. Billy entered

Mr. Billy shook Andrew Corbin's hand. The two friends had never been more glad to see one another.

They began with one voice to praise John Soper. " He be a good workman," they remarked to Mrs. Cuddy. Very soon Andrew Corbin remembered the lame cow. " He feared he must be going," he said. Mr. Billy rose together with his friend, and they both went out into the road.

Mrs. Cuddy watched them from the window, then she turned away and sighed.

CHAPTER XX

THERE had been gales in Madder. A great many of the leaves of the tall elms had fallen and lay thick in the lanes.

Farmer Mew walked in the village. He walked by the side of the road and kicked up the dead fallen leaves. As the trees were all his, he only kicked his own property. But even though he kicked them the dead leaves tormented him in a queer way, as in the summer the flowers had done and the butterflies.

Mr. Mew had read somewhere in a farmer's paper that in the autumn all the life-blood of a leaf is drawn back again into the parent tree, in such a way that, though the leaf dies, its life goes back again into its mother.

Mr. Mew saw the dead leaves cheating his very feet as he kicked at them.

He took the lane that led to the churchyard. He entered the place of the dead.

As he was churchwarden, he regarded the dead in the same sort of way as he did the rest of Madder, as his property. He believed the dead belonged to him. They had helped to make his farms what they were ; they had helped to gather his possessions, and now they were destroyed. He lived by their destruction.

Farmer Mew kicked the grave mounds as he had kicked the leaves. He was elated. He called out aloud :

"I possess all things ; at my will I destroyed Mrs. Patch and took her cottage and I have removed Jar's stone."

Mr. Mew stood over Mrs. Patch's grave. He shivered with a new fear.

"Is it true," he asked himself, "that life leaves the corpse and returns into the great tree, the giver of life? Hath this one then escaped?"

Some little birds twittered on the yew tree.

Mr. Mew looked at the tree with anger; he wished he had a gun in his hand so that he might destroy the birds. He bethought him that once he had tried to kill all the little birds in his stack-yard. He had shot at them for all one day. Some he killed, but certainly not all. For the next day there were quite as many.

While Farmer Mew stood beside Mrs. Patch's grave, a figure with an untidy beard and soiled hands passed by him, going towards the elm tree. This was James Gillet, who had come into the churchyard to pray.

James Gillet knelt between the roots of the great elm. Above him, formed in the bark, was the rude face somewhat resembling Mr. Jar the tinker.

Farmer Mew came up to where James Gillet prayed. He watched him for a while in silence.

James Gillet hardly noticed him, but prayed on.

Farmer Mew spoke.

"What is it you are asking for?" he said. "You can own nothing in Madder—I have all. Mary is mine. All Madder is mine, and I have never said a prayer. What do you do here? You had best go back to the ditch and rake out the mud."

"Yes," answered James Gillet, "you have all Madder; you have oxen, sheep, fields, servants, but there is something of more value than all these. There is God."

"What is God?" asked Mr. Mew. "Can you hold Him in your hand, can you send Him to labour in the fields, can you enjoy Him as a woman? What is God?"

To this question James Gillet did not reply, only he bent lower.

Farmer Mew trembled. He was aware that his question had been answered. The leaves under the elm were driven by a sudden gust of wind; they formed circles and danced and lay still again. James Gillet had bent his head so low that he became almost like one of the roots of the tree. Had the great tree sucked him into its heart as it sucked in the life of the leaves?

Was that the answer?

Leaving the churchyard, Farmer Mew walked slowly to his home. There was soft mud in the lanes. When he reached the farm Mr. Mew wrote a note. This note he gave to Naughty Nellie to carry to Love Cottage. In the note he commanded Mrs. Cuddy to be at the farm at eight o'clock that same evening, or otherwise he would take Love Cottage away from her.

CHAPTER XXI

AT the back door of the Madder Rectory a knock was heard.

Susan Summerbee was making the tea, but she at once left the kitchen fire and opened the door.

Mr. Jar, the tinker, stood outside.

Mrs. Summerbee looked kindly at the man and invited him to come in. No doubt he had come to beg for food. Susan Summerbee placed a chair for Mr. Jar, saying as she did so, that her husband had gone for a little walk but would soon be back. Mr. Summerbee had gone to the church with some winter roses. After a few moments he returned.

He found the tea laid in the kitchen and Mr. Jar sitting by the fire. Susan Summerbee was talking to Mr. Jar about kittens, and laughing at what he said.

Mr. Summerbee was pleased to see an old man clothed in rags sitting beside his kitchen fire. He shook Mr. Jar warmly by the hand and sat down by the fire too.

" Mr. Jar says he loves kittens," said Susan Summerbee, " and I shouldn't be a bit surprised if he doesn't love babies."

Mrs. Summerbee had made this remark without thinking what she was saying. She blushed when she said it, and turned to poke the fire. She felt sure that her husband had begun to wonder.

*   *   *

Mary Gillet sat alone in her cottage. Something moved within her like a little bird caught in a dark trap.

A feeling of faintness came over her; she went to the door.

Mary stood outside the door. Though it was just a usual autumn evening the wind blew queerly. Wild gusts beat upon the bare Madder trees, and the sound of the wind was like the sound of heavy footfalls,

Darkness was falling, and the wind still blew. Mary looked over the valley to see who had lights in their houses.

In the village there was one very bright light burning, the sort of bright light that welcomes every one. Mary knew that this light came from Love Cottage. Though she felt so lonely she smiled. She knew that Minnie Cuddy was always entertaining, always giving suppers and such things. Mrs. Cuddy would get all the little children to come in and make them eat rich cakes. She never forgot Mad Button. When she saw him by her gate she would ask him to come in too. When invited to enter Love Cottage, Tom spent all his time in eating. He never dreamt of telling her about his secret : before such a well-laden table his thoughts were all occupied in other matters.

Mary looked away from Love Cottage. Near to Madder Church there was another light burning. This too was a friendly light, dimmed a little by pink curtains, perhaps, but still friendly. No doubt behind the pink curtains Mrs. Summerbee was filling up good George's teacup with cream. Perhaps Mr. Summerbee was wondering. All the village knew how George Summerbee wondered. For a moment Mary smiled again.

She thought about her father. Where was he ?— praying in the churchyard most likely. Oh, but even with all this praying a hawk had pounced upon her. Mary shivered. She heard strange sounds far off. Was some one walking upon the hills of God's Madder ? The wind blew again in wild beating

F

gusts—like the beating of huge wings upon the roof of heaven, or deep steps in the sky.

Some one in the village was calling.

It was Mad Button calling to some stranger, perhaps: Mad Button always called to strangers. Mary went in again, closed the door, and began to lay the tea-table. The kettle was beginning to sing. She wondered how far the light from her candle shone out into the darkness.

She sat solitary with her one candle still burning. Her father was still out.

The Squibb family were collected in their cottage. Farmer Mew had been more than ever gloomy of late. He often locked and bolted all his doors. He feared a thief, he said.

The Squibb girls blamed Mary Gillet. They babbled one to the other, and then they sat down to make a doll out of old rags.

When they finished the doll, they called to Naughty Nellie who had gone out to play in the dark lane. Naughty Nellie came in, and they gave her the doll and told her where to take it.

When Nellie was gone they talked about Minnie Cuddy being turned out of her house by Farmer Mew.

They laughed coarsely about John Soper. . . .

Mary Gillet sat lonely. She supposed her father had gone out to talk with God.

She opened the cottage window and looked out. There was a moon, but clouds were drifting over it.

She sat down again. Something came through the window and dropped on the table near to the candlestick. She took it up; it was the rag doll the Squibbs had made.

Round the doll's neck was tied a label on which was written: "Farmer Mew do good work, 'e do."

Mary went to the cottage door and opened it. The clouds were moving fast over the face of the moon.

Mary felt it was time for her to move too. She threw a scarf over her shoulder and went out into the lane. A gust of wind blew her scarf into a thorn-bush. In searching for it she scratched her hand. She could see the red blood on her white scarf, and that troubled her.

She walked down the Madder lanes and entered the fields that had once been her father's.

Mary thought of Mad Button; she smiled. Mad Button used to try to play with her, but she would never let him. And yet she had been taken like a bird in a snare. And now the little hills would never see her any more.

She wondered what Mr. Jar was doing. Had he gone away for ever? Her father used to laugh with her sometimes about Mr. Jar, before he was taken up so much with God.

Who would wear her Sunday dresses when she was gone? The pale-blue one with the butterfly— she hoped her father would give it to Naughty Nellie. Naughty Nellie always wanted clothes, underclothes most of all, perhaps?

She felt the little caged bird flutter inside her body. Why did it move just then? Did it want very much to leave its dark prison? There was that thrush caught in a net at Mr. Mew's. She had tried to let it go, only Mr. Mew came out into the garden and wrung its neck. Mr. Summerbee had once let one go that had got into a church lamp, and then the bird flew at once into Mr. Summerbee's gooseberry bushes.

The bird she knew of was not in a lamp but in herself. She could kill too as well as Mr. Mew. He had taught her, by forcing creation upon her, to kill.

It was too early yet for the tadpoles. But the pond was there nursing the shadow of the elm, and no doubt there were sleepy toads under the weeds.

She had been crushed upon Jar's stone, and that had taught her what life was.

As she stepped into the water, she frightened a moorhen that flew away in a hurry. . . .

*   *   *

A shadow followed Mary down to the water. The shadow was shaped like a pillar of cloud—sometimes the cloud became an old man. Near to the pond the moving cloud became Mr. Jar.

Mary gave a low cry when Father Jar took her out of the water. She had only disturbed the weeds under which a toad lay asleep.

The toad dreamed of snakes.

On the way home Mr. Jar talked about squirrels and nuts. He carried a stick in his hand.

The old man made himself at home at once. Though he was so tall the low room suited his presence. He sat down beside the fire.

Presently James Gillet came in. He sat down dejectedly, taking very little notice of Mr. Jar.

" I never heard in the village that you had returned to Madder," he said, " and I have come straight home from the church."

Old Jar warmed his hands at the fire and chuckled.

" I never go near a church," Mr. Jar remarked. " But I met Naughty Nellie by the well, and Tom Button called to me.   While on the hills I was hidden by a cloud of mist."

Mary looked at the old man with pity ; she noticed his soaked rags, as wet as hers.

" You must be wet through," she said timidly.

The old man looked into the fire.

Mary, though sad at heart herself, wished to cheer him.

"Silly Button always said you would come one day ; he believes in you, you know " ;—Mary smiled— "and I'm sure Minnie Cuddy will be glad to see you.   Besides Minnie there's Mrs. Summerbee too. Only the other day she said : 'Oh, if Uncle Jar were here, he'd love this apple jelly ; I will give him a whole pot for himself when he does come."

" All Madder belongs to Farmer Mew, now," said James Gillet.

Father Jar sat beside Mary, holding her hand.

Suddenly Mary Gillet began to weep.   While she sobbed her hair fell loose and hung over her face.

When she grew quieter, Father Jar stooped over her and wiped the tears from her eyes with her hair.

*   *   *

Mr. Jar rose to go.   When he stepped out into the night a low moaning came from far away ; it was the wind awakening again.

The wind came and moaned through all the empty places in Madder; it moaned in Farmer Mew's barns; it moaned in the bare leafless elms.

Mr. Jar moved with the wind.

He stood in the Madder lane and waited. He appeared to know all that was happening in Madder. Old Jar expected Minnie Cuddy to come by.

Though Minnie Cuddy lived in Love Cottage, she had no love for Farmer Mew. She did not like the way he had treated Mary Gillet. Minnie was willing in a womanly way to help any man, but she allowed that others had a right to think differently upon this subject. Minnie considered Mary as the sort of a girl who should be decently married. Farmer Mew had made Mary's case a bad one.

"Well," said Minnie, speaking to her best china teacup, "well, I suppose I must go to Mr. Mew's. I don't want to be turned out of my home. Love Cottage suits me so well, and Mr. Billy is not quite so nervous as he used to be; besides, there's Andrew Corbin, who smiles sometimes. I'm sure I ought to stay." Leaving her light burning so that it might lead any poor traveller who passed, Minnie Cuddy, wearing her warmest coat, hurried along the Madder lane. She all but ran into Mr. Jar.

"Oh," she said with a little scream, "I thought you were John Soper."

"There is no hurry," said Mr. Jar in a kind tone. "I am going to Farmer Mew's too, so we may as well walk together."

"You must come to Love Cottage," she said, "and I will give you some new-laid eggs; even though it's winter now, you know, my white hens lay."

"We will go to Farmer Mew's first," said Mr. Jar, allowing the lady to hold his arm.

At that moment they heard a voice calling by the Madder well. It was Mad Button.

"Wold Jar be come, wold Jar be come," the voice called.

"Who be wold Jar ? " the voice asked itself.

"'E be the leaf that do drift in the wind. 'E be the cloud that do cross the moon at night-time. 'E be the stone that a poor man do take up in road to throw at 'is dog. 'E be the pond weeds where do bide the wold toad. 'E be the bastard child before 'tis born. Wold Jar be come."

Tom Button's calling was answered by a laugh near to the well. The laugh came from Naughty Nellie.

Minnie Cuddy and Mr. Jar began to walk through the darkess.

"John Soper makes such beautiful fowl-houses," Minnie Cuddy said.

"And Andrew Corbin ? " asked Jar.

"Oh, he doesn't make anything at all."

"Well, there's Mr. Billy."

"Mr. Billy helps me with my accounts sometimes," answered Mrs. Cuddy coyly. "He counts up how much I get for my eggs."

"You are a good woman, Minnie Cuddy," said Father Jar.

"Oh no, I'm not," Minnie answered, "I'm very bad."

They reached Mr. Mew's door. Mr. Jar knocked. While they waited for the door to be opened, Mr. Jar walked round his stone three times.

The visitors entered Mr. Mew's house.

Farmer Mew had expected Mrs. Cuddy. He had drawn the sofa up to the fire and had placed a bottle of wine and glasses upon the table.

Minnie Cuddy looked at these preparations with approval. After all, Farmer Mew was a man.

"I am come too," said Father Jar.

"What do you want here?" Mr. Mew asked. "Have you come to steal?"

"Yes, I am the thief," said Mr. Jar, "the thief that comes in the night."

Mrs. Cuddy wished herself in Love Cottage.

"May I go?" she asked Farmer Mew.

Farmer Mew did not answer, but Mr. Jar spoke.

"Minnie," he said, in a tone that a father would use to a child, "go to James Gillet and tell him to harness a horse from Mr. Mew's stable and to take a light wagon and to load up his furniture ready for departure. By the time all is ready I will come to him."

Mrs. Cuddy looked nervously at Farmer Mew as though she expected him to contradict this new master's order. But the farmer remained with his eyes fixed upon the floor, reminding Minnie at the moment of a tree that is partly cut through and leans a little before it falls. Mrs. Cuddy looked at the sofa and the wine and sighed a little, but she went all the same.

She was frightened; she wondered why old Jar had

called himself a thief. "Of course, tinkers are often thieves," thought Minnie. As she walked down the lane she decided that she would treat Mr. Jar very well and let him eat of all the good things that she had, so that he should have no temptation to steal anything.

In the lane she came upon Mad Button. Tom came near to her and whispered in her ear. "Where be wold Jar a-walking to?"

Minnie Cuddy pointed to the light that burned brightly in the farmer's room.

"'Tisn't there wold Jar be gone, be it?" asked Tom.

"Yes," said Minnie nervously, "he's in there, but I have a message to give to Mr. Gillet, so I mustn't stay. To-morrow, Tom, if you come to Love Cottage you can have some dinner."

Mrs. Cuddy disappeared into the darkness.

Tom Button couldn't take his eyes from the light that shone from the farmer's window. He drew near to it. Now and again as he moved he looked up at the sky. The driven clouds opened as he looked and left a narrow clear space in the heavens. Tom saw no star.

"True enough," he muttered to himself, "I do know now that Jar's star be come down."

Mad Button cautiously entered Farmer Mew's garden. He knew that Jar's stone was only a yard or two from the window.

Tom climbed upon the stone and looked in. What he saw in the room frightened him, so that he crouched down upon the stone and began to talk to it as though the stone could hear.

" Do 'ee mind what I do say," whispered Tom, " 'twasn't I that did move thee, 'twas Farmer Mew."

Button peeped again. Farmer Mew's lamp shone as never lamp had shone before in the farmer's house. But though bowed down Mew still faced Mr. Jar.

Father Jar looked at him sternly, though not with anger.

Mew straightened himself and spoke, but too low for Tom to hear what he said. He appeared by his gestures to be ordering Jar out of his house. Then, as it seemed to Tom, Mr. Jar stretched out his hand over the table and took up the decanter of wine and poured out a full tumbler.

"Wold Jar be thirsty," whispered Mad Button to the stone.

But Jar did not drink. He dipped two fingers into the glass, and leaning forward he wrote upon the table.

Farmer Mew raised himself to his full height. On a side table near to him there was a heavy Bible. He took the book up as though to cast it at Mr. Jar, who still stooped, writing with the wine upon the table. But Farmer Mew's arms had lost the power to strike, and the book fell to the floor.

Mr. Mew stood with his teeth clenched, and in his might he cursed Jar.

Tom Button looked at Mr. Jar. The tinker had covered his face with his hands. Tom thought he wept.

" Poor Jar be a-crying," he whispered. " Poor Father Jar ! "

Mad Button looked at Mew. The figure and

the aspect of the man were terrible. He stood as though he were resisting to the uttermost a huge force. With every sinew he fought Jar.

Mad Button slipped down from the stone. He went out into the lane. But even there his crazed imagination could not resist the pull of such exciting events. He came nearer to the garden and hid in a safe hedge, but this time at some distance from Jar's stone. Soon he saw the tinker leave Mr. Mew's. Jar walked as a man does who has suffered defeat. His head was bowed low as though he sorrowed— and now that he was gone the light in the room shone less bright.

Tom Button began to feel sleepy ; he closed his eyes. Soon he was awakened by the sound of a pick-axe. Mr. Mew's room was still lit up, and Mr. Mew was digging under Jar's stone. He had already made a large hole. Tom watched. Farmer Mew shovelled out some more earth from under the stone. He then went round to the back of his house, but soon returned pushing a large barrel. He rolled the barrel into the hole that he had made and, standing back a little, he broke the top of the barrel through with his pick.

"Farmer be giving drink to stone," thought Tom.

Mr. Mew went into the house.

Tom crept from his hiding-place and ran to the stone ; he wondered if there really was beer in the barrel. Taking a little of the contents of the barrel in his hand, he returned to his hiding-place rather mournfully. In his hand he held soft black stuff like coal-dust.

"What be Farmer Mew a-doing?" he said to himself.

Mr. Mew did not stay in the house long. "He must," Tom thought, "have gone out of the back door," for he came to the stone again by another path, carrying this time some dry sticks and straw. This fuel he heaped upon the barrel. After doing so Mr. Mew paced up and down before the stone.

Mad Button closed his eyes again.

CHAPTER XXII

WHILE Mr. Mew was preparing to blow up Jar's stone, a wagon loaded with furniture was standing before Mrs. Patch's cottage.

The furniture was James Gillet's. Jar, the tinker, helped Mary to climb into the wagon.

James Gillet took a place beside Mary, for he had learned to do the will of Father Jar.

Father Jar led the horse on. They went through the Madder lanes and slowly climbed the hills.

They reached the top of the Madder Hills.

The gorse shadows lay very still, as though they prayed.

The wagon moved in a very great stillness, while behind it there was the roar of a mighty wind.

Mary nursed a kitten in her lap, who purred contentedly.

The wagon rumbled on through Mr. Pye's lanes and past his great barns and houses.

Mr. Pye's shepherd was out with his flocks, for it was lambing time. The shepherd heard the wagon go by and hurried to the gate in order to see who it was. His lame leg prevented him reaching the gate in time. He blamed the moon.

The wagon went on. It left the lands owned by Mr. Pye and passed over a wide heath. Again it climbed some more hills and went through the silent street of a little town. The town clock struck four in a sad tone, as though it thought the winter's night would last for ever.

They still went on, and the sweet scents of the night met them as they travelled. They came to a river that passed sleepily through some peaceful meadows. They crossed the river by a stone bridge, and the wagon dipped into a cloud of dust.

But still Father Jar led the horse on.

During the night Mary slept a little; but when the horse stopped to drink at a shallow brook that ran over the road, she awoke.

The morning was still dim and half-awake. She found herself looking at a cow who was standing beside the wagon and drinking from the brook as the horse was. The cow had a thin string tied round its neck. Mary's eyes followed the string to see who was holding it. The string was held by an old woman who wore a black shawl and a summer straw hat trimmed with flowers. The old woman was talking to Mr. Jar and proudly watching her cow drink.

" T'other beast be dead," she was saying; " 'twas its leg that killed en, and now there be only this one to milk."

Jar led the horse on. A frightened blackbird flew across the road. They passed by a cottage completely covered with ivy. Through the ivy leaves a grey head appeared.

"Thee bain't Farmer Spenke, be 'ee?" the head inquired. It nodded in a friendly way, and as it disappeared it called out, "No, I do see thee bain't."

The next thing that appeared alive in the road was a little pig. The pig fancied that all the world was after it, and ran up a side lane grunting and rustling the dead leaves.

Farther on there were large green bushes by the side of the road of a kind Mary had never seen before, and before the travellers the road began to open like a book of pictures.

"Round the next turning there may be another little pig or a cottage," thought Mary.

They turned the corner and met a man carrying a roped bundle of straw. He looked up at Mary in such a cunning inquisitive sort of way from under his bundle that she laughed aloud.

The next thing she saw was a heap of large stones by the wayside, and an old man standing beside them with a hammer in his hand who looked at the stones as though he counted them.

As soon as the wagon came by him he stopped counting the stones and peered up at Gillet's furniture. "Be thee from Pidden Gap?" he asked the table.

Mary laughed again because of all these strange new beings. But still Jar led the horse on. . .

*　　*　　*

In God's Madder Tom Button still slept under the hedge near to Mr. Mew's house.

The night had grown very still; the winds that

had raged in Madder were quiet; the clouds hung low and heavy but very still.

Farmer Mew walked in Madder. He wanted to see some of his possessions for the last time. He climbed the gate into the meadow where the herd of milch-cows were sleeping. He heard their breathing. In the midst of them lay a great bull. He called the beast by name, but the bull gave no heed to him.

The farmer left the herd and passed on to the sheepfolds. The sheep too were sleeping, for none of all his possessions would watch their master during his last agony.

Would nothing wild meet him in the night? Was there no demon in Madder to rage as he raged? Was there no tortured one who dared to curse Jar and could die in the daring?

Mr. Mew remembered the Squibbs. Why should his slaves sleep so snug under their thatch when their master was abroad. They should be at the plough. What though the night be dark. Why should they idle?

Mr. Mew went to their house. He beat at the door with his fist. All was silent within. He might as well have beaten the grass above their graves for all the notice they took of him.

Mew left the Squibbs and went to Mrs. Patch's cottage where the Gillets lived. All was quiet there too. Perhaps Jar was asleep there, who could tell? He would smoke him out, this old wandering beggar, for hasn't a man a right to set fire to his own?

Mr. Mew set a light to the thatch. The eaves smouldered first, then caught fire A tongue of flame lit up the night.

Farmer Mew laughed.

Here was a slave who could give him back word for word, answer for answer. Here was one as wild as he, one he could laugh with in the night, a pretty playmate.

Those sleeping Squibbs, those tame kine and silly sheep, what had he to do with them? Here was one who could roar and make the black clouds glow red. Could he not burn Jar with fire?

All the village still slept, and Farmer Mew walked in his own garden again. He took the path to Jar's stone. On his way he met a company of brown rats that were hurrying from their holes near the stone. Instinct had told them to flee.

Farmer Mew laughed. He stood upon the stone and cursed Jar.

The black clouds in the sky were beginning to grow grey, for the dawn was near.

Farmer Mew lit the dry straw that he had placed over the barrel of gunpowder.

He stood upright upon the stone and cursed Jar. . . .

*   *   *

One reason that Mad Button had for staying out all that night was his mother. At teatime Tom's mother had named work again, so that Tom was unwilling to go home.

When he left the cottage he told his mother that he was sure to pick up something in Madder. " If one looked about," he said, " one could always pick

up something from the ground.   Stars fell sometimes
and pennies. . . . ”

*   *   *

Mad Tom awoke thinking that the end of the world
had come.   He had gone to sleep on his back, but awoke
on his face.

An immense cloud of smoke hung over Farmer
Mew's house.   Something fell from the sky beside
Tom.

Mad Button stooped and picked up the thing that
had fallen.   It was Farmer Mew's left leg.

Grey light was beginning to come in the sky.

“ Poor Farmer Mew,” said Tom softly, “ 'ave a-
lost 'is leg.”

Mad Button felt both his own legs to see if they
were safe.

“ But 'tisn't a leg that I do want,” said Tom, and
went his way, thanking Mr. Jar for his gift, though he
did not need it.

> *There I met an old man*
> *Who would not say his prayers ;*
> *I took him by the left leg,*
> *And threw him down the stairs.*

G

HESTER DOMINY

TO
DAVID GARNETT

CHAPTER I

ST. LUKE'S BELLS

OUTWARDLY the sound of St. Luke's bells touched nothing in the town of Eveleigh. Inwardly they touched certain human motions, motions that became intensified on the seventh day, and then died away to a mere nothingness in the week. They were not quiet bells and they were not too noisy; they were meant to be what they were—mere sound.

The sound they made was ugly. It was as far from true music as any sound of bells could be. They were intended to be rung in this dull fashion, in order to be as near as possible like the dull church wherein they were hung.

No other path in life was left for these tuneless bells. They were the chief bells in Eveleigh because they so exactly expressed the religious effort of the town. But they had their place, they performed a part, they condoned a usage.

In the dreary monotony of the town life, they exceeded the most forlorn hope of Eveleigh. Their purpose was death in life, to be dead sound was their mission.

One could hear them or one could let their sound alone. It was quite easy to walk along the front, as though there was no such thing as a church bell in the world, even when they were ringing at their loudest.

You could lie at your ease in the summer gardens, and watch at your will the white frocks and summer sashes of the girls, and take no thought of the bells, that might be, for all you care, ringing at the bottom of the sea.

But think as you might about them, they still would ring in the steeple of St. Luke's in order to remind Eveleigh of the Sunday children.

Do not mistake me. I do not mean those dainty petted ones that run so gaily in the streets, but those other ones whose minds were toned down under the bells, and who were taught in the St. Luke's Sunday School by Hester Dominy.

Yes, however hard it is to believe the fact I am stating, there were children that attended St. Luke's Church on the Sabbath day.

There were also old women. In the old women's ears the bells sounded, and moved them along. Those who had once other thoughts in their minds, in times past, now with black books and black bonnets passed in under the bells.

To walk along the pavement when they rang, meant that one crossed off in gloomy ink all one's youth and gladness, and took up instead a meagre covering of dull sound as a vestment suitable to steps that go down to the pit.

To fall in complete tune with the bells compelled a gloomy tone of mind, a sad drooping of vitality, a passing away from intense life, a drifting downwards, a carrying of one's soul in a black book.

It is necessary for us to pry and to peep, and to look under a good many other matters, in order to see what really went on when those bells rang. If we take the surface of Eveleigh merely, we shall see nothing. Upon the surface of the town other things mattered. There was the sunshine on the roofs, there were the red fronts of the old Georgian houses, there were the waves splashing in the sea.

This was the surface of Eveleigh.

There were also the usual sounds, the laughter of sailors, the fanciful chatter of young people, the whistle of a steamer.

To the ordinary person there existed no such thing as a church bell.

The surface of Eveleigh never heard them, the surface of Eveleigh had other things to think about. To follow the sound of St. Luke's bells one has to go deep down and below the surface. One has to dip into the dim places, wherein the human mind is illuminated only by lights that come from afar.

The merry thoughts, the holiday thoughts we dig through, they are not hard to move, they lie shallow. Even your friend that you are to meet to-night by the town clock, we must pick below him. And the lady that you saw yesterday in the gardens, we will pass her by. We will follow the bells. We will approach the matter of the bells by a side lane, a by-alley.

To Eveleigh the bells were as nothing, to the ferry-men nothing, to Mr. Pardy, the people's grocer at the stores, nothing—unless pure boredom—but to Hester Dominy they meant a great deal.

To find out what they meant to Hester we must delve below the waves of the sea, below the laughter of folly, below the call of the crier, below the usual town noises.

From childhood Hester's soul had been fed upon

the bells, their ringing had been her food, their tolling
her drink. She heard them always. She lived within
their sound.

Hester Dominy was the interpreter of the bells of
St. Luke's.

Hester knew more about the bells than anyone
else had ever known ; she was their sister ; in her alone
they rang harmoniously. When she combed her silky
brown hair, the comb moved to their sound. As her
youthful limbs moved in the street, her feet rang upon
the pavement like the bells.

The bells had always been her life and she was
theirs. She mingled her hours with their sound, and
to her seeming all the world was touched by the sadness
of their empty clang.

Through Hester Dominy the sound of the bells
reached to her following—the St. Luke's school-
children.

Without Hester Dominy these odd out-of-the-way
imps of the town would have been dead and unnoticed
by any human being, here or hereafter. They would
have been nowhere existent save as mere stones in the
street, mere mites in the cheese. The bells rang in
Hester, Hester created life in the children. The
members of the St. Luke's Sunday School were children, so one supposes, though in truth they were
more like the echo of the bells. They might each
have been a little fly above the clapper, or else a small
portion of dust in the belfry.

One may take it for granted that none of the fashionable people who moved in the streets of Eveleigh, and
who sometimes even went to St. Luke's Church, had

ever seen or heard of these impish school-children. Neither is it likely that they had either seen or heard of Hester Dominy.

No fashionable person would have thought it possible that the sounds of the bells could so enter into the life of the town as to march two by two from a back-street Sunday School to the low back forms of St. Luke's Church.

And now for a word in season.

In order to find a blind alley one has first to go through the wide streets, and then take the dingiest turning we can see, and from the turning dip lower into the slums and so on.

This we will do. We follow our clue, we go down until at last we reach the echo of St. Luke's bells, the place of the echo.

And now for the division.

We will divide into two portions the congregation who attended St. Luke's Church; we will divide them into the initiated and the uninitiated.

Hester Dominy was one of the initiated: she knew the bells.

CHAPTER II
BACK SEATS

HESTER DOMINY walked in her usual quiet manner by the side of the children.

The St. Luke's Sunday School was marching to Church.

In Hester's soul the bells were ringing. People

passed, hardly looking ; the children shuffled moodily
on and Hester listened.

The bells had taught Hester so much wisdom;
they had, by dint of their monotonous ringing, made
her tire of her own prettiness, they had coated her
soul with an iron substance. The bells had led
her into a blind alley from whence there is no turning.
They had dimmed her light, they had increased her
darkness, they had only left a little opening in her
heart for love to breathe.

*   *   *

And this breathing-place they had hidden with a
heavy cloak. Hester had all the seductive allure-
ments of youth and girlhood. Her figure was charming, but even when before the glass, she did not think
of her whiteness and beauty, she thought only of the
bells. They had set their dull sound upon her ripe
lips instead of merry kisses.

Hester walked on slowly with the children.

The day was silent, the atmosphere calm and
quiet, and the bells sounded more than usually loud.

The ferrymen at the Quay thrust their hands deeper
into their pockets and their pipes deeper into their
mouths. Mr. Thomas said that he expected a storm.

It was Hester's custom to take the children very
early to the service at St. Luke's.

The Rev. Mr. Haysom, whose importance in our
story is due to his being the friend of Mr. Earley, of
Enmore, did not wish the children to delay the entrance
of the other worshippers at St. Luke's. Good man
that he was—as one would expect from his being a
friend of Mr. Earley's—he saw no reason why his

livelihood as a clergyman should deprive him of food. His customers, as we must mentally call them, did not like to be touched by the children when they entered the church.

They had their reasons.

The outward troubles of Mr. Haysom had always hemmed him in and prevented him doing as he wished in the world, but he had always felt the impossibility of trying, even, to be as good as his friend, Mr. Earley.

Mr. Haysom could face no one's dislike ; he knew he was never meant to be a martyr. He felt it was not for him to alter or disturb any custom that ruled in the parish.

The St. Luke's school-children sat at the very back of the church upon low forms.

The church-cleaners—noticeably for those who sat near—left the forms alone when they cleaned the church : there was no chance of a sixpence being dropped there.

Mr. Haysom tried not to think about the children, the curate tried not to think about them, the sidesmen never thought about them at all. No doubt every one believed that the children were very well seen to in the hands of Hester Dominy and the bells.

Mr. Haysom, who lacked the realistic outlook that helped Mr. Earley in his duties, almost came to believe that Hester, through some magic art, actually turned the wayside stones into Sunday School children. Why they were all girls he never tried to understand. He knew he could never think things out like his friend.

Those almost too simple words, "Suffer little children," Mr. Haysom passed softly by, hoping at the same time that the Divine Master would realize how impossible it was for him, a poor priest, who liked brown bread, to make the Pharisees of his church understand their meaning.   Mr. Haysom knew his limitations ; he was not Mr. Earley.

Hester Dominy sat upon a chair near the forms. When the time came for kneeling, she gently placed her knees upon a small hassock ; this hassock she carefully placed under her chair after the service. During the sermon she would often look at the two rows of children who were in her charge.

When they waited for the service to begin, a strange feeling of unreality was wont to hang about Hester. She appeared to be enveloped in a dull-coloured smoke ; the smoke was the children ; it took its colour from the sound of the bells.

No one ever looked at Hester or her charges.   The rich well-fed people and their families walked into the upper pews.   No well-to-do child ever sat upon those back forms near to Hester.

The difference was plain ; between the forms and the pews there was a wide gulf.   Mr. Haysom thought, hoped even, that Hester was the bridge ; the kindly mothers of the other pretty children thought of her as merely a prison warder.

The rich children were like the gay town ; the poor children were like the ugly bells : no one thought of the bells, and no one looked at the Sunday School children.

In the blind alley of Eveleigh dwelt these poor

Church children ; the keeper of the alley was Hester
Dominy.

There was no love lost between the Church and
these children. The children hated the bells, and
the bells hated the children, and each side of the hatred
strove to annoy Hester Dominy.

And here was a battle that no one watched—it was
a battle in a blind alley.

The forms at the back of St. Luke's Church were
as uncomfortable as any forms could be : the girls had
to lean forward in order to ease their tired backs.
Mr. Haysom was sorry. He would have liked the
children to have had easy chairs, but Mrs. Pardy, the
churchwarden's wife, thought otherwise. And Mr.
Haysom was no Mr. Earley to correct her faults.

CHAPTER III
RATS

THE service over, the Sunday School children of
St. Luke's followed the rest of the congregation
out of the church. Once outside they marched down
two streets under the care of Hester Dominy and
then they broke up and departed, or, to put the
fact of their deliverance more truly, they dissolved.

Where they went to Miss Hester Dominy never
knew, no one ever knew. Mr. Haysom, who had
indeed learnt from his friend how a parish really ought
to be managed, had wisely entered all their names in a
book, and Hester used to mark mystic numbers upon
cards that concerned the children. What the signs
she marked were all about Hester never knew.

The children neither laughed nor cried as they moved out of the church, which fact alone, if one thinks of the uncomfortable forms, was enough to class them as child-shadows bereft of proper feelings. As they walked they murmured, and that was all. When the time came to disappear they simply went. They stopped like the bells, the sound of their murmurings faded into thin air, they were gone.

Miss Hester Dominy walked to her home.

There were two ways that Hester could go : she could take the garish way along the front, or she could go the shadowed way along the back-street. Hester always chose the back-street, and walked near to the houses. She had walked thus in the same way every Sunday for years. She could remember when she was very young—and she now almost despised the remembrance—that she used to step along upon the very edge of the pavement, balancing herself prettily as she walked. She now utterly disregarded such childlike wantonness and walked under the houses.

The bells went with her ; they had guided her always under those very houses and away from the grand parade. With the dull tone of those bells in her heart she could never face the smiling young men. Hester knew that her meaning to herself was a very different thing to what her meaning would seem to be to the young men. Her name was written upon the bells, and was never carved upon the town trees by the young men. Hester thought of herself as mere iron sound.

She walked slowly along the dreary pavement under the houses.

Old women passed her, those old spider-like women

whose trade, like Hester's own mother's, had to do with the visitors. A little pert boy upon roller skates brushed Hester's frock. One or two aged faces peeped from the windows.

Hester Dominy reached No. 3, Ridgeway Street, and opened the door. There was no pleasant fresh-scented gladness about Hester's home. She smelt burnt cabbage and pork.

Mrs. Dominy sat in the kitchen that was their usual living-room, watching a saucepan. Her white face and heavy flapping cheeks had become a part of the cooking. She was like the sausage in the story that stirred the soup from its own body. She stared with glassy soupy eyes into vacancy, in the vacancy there lived for her an eternity of eaten dinners. The lady had disbanded all her senses except the sense that smelt the burnt cabbage.

As soon as Hester entered, Mrs. Dominy began to speak, though she still looked at the saucepan and still drank in the odour of the soaked cabbage and boiling pork. The words came greasily from her mouth, without emphasis, as though all her thoughts had been soaked like the greens; her words had a culinary sound. They escaped out of her mouth as the evil odour of the burnt cabbage escaped out of the saucepan.

"The rat," she said. Hester placed her prayer book upon the table. "I've seen the rat; Antony Dine lets the rats live, 'e don't mind what 'arm the rats do to us."

"But, mother, how do you know that the rat comes from Mr. Dine's house?" Hester asked wearily.

" ' E never kills a rat, 'e never kills a rat, 'e saves the rats." Mrs. Dominy panted, she was not used to saying so much.

Hester sat down upon a wooden chair near the closed window. Mrs. Dominy moved from her place. As she moved she disturbed the odour of burnt cabbage, that now more than ever pervaded the room.

Reaching up with her hands; Mrs. Dominy took from a side shelf a silver teapot; she placed the teapot upon the table and began to rub at it with a cloth; while she did so she still looked at the saucepan.

Hester sat silent for a while, and then she said suddenly :

" I hate the bells, mother ! "

Mrs. Dominy dropped the duster and looked at her daughter, her eyes becoming more than ever like the eyes of a stewed fish.

" I hate the bells," Hester said again.

Mrs. Dominy sat down upon her chair near to the saucepan, and placing the teapot upon her lap she slowly rubbed it up and down.

" ' E 'adn't got those springs, and you couldn't 'ear what 'e preached about."

" Why, of course he hasn't springs, mother ; Mr. Haysom has his own teeth."

The stewed duality of Mrs. Dominy's mind proved that she understood the higher phrases of philosophy. Two ideas had bitten into her mind like maggots into cabbage—rats and false teeth.

" Don't you believe it," Mrs. Dominy said more

sharply. "Mr. Haysom can't afford springs, that's why 'e 'asn't got them, and 'e can't preach proper without springs, poor man. You must tell 'im to 'ave springs put in, 'Esther; I'll show 'im 'ow easy they are to manage if 'e comes to me."

"Don't be so foolish, mother; you know very well Mr. Haysom hasn't false teeth."

Mrs. Dominy took the saucepan off the fire; she allowed the subject of teeth to soak into her mind again.

She sat down and rubbed the teapot. Her cheeks moved, she was speaking again.

"The rat ran along the wall. Antony Dine saves the rats, and she, she, what is she with all 'er 'ouses? Mrs. Dine, she's a nice one, it's always 'ouses with 'er. Only yesterday, when I stood at the back door looking out for the rat, I could 'ear she in the back road talking about those 'ouses."

Hester frowned, her full lips pouted; she said nothing. In her soul she was trying to break away from a cruel evil spell, the spell of the bells.

CHAPTER IV
A CHANCE FOR HESTER

THE evil spell of the bells hung around Hester Dominy. It seemed to her impossible that she should have any other kind of life than the life the bells gave her; her life was their life, and her soul theirs.

The bells of St. Luke's were her real parents: they fed her with grey shadows, grey sound, grey gloom;

they crept into her body by every pore ; they muffled their sounds in her being ; they drank of her blood.

The dim stuffy kitchen, her mother's fishy eyes and floppy cheeks were all served up in the sound ; they were in the dish that the bells gave to Hester. When her mother had springs made for her false teeth, the very springs became part and parcel of the bells. The bells never left Hester alone ; they rang on, on, on in her life ! The bells gave the note to the Sunday rat as he ran up the wall ; they helped to shine the teapot that had been given to Hester by the clergy of St. Luke's. The bells became the dinner of pork and cabbage that was ready to be eaten upon the plates.

Hester saw her own life reflected in these sodden appearances. The true glass was there, the false was over the mantelshelf. The false reflected something quite different to what the real glass pointed to. The girl Hester, the woman, so rounded off, so waiting, was utterly dulled over by the life that she led, and was made to love, by the grim process of necessity. Why did the glass upon the mantelshelf lie so. Why did it lie ? To what natural purpose did it lie ? Hester did not know.

There were the rat, the teeth, the teapot ; there were the school-children on the one hand—and Hester. On the other hand there was a Hester too—but so different. Her life that touched the pavement with her Sunday shoes—she was aware of its existence. And beyond the sound of the bells she knew nothing —save only one little fancy.

Mrs. Dominy was still rubbing the teapot, for

H

the moments of living passed slowly in that kitchen.

"Mr. Haysom ought to have those springs," she muttered as she rubbed. "He can't afford them, that's 'ow it is with 'im."

"Don't be foolish, mother," said Hester.

Mrs. Dominy's watery eyes looked at the dinner table. She raised her white face to Hester's.

"'E spoke to you, didn't 'e?"

"Oh, I don't know, mother."

"But the teapot, 'e gave you the teapot; every one subscribed for it, even Mr. Pardy gave something, and all because you taught so long in the Sunday School." Mrs. Dominy smiled. "You 'ave only to go on teaching and 'e will want to give you 'imself, or else there is 'is friend, Mr. Earley." Mrs. Dominy's face bent like a white sickly moon over Hester. Her dull eyes showed a queer combination of disgusting maternal lasciviousness and a natural love for her child.

Seeing no reply in Hester's look, Mrs. Dominy dropped into her own chair again. Her thoughts slid back to their usual trend.

"Antony Dine don't kill the rat; the thing climbs up the wall; it's a great brown rat, a rat with a long tail."

"Of course the rat has a long tail, mother."

Hester placed the dishes for the meat and cabbage upon the table.

"Then you 'ad better tell Mr. 'Aysom to 'ave springs. 'E won't 'ave to pay at once for springs. Don't 'e look at you when 'e preaches? No, no, I suppose 'e don't, because 'e must be afraid of 'is teeth dropping out.   Yes, it's a pity Antony Dine saves the rat."

Hester sat down at the table ; the cabbage was horrible, she could not touch it ; she ate a little bread and. meat, that was all.

At half-past three there was a knock at the street door.

Mrs. Dominy shuffled out of the kitchen.

Hester still sat in the kitchen.   She heard Mr. Haysom's voice in the parlour, became mildly interested, and began to wonder what the Vicar of St. Luke's had called there for.

After waiting a little while Hester heard her mother's voice calling her.

Hester went into the little parlour.   Mr. Haysom shook her by the hand, and Hester fancied that she was shaking hands with the bells of St. Luke's.

Mr. Haysom inquired of Hester whether she would care to go to Enmore, a little village about ten miles from Eveleigh, to take the post of assistant teacher in the Church school.   Mr. Haysom explained that he had been asked by his friend Mr. Earley to find a suitable girl.   He said he had thought at once of Miss Dominy, who he knew would fulfil all the hoped-for expectations of his friend.

Hester had never heard before the sound of her life's bells breaking into so loud a clatter.   They burst into real tune like the birds.

If she had happened to hear that St. Luke's was struck by lightning and all the children burnt, she could not have felt more pleased.

She said quietly that she would be happy to go.

The sober bells still ruled.

The Vicar of St. Luke's opened the door himself and went out. Mrs. Antony Dine saw him in the street and said to herself, "What is 'e doing there, I wonder; there's always a girl where they clergy do go!"

Mrs. Dominy was so overcome by the visit that she still sat in the parlour, a room that she only frequented during the limited stay of any visitor.

Hester sat on the edge of the sofa nursing her own thoughts.

Even into the parlour there had filtered the afternoon smell of stale cookery. The woollen covering of the sofa, the silk cushions, had soaked up the odour; it remained in the hanging curtains and in the table-centre; the very glass in the window appeared to be beaded with the lingering perspiration of the midday meal.

The steps in the street sounded dull and heavy, as though they were clotted with the waste garbage from the dinners that had been eaten all along the row of houses.

"If only poor John had worn springs he would never have died," whimpered Mrs. Dominy

"But father died of consumption, didn't he, mother?"

The mother's thoughts had gone elsewhere.

"Mr. Earley's a widower," she said.

Hester moved from the sofa to the window; she was afraid the springs would come again into the talk. As a Sunday subject of conversation she preferred the rat.

CHAPTER V
HESTER'S FRIEND

THE next day Hester Dominy went to see her friend.

Hester's friend was the only matter of importance to her in Eveleigh beside the bells.

The two had grown up together in her life, the bells and her friend. They merged, they became almost as one sound; at times they quarrelled over her like a father and mother who each wants the greatest love from their child.

Through long hours of sitting in her stuffy home kitchen, Hester had heard the one and thought of the other. These two matters made the only sounds in her life—the bells and him.

He was the narrow aperture in her heart through which love breathed.

Hester Dominy went out into the street. She closed the door behind her. As she did so she saw her mother's white face peeping from behind the curtains that hung in the parlour. Hester went to No. 1, Ridgeway Street, and knocked. A lean old woman opened the door. Hester stepped in.

" How are you, Mrs. Dine ? " Hester asked cheerfully.

Mrs. Dine coughed impressively, as though she had saved up some very important information till that moment.

" Our new 'ouse," she began.

"You've surely never saved enough to buy another house ? " Hester inquired.

Mrs. Dine smiled. Her smile made her look horrible.

"Oh yes," she said, "we've bought another, and Antony's saving for the fourth."

Mrs. Dine looked greedily at Hester, as though she were a house to be bought. She then went into the kitchen and began to sweep. Hester knew her ways, and did not expect any welcome beyond the remarks about the houses. In the dim light of the back kitchen Mrs. Dine's sharp bare elbows protruded beyond the brush handle.

Hester walked upstairs. She opened the door of a back room and entered. This room was a tailor's workshop.

Antony Dine was sitting cross-legged upon the tailor's board working his machine. By his side were beeswax, thread, a tape-measure, a lit stove with an iron upon it, and scissors. About him were pieces and chips of stuff, and the atmosphere was thick with fluffy dust that rose up all around him as he worked.

The window of the room was tightly closed, and the cracks stuffed with pieces of cloth.

Antony Dine was a small grey man. When one watched him working, his personality would appear to fade away and to leave only the sense of eternal labour instead of anything really human. He was more like an ant or a bee than like a man.

"You'd better not stay here, Hester," Mr. Dine said as the girl entered. His head was bent over his work ; he was like a drudging goblin, and did not look at her when he spoke.

"You don't want me to stay, then ?"

"No." The machine quickened. "Why don't you go? Why don't you go?"

"You needn't be so cross, Mr. Dine."

"You had better go."

"Well, if you must hear it—I am going. I'm going into the country."

"Going soon?"

"Yes, next week."

The voices could only just be heard.

There was one sound in the room, the sound of the machine. It was a sound exacting and toilsome, a sound that filled every cranny of the room with the supreme dreariness of labour. The sound droned on as though eternal. It was of a heavy stone-like sound-substance. It pressed all goodness into the bare boards of life, it broke all gentle joys, it tore up harmless leisure by the roots, it rent all serenity to pieces, it dashed all hopes to the ground.

Hester Dominy watched the machine. Was it turning faster than it had ever turned before? Was the needle biting at the cloth more fiercely? Was the hand of the man who worked more closely clenched upon the handle of the machine?

"What did she say when you came in?"

Antony Dine had ceased to turn the machine, and was closely examining the trouser leg.

"Oh, she spoke about your houses. You know very well, Mr. Dine, that it's always about the houses that she talks."

Antony Dine took up the scissors : he was unpicking the leg that he had just sewn together. Hester looked at him with astonishment.

"What are you doing, Mr. Dine?" she asked.

"You can see what I'm doing."

"You are unripping all your work——"

"Yes, I've made a mistake."

"You—a mistake, Mr. Dine?"

"Yes, why not?"

"Why, you never do your sewing wrong."

"It's wrong this time."

He fixed the cloth into the machine again. Hester watched him. The evil noise began again as though it intended to grind all beauty into the dust with its dreary sound. Fluffy bits of cloth swam in the air of the room like feathery moths. They were the smoke of the incense that rose from this altar of labour.

Antony Dine went on working as though he were alone. Hester sat on a stool near to his board, and watched him; she was hoping that he would speak more kindly to her.

"You had better go out into the street," he said. "Why don't you go?"

"But I like to be here, Mr. Dine. I like to see you working."

"Work, do you speak of work? Work, my God!"

"Oh,"—Hester gave a little quick cry—"you've broken your needle."

The machine had stopped.

"What's she doing now?" Mr. Dine said quietly.

"She's sweeping the kitchen."

"What are you doing here?"

"Oh, I'm watching you."

"No you're not"—the man's voice was raised angrily—"you're watching toil, sweat and toil, eternal labour. It always goes on, on, on. It never stops, it's a God. And she sweeps the kitchen and talks of the houses, she sweeps and talks. Do you know what you've just seen me do?"

"Yes, break a needle, Mr. Dine."

"That's true. Now tell me how often you've sat upon that stool."

"Oh, hundreds of times. Why, I used to come and watch you working when I was six years old. I've come ever since then. I remember you sometimes used to let me have the beeswax to play with when I was a child. But since I've grown up, I've only watched you at work."

"Yes, you've always watched me working, that's true—now count those." Antony Dine reached under the board and picked up a bag filled with little chips of cloth. "Count those," he said, and without looking at Hester he busied himself about putting a new needle into the machine.

Hester obeyed.

The machine worked on, the minutes passed, the bits of fluff strayed about in the room; they were caught in the cobwebs in the corners. The tailor watched his work as though he were a part of the machine.

As soon as Hester had finished she looked up at him and waited.

After a few moments the machine stopped.

"There are one thousand three hundred and forty-five," Hester said.

"Yes, that's about right—and now add this"—
Antony threw to her a little chip of cloth.

Hester put it with the rest into the bag.

"You know now how many times you've sat
upon that stool—now go!"

"I will run in to say good-bye, Mr. Dine."

"I would much rather you kept away."

The machine hummed again.

Hester rose to go.

"Good-bye, Mr. Dine," she said, "I've liked
coming here."

Her words were lost in the noise of the machine.
Antony Dine did not look up at her; he merely with
deft fingers shifted the cloth under the machine and
turned the handle more rapidly.

Outside the door of the work-room, Hester found
Mrs. Dine sweeping the stairs.

"You mustn't forget to tell Mrs. Dominy," Mrs.
Dine said, as Hester passed her.

"What shall I tell mother?"

"Oh, about the new 'ouse we've bought; we 'ave
four 'ouses now and 'e's getting money for the
fifth."

Mrs. Dine held Hester by the arm. "See 'ow 'e
works," she said, "Sundays and weekdays—day and
night the machine goes. He never stops working."

Hester still heard the sound; it increased in volume,
it became all-powerful. The noise grew, it beat in
her heart as she entered the street. It became alive,
it became sad and sorrowful, it became like the
bells.

CHAPTER VI
NO REPLY

THE day before Hester's departure for Enmore she went to No. 1 Ridgeway Street in order to bid Antony Dine good-bye.

She found Mrs. Dine busy dusting the front room. Mrs. Dine at once began to talk of her houses.

"They are large 'ouses," she said. "One is let at 15s. a week and another at 12s. There'll be the fifth soon—don't forget to tell Mrs. Dominy!"

Mrs. Dine's bare elbows looked sharper than ever.

Hester went upstairs to the work-room. She knocked at the door. There was no answer. Inside there was only the noise of the machine.

Hester turned the handle and pushed. The door was locked.

"Please may I come in, Mr. Dine?" she called.

No reply came to her question; there was only the sound of the machine. Hester waited for a few moments before she turned away.

As she walked slowly down the stairs she touched her cheeks. Her cheeks were wet. At the bottom of the stairs she heard the voice of Mrs. Dine speaking to her.

"One 'ouse is let to a lawyer—a good tenant 'e be. "'Tisn't every woman in Eveleigh who can 'ave a lawyer paying rent."

Mrs. Dine grinned; she expressed in her grin the views of a world of greedy folk, all wishing to gain possessions and to overreach each other. All greed was echoed and re-echoed in Mrs. Dine's smile   It was conscious nature smiling in malice.

Hester walked out of the house.   Two young men passed her on the pavement ; they looked at Hester, but she took no notice.   Hester could only see a lone man sitting upon a tailor's board and working a machine.

She opened the door of her home and went up to her room to pack her trunk.

CHAPTER VII
MR. EARLEY

THE Rev. Albert Earley was digging in his Vicarage garden at Enmore.   Mr. Earley dug in his garden in order that he might dispel the gloom that had so sadly overcast his mind.   It was a mistake of his to think that the gloom had come because of the death of his wife, though she had in some ways kept his melancholy from him.

But in reality grief had been a new experience, a new sensation to Mr. Earley.   His sorrow had come to him in the midst of his usual daily experiences and there was excitement in the manner of its coming. Besides, to see one who was so lately in such pain quietly laid out—a marble figure—with hands crossed and sweet-smelling flowers all about her, was in itself a sacramental sign of blessedness.   And when Mr. Earley prayed by her bedside and called his God to witness that he would never marry again, he felt a tingling sensation all about him, as though he were assisting at the high festival of a saint's welcome in Heaven.

It was so easy for Mr. Earley to see it all in the dim mystic light of the drawn curtains, her dying so peacefully upon the bed. It was all done so quietly, the lady's soul passing like one of Mr. Earley's own happy dreams. The nurses had such gentle voices, and they spoke so like ministering angels. Death himself was almost like a kind nurse in clean starched linen who kindly came to give a helpful word.

Even the arrival of his wife's aunt brought to Mr. Earley the same proof of consolation, showing above all things the value to the world of old women. The aunt came in, or rather appeared, out of a closed carriage, and settled everything about the funeral so promptly, so convincingly. The good lady even took Mr. Earley by the hand and led him away from the graveside, into which grave he had been peeping, she feared, a little too long for his soul's good.

When the old lady went back to her London house, Mr. Earley felt how comforting her presence had been, because there was just that touch of worldliness about her that helped to bring his soul away from the unearthliness of it all into the daylight of more common things.

Mr. Earley expected to feel broken-hearted, and indeed he felt a curious sense of surprise that his friend, Mr. Haysom, who took the funeral, wasn't shedding as many tears as he himself was doing.

And then there were her clothes. He could not touch any of her garments without feeling an almost heavenly bliss. And when he gave her things away in the village, how indeed could he prevent himself from bursting into tears at each cottage door ? Of course, when he wept, the women to whom he gave the clothes looked at him with astonishment, as though they thought him utterly naked and foolish, so that when the clergyman had finished crying they hardly thanked him for the clothes.

The same well-paid elderly servants remained after Mrs. Earley's death, and however much Mr. Earley tried to fancy that there was a difference, the thick cream and breakfast porridge always tasted the same as of old.

It would not have been easy for Mr. Earley to explain why the lone clouds of melancholy had fallen upon him. He could not explain why.

He tried to persuade himself that his sadness had come owing to the love that he bore to his wife, but in his heart he knew very well that this was not the case.

Mr. Earley had never seen his wife as a girl, all her girlhood had been schooled out of her long before he saw her first.

The lady had died from a chill taken from the dampness of the grass upon which she had been incautiously sitting when out painting one October day. The chill had attacked her lungs with a sudden and vindictive malice, laying her very rudely at death's door and even carrying her quite through.

If some demon had whispered to Mr. Earley that he had not loved his wife he would have been most profoundly astonished, but for all that there was something in his soul that had never cared for her so very deeply—until she died.

After Mrs. Earley's death the bereaved husband applied himself to his parish work with all the soul that he possessed. In so doing he followed the advice of his friend, Mr. Haysom. He went about as he hoped and believed, doing good—and very naturally redoubled his efforts to get the folk of his village to come to church.

But alas, for his fair hopes ! The stagnation that always shrouds a country village—except for the funeral sermons—soon fell upon this one, and in desperate need of an outlet the good priest began very seriously to read the writings of St. Paul as he found them written in the Bible.

He found them unsatisfying.

Setting St. Paul aside, Mr. Earley began to read a translation of Dante, and was horrified to find that the very first company of the damned seen in Hell by the sombre-minded Italian would undoubtedly have included himself.

This illusion of the lost was the proper effect of the gloom that slowly but surely began to settle down upon the parish priest of Enmore.

Mr. Earley was honest ; he loved his friend, he hated the devil and the drink, and he saw almost tearfully that the abundance of little church matters that he spent his time in doing—the vicar of St. Luke's would have called it spade-work—in reality spelt the plain words, nothing at all.

Mr. Earley had gone abroad for three months after his wife's death and the priest from Shelton—the nearest village to Enmore—took charge of the services.

When Mr. Earley returned, he found everything exactly the same as when he went away. No one in the village had committed any very grave fault, and no one had left the tenor of his or her way to be over-virtuous.

In Enmore the same stagnant influence remained always the same, and, with the exception of the funerals, this influence was the people's master and the priest's master.

When, after his somewhat sadly-coloured holiday was over, the good man bestirred himself and gave the people a more than usually tearful sermon, the congregation only looked up at him in grave astonishment not unmixed with shame. They had only caught at some aside expression that was quite unimportant, so that they might carry something of the sermon outside in order to make fun of it, just as they made fun of old Betsey's shoes.

Mr. Earley now saw Enmore as being neither good nor evil, but only lost in just that apathy that filled the lives of the sad spirits who dwelt close inside the gates of Hell.

It was when he felt his failure so completely that Mr. Earley began to dig in his garden.

He began also to fear that true goodness was something impossible to get near, like a white star far up in the sky, or as a fair cloud that never rests in one shape, but is always changing its form in the upper airs.

It was at this period in his life's history that Mr. Albert Earley began to be a real trouble to the people of Enmore.

He turned reformer. He became more filled with zeal than Martin Luther or Mr. Johnson. He compelled the choir to turn to the East when the belief was being said, a manner of church behaviour that had never been used by the Rev. John Jassamy, the late Rector.

In doing so, Mr. Earley had but followed the advice of his friend, Mr. Haysom.

But he went still further. He shut up the inn. He represented to the magistrates that the inn was not necessary. He opposed the renewal of the licence, and won the case.

The magistrates closed the inn.

The good people of Enmore were troubled by such conduct; but they never complained.

Mr. Matterface, the evicted landlord of the hostelry, retired to a small Enmore cottage to brood over his woes. His old-time customers moped like sad un-nested owls in sad corners.

CHAPTER VIII
THE ENMORE POUND

THE Enmore Pound stood solitary, silent, and unused in the middle of the village, a relic of more stirring times. It consisted of four rather crumbling walls and a broken-down gate.

From the outside the Pound appeared to be a mere monument of old-time decay. It had no features to be admired. The architecture was crude. The bricks were rubble. It was a forgotten stagnation amongst buildings, a building that clung to its old

I

spot only because it could not fall to pieces any faster.

The inn had been shut for some weeks when a curious fact came to be noticed by the dogs and cats of Enmore that concerned the Pound.

The curious matter was that a well-trodden path had come into being leading into this old-time prison of strayed cattle.

It was a path not trodden by the beasts of the field, but by man.

The stray Enmore cats began to avoid the Pound.

The ways of men are always curious, but that anyone should have chosen the Pound as a resting-place was certainly a mystery that needs an explanation. Let the Enmore Pound tell its own story.

The Pound had been happily discovered by Mr. Poose, the shepherd, and not without a reason.

The manner of the discovery was as follows :

The Enmore Inn had been closed for some weeks. Cats frequented it, but no men. One day it chanced that Mr. Poose, the shepherd, drove a few sheep to the Eveleigh fair. It was a moonlight night when Mr. Poose returned. The shepherd was in luck, Mr. Warry, the dairyman, had given him a ride in his cart. On the way home Mr. Warry and Mr. Poose allowed the horse to feed by the side of the hedge. The two companions climbed through the hedge. They drank beer in a field. They found the bottles of beer in rabbit holes. This was Mr. Warry's wayside cellar. Mr. Poose secreted one of Mr. Warry's bottles in his coat pocket. They climbed through the hedge again and the cart moved on.

Beside the little Enmore brook Mr. Warry turned aside to pass through a field that led to his home. Shepherd Poose stood still and pondered. He wished for a snug corner wherein to drink his beer.

Passing over the little brook, Mr. Poose carried his bottle of beer into the Enmore Pound. Mr. Poose observed the four crumbling walls with interest.

The shepherd was tired ; he had risen at two o'clock that morning and wished to take his last drink in contentment and peace. Mr. Poose looked around him—the moon whitened one wall of the Pound. Jock, the dog, lay down in a corner and went to sleep.

The moon shone above. Mr. Poose felt lonely and inspired ; he looked up at the moon. He did not curse Mr. Earley—he blessed God.

The shepherd placed his bottle upon a stone in the middle of the Pound.

He saw consolation. Though Mr. Earley had shut the inn, Mr. Poose had opened another tavern. Mr. Poose looked at his sleeping dog.

" Thik dog do know more than thik parson," said Mr. Poose.

The shepherd began to place large stones around the walls suitable for seats.

Mr. Poose smiled under the moon because he had created a new inn.

After drinking his beer, Mr. Poose went to sleep with his head upon one of his stone seats. In the early morning he went to look after his sheep.

These important events all happened during the summer that preceded the opening of our story.

After Mr. Poose had looked to his sheep, he went

into the fields to help to make Farmer Hart's hay.

Mr. Poose felt pleased with his night's work.

"Thik parson Earley, 'e don't like they inns," he said sagely to Chipp, the rabbit-catcher, who was also helping in the same field. This remark seemed to lead nowhere, but Mr. Poose's smile went a very long way.

"'Tis they 'omen that 'ave done it," remarked Mr. Pike, the road-mender, who always blamed the women for every calamity.

"No, no, Pike, me lad, don't 'ee blame they 'omen," said Mr. Warry, the dairyman.

The haymakers laughed.

Mr. Warry, though married, was the Don Juan of Enmore. The opinions of Mr. Warry and Mr. Pike were wont to clash when women came up in the workaday conversations. They always agreed about pigs and ferrets, but about women they thought differently.

"I do know somethink," Mr. Poose said mysteriously as he turned the hay. Mr. Poose looked as though he knew. He was smiling and moved his fork thoughtfully.

"Thik shepherd, 'e do know," echoed Mr. Chipp.

When the day's work was over and the evening was come, Mr. Poose was seen to be slowly walking down the lane in the direction of the village Pound. In more than one respect the men of Enmore were like Farmer Hart's sheep: they followed the old rams. Mr. Poose often led his friends in this sheepish way.

Chipp, the rabbit-catcher, followed slowly in Mr. Poose's steps.

Chipp passed Mr. Pike's door.   Mr. Pike was at the moment giving a word of counsel to his wife; he looked up and saw Mr. Chipp go by.   Throwing out a last word at his wife, the road-mender stepped into the street to see where his friend was going.   He saw him enter the Pound.

Mr. Pike moved into the middle of the way and spoke to Dairyman Warry, who was employed at the moment in watching a girl cross a field.

"Where be going?" inquired Mr. Warry.

"To Pound," answered the road-mender, and proceeded thitherwards, accompanied by the dairyman.

CHAPTER IX

MR. MATTERFACE IS PLEASED

THAT very same evening the retired Mr. Matterface was walking with dismal steps up and down in front of the closed inn.

His new cottage was situated about a stone's throw away from his old home.

Mr. Matterface walked up and down with his head bent low to the ground.   He was looking back into the past; he was thinking of the days of his lowly kinghood; he was thinking of the merry evenings that were gone.

Mr. Matterface could see the mugs upon the table and the drinkers sitting around on the forms.   He could hear the old disputes that always used to be carried on between Pike and Warry about the women. He could hear the two doughty combatants make up the quarrel and turn to praising the pigs. He could hear the stories of Mr. Chipp and the laughter of the shepherd. But all was now over, for the windows of the inn were boarded up.

Mr. Matterface sighed dismally. His life had been one long, kindly, good-tempered listening. A listening that seemed to be able to provide each customer with thoughts to express. A listening that every evening was obliged, like fate, to sum up all, even when all wished to prolong the feast, in the one final and God-like word, "Time."

Mr. Matterface had a small pension. This was pressed upon him by Mr. Earley, "who felt," he said, "for the poor landlord's trouble." Mr. Matterface thought nothing of his pension; it was mere dirt to him. Mr. Matterface had a soul.

He had never, this old Enmore time-piece, lived by bread alone. His life had been enlivened by quips and jests, by joke and by banter. He was wont to live by merry country words, by polite social talk.

Mr. Matterface used mechanically to draw the drink and take the money, but his real interest was in the conversations that always went on.

It was now all over.

The sun-browned faces, the hoary hands, the homely tones of the well-known voices, were passed away from the landlord's ken. A fateful angel with a sword, in the shape of Mr. Earley, had thrown our honest Enmore Adam out of the garden of his tap-room into the empty and thirsty desert. Mr. Matterface had always loved life; he now began to hate it.

He had bread and butter to eat, he had tea to drink,

and yet he was thirsty and starving. He was getting thinner each day.

After walking a score or more times up and down past the closed inn, Mr. Matterface directed his weary steps towards the little Enmore brook ; the honest goodman wished to hear the melancholy sound of running water. Beside the little brook Mr. Matterface looked sadly into the water.

As he looked he listened.

Was he dreaming ?

Somewhere quite near to him he heard a conversation being carried on between two well-known voices. The talk was about women.

" Don't 'ee now say nothink again they 'omen "— Mr. Matterface recognized the voice of the dairyman —" vor where indeed would us men-volk be wi'out they 'omen ? I do a mind putting me arm around wone of their waisties only last Sunday in Meadow mead. She were a pretty maid too to catch 'old on."

" Don't 'ee tell me nothink more," said another hidden voice. " They 'omen-volk don't do no wone no good ; they be liars, they be rogues, they be stealing thieves——"

"No, no, John Pike, thee be wrong ; they bain't nothink so bad as thee do say, vor only yesterday I did take a pretty fair maiden into wold barn, and did kiss she's pretty lips, and will do same again, God willing."

" These both be wrong, both one and t'other of 'ee," came the peaceful voice of Mr. Poose, the shepherd. " But all same 'tis me wone belief that none of they 'omen be as good as me dog Jock, that do lie asleep in corner. 'E do thinkie, do me dog. An' never 'ave I met a 'oman that do thinkie. Maybe they 'earken catty-like and speak sour, but they don't thinkie like a dog they don't. Me dog do know when a sheep be lost, me dog do——"

Mr. Matterface looked this way and that. Was he dreaming ? Was he under a barrel with the beer running well into the big jug ? Was he handling the silver and the coppers ? Was he wiping with an old duster the bar-room table ?

Mr. Matterface wondered, had he gone mad ; would he want the next moment to bite his own finger ? The lane was empty, the brook trickled by. Except for the weird voices, the evening was unusually silent. The delicious scent of newly-made hay was in the air ; there was a stack not far away and a loaded wagon that awaited in a humble silence the haymakers of the morrow to unload its burden.

Mr. Matterface heard the sound of village voices. Mrs. Pike was talking to Mrs. Poose by the village well. Mrs. Pike was complaining of the price of candles.

The voices crooned on and then died down into nothingness. Far away on the upland downs a fox barked.

Mr. Matterface listened again. The spirit voices continued to speak. Mr. Matterface looked towards the Enmore Pound.

He moved softly in the direction of the Pound, his steps guided by the voices that he heard. Mr. Matterface entered the Pound. In the Pound, sitting upon stones with their backs against the crumbling walls, were his old boon companions.

Mr. Matterface sat down amongst them. He became their chief, their chairman ; he had the largest stone.

"Well, landlord, an' 'ow be thee these days ? " was the welcome that Mr. Poose gave to him.

An hour after, when Mr. Matterface returned to his home, his steps were lighter and gayer and his heart more happy—the situation was saved. The figure of the man was fixed again in its right groove. He knew that once settled so contentedly, the gossips of Enmore would never leave the Pound. Mr. Matterface had found a new salvation to replace his old lost happiness. In his cottage bed he smoked a last pipe of content as he thought of the Pound.

He went there, again and again, as did the other companions. The homely place that had in former times been the prison of many a weary donkey and straying cow, became the evening club of the Enmore companions.

They met there as they had formerly met at the inn ; they bandied former jests and old-time merriment.

Mr. Poose praised the unique wisdom of his dog. The rabbit-catcher told stories of snares, badgers and foxes. Mr. Warry, the lover—though somewhat old and married—spoke in praise of women. Mr. Pike, the hater of the sex, discounted them all ; and Mr. Matterface pronounced gravely the final and significant word " Time," as of yore.

CHAPTER X

OCTOBER WINDS

THE October winds raided the town of Eveleigh. The ferrymen, on pretence of lighting their pipes, moved on one by one under the shelter of the ancient wall near to the quay. In the wall above the heads of the ferrymen was a cannon-ball that had been shot into the town during the time of the civil wars.

From the shelter of the wall the ferrymen watched pieces of dirty paper being blown by. The men were cold, but with the usual sturdiness of fishermen they said nothing about it. They lit their pipes and put their hands into their pockets and watched the rain.

The old women of Eveleigh acted more strenuously ; they became at war with the wind, they fought the elements.

To make a beginning, the old women filled up all the cracks and crannies of their houses with old rags. They then looked through the closed windows. Although they felt cold one winter, happiness always came to them. The pretty girls of the town could wear white frocks no more that year. The old women were glad.

From the wild west the rain came, and ran down the windows and blew in under the doors. When this happened, Mrs. Antony Dine felt glad that the front doors of Ridgeway Street faced the north.

It was otherwise, however, with Antony Dine's workshop window, down which the rain-drops ran merry races. Did these very rain-drops perhaps wonder why Antony was not at work ? After he had heard Hester's knock, he had worked for an hour or so, and then he ceased. He allowed his hands to rest idle for the first time for forty years. The stove went out, the machine was silent, the beeswax and thread untouched. The little bits of stuff settled upon the tailor's board ; they found resting-places in the corners upon the floor. The room became ominously silent. Even the very spiders felt as though something strange and woeful had happened. With the noise of the machine always going, they had been easily able to catch the flies that have always, from time immemorial, been known to frequent the room of a tailor ; they now crept into their inner parlours.

Antony Dine sat still and looked at the stool. He had remained there for three days. After Hester had finally departed he had done nothing ; he spent the time in looking at her stool.

The child had grown up there, grown up as though she were a flower and the stool legs her roots. While she watched the machine, Antony Dine had watched her, his clever well-trained fingers doing the necessary work without the help of his eyes always guiding them. Hester was entranced by the machine, Antony Dine was entranced by Hester.

From the very first she had been fascinated by the machine, by the busy scissors, by the innumerable buttons. She watched and grew.

Antony had seen the little legs fatten out, grow larger, until the child grew into the wonder of woman-hood.

To begin with, the stool had been almost too large

for her, for Hester was very thin in those early days ; but soon the child began to grow out beyond the stool. Thus Hester Dominy grew up under two sombre clouds—the bells of St. Luke's and the love of Antony Dine.

One of the clouds was soon to burst. From the other she had flown.

When Hester was gone, Antony Dine's life caved in. The cloud burst. He became a broken harmony, a vial in two halves, and, though he tried to hide from himself the reason, he felt that he could work no more.

Antony had always fancied that work was his sole master ; he was now undeceived. Suddenly his work had become as nothing to him. The golden tint that had at first merely touched his life had grown into vast proportions. It had become a sun. The sun was Hester.

CHAPTER XI

ANTONY WISHES FOR AIR

IT was late afternoon ; Antony Dine sat still at his tailor's board.

Sometimes in human life a prison so thickens with darkness that the gloom itself acts as an explosive and bursts open the doors.

Antony's prison was becoming darkness itself.

Outside Antony's room there were steps. Mrs. Dine opened the door.

All down the front of Mrs. Dine's skirt there were spots of grease ; her blouse was soiled and untidy ;

her thin grey hair looked like badly swept cobweb.

For some moments she did not speak ; she merely looked at her husband. At last she said : " But you're doing nothing, nothing ! "

Antony looked at her thoughtfully ; it was the first time in his life that he had looked at her in that strange way.

" Yes, I've finished," he said quietly ; " I've finished working."

" But the 'ouses, the 'ouses," Mrs. Dine wailed. " We've so little in the box, so little saved for the next. Oh dear, oh dear ! "—she almost prostrated herself before her husband—" every one knows 'ow the price of 'ouses 'ave gone up ; we need more than ever to buy a 'ouse now. An' 'twas only yesterday that Mrs. Dominy called out that Mr. Pardy, the grocer, has twenty 'ouses."

Mrs. Dine sank down in a corner.

Antony rose wearily from his board. He stretched himself, and went downstairs into the narrow sitting-room ; his wife followed him.

" We'll see how much we have saved," Antony said.

Mrs. Dine was glad that he wished to look at their savings ; she hoped that when he saw how small the sum was, he would at once go to work again. The cash-box was taken out and opened ; it contained twenty-three pounds, seven shillings and sixpence.

Antony Dine took the money off the table and put it into his pocket.

Mrs. Dine sobbed dismally.

" What are you going to do with all the money ? "

she whimpered. "You 'ave never taken the money like this before ; you know it's saved—saved——"

"I am going away," Antony said very quietly, hardly believing himself the words that he spoke.

Mrs. Dine was so astonished that, for a moment, she could say nothing ; at length she found her voice :

"But Mrs. Dominy, Mrs. Dominy," she sobbed. "She'll say we've never bought any 'ouses at all ; she'll say you've run away owing people money——"

"Let her say what she likes," Antony replied. "I'm going into the country. I want air, air, wide spaces, trees, hills."

Antony Dine trembled. He had never spoken like this before ; he felt himself carried away by his own words.

Mrs. Dine still sobbed pitifully. His act, in taking the money, was to her as though he had torn out the very heart's blood of their lives.

Antony Dine did not look at her. The total darkness had suddenly become a glorious light ; the cloud had burst.

The stuffy tailor's workshop with its dust and its flies had been the battle-ground of two terrible forces. For a while they had lived at peace, as children will sometimes do before they are roused to hate by a subterraneous burst of passion.

The crux of the battle was when Hester was gone. The force of love then struck harder than it had ever done during her visits. The work force was defeated, love won.

Antony Dine wished for air.

Mrs. Dine looked at him as though he raved. She

had ceased to sob ; her thoughts had taken a new turn. She was counting up in her mind how long it would take to buy another house with the money that she hoped to save from the rents of the ones she owned. She hoped to be able to buy another house in two years' time.

Antony Dine put on his overcoat and went out into the rain.

CHAPTER XII
MR. WARRY'S CELLAR

ANTONY DINE had never walked more than two miles before in his life. This two-mile walk he had usually done on Sundays, going with his wife as far as the Eveleigh coastguard station.

During the Sunday walk this peaceful pair of sober citizens were wont to discuss the different merits of the houses they had bought.

To Mr. and Mrs. Dine the Eveleigh coastguard station had always been the uttermost end of their known world. To walk beyond that point, to pass the milestone that stood there, would have seemed to them as though they advanced into sheer space.

They would generally stand for a few moments at this uttermost limit of their Sunday's excursion and look back at the town before they proceeded thitherwards.

Mrs. Dine would view the town as unbought houses; Antony would see only his labour and a girl.

Antony Dine now walked past the coastguard station. He was like a person suddenly projected into a new world. He began to take pleasure in noticing little things. There were puddles of water in the road; Antony found himself taking an interest in the puddles.

The hedges in the dim evening light pleased his fancy; the very sound of his footsteps upon the hard road made him glad. A dog barked at a distant farm. Antony stopped; the sound made him glad.

He walked on again.

About three miles from Eveleigh he came to a hay-stack that had been placed by the farmer for convenience near to the road-side. An open gate invitingly led to the hay-stack. Antony went in under this kindly shelter. He smelt the hay; it was the first time in his life that he had smelt hay, for no farmer had ever placed stacks along the coastguard's road.

After sheltering a little while, he thrust his hand into the stack and drew out some of the sweet hay. For the first time in his life he had done something of his own willing, an act entirely individual. Before now there had always been forces behind him that drove him on—forces that directed his feet, his hands, his thoughts—forces that bullied, pushed and grumbled.

But now something had happened—something had broken.

Antony was beginning to act as though he were free born. He had thrust his hand into the hay-stack out of pure wantonness. This was a new way of living. A heavy burden had been lifted off his back. Antony Dine was beginning to live.

Even in his workshop he had not given in to the
greatest tyrant without a struggle. He had welcomed
the child Hester as a way of escape rather than as
another foe. But slowly he had grown to see her as
the most dangerous. He had sewn the faster, and
worked longer into the night. But when she came
again, he was forced to look at her. The two terrible
ones strove for his blood. The second child grew
into being the more terrible ; it overcame the other.
Antony had fought hard. The two clouds became
as one ; they burst. Antony had fled.

A rift came in the heavens. Antony looked up into
the sky. Bright stars shone cold and clear. A cool
wind from the west had driven the rain off and
at the same time had uncovered the beauty of the
heavens.

Antony was glad of the change ; he had discovered
new and wonderful friends—the everlasting elements.
He had only thought of them before in terms of mere
weather talk, but how little had he known of their
power or of their glory. He had their consciousness
now as they had his ; their beauty became his beauty,
their living-room, the uttermost firmament, became his.
A tiny spark in his soul had begun to burn, to grow.
The Almighty fire of the spirit ran through his body ;
it joined the fields beyond ; it became one with the
universe. Antony Dine looked upwards longingly,
exultantly.

Antony left the stack and walked along the road
again. The night was become clear and wonderful ;
the stars shone brighter than ever. There was one
that seemed to move before him as a guide. It was

K

bright and luminous. For the first time in his life Antony Dine was made free of the firmament. This consciousness is the uttermost wonder that a man can reach to. Bathed in it man becomes God.

Antony walked on gaily. He laughed at labour ; he laughed at love. Life leads a man on from contrast to contrast. From the top of the heavens one is often moved to the bottom of the earth. After conversing with stars one often finds oneself talking to little men. Antony Dine experienced this sudden change. It did not disconcert him, for the grotesque and the wise, the jester and the king go well together.

Coming round a corner of the road, Antony found a horse and cart by the wayside. The horse was feeding contentedly ; two of the cart wheels were in the ditch.

Antony walked in a merry mood. Having gone so far up into the beauty of the night, he was ready to meet the merry animal, man. He expected to see something between a fish and a monkey, something grotesque and queer. His own burden having fallen, he was ready for merriment.

There was a gap in the hedge. Antony peeped through and dimly saw the figure of a man sitting amongst the rabbit burrows. The man was holding up something in the air ; he looked as though he were aiming a small gun at the stars.

Antony Dine crawled through the gap in the hedge.

He found a man in the field drinking out of a bottle. As soon as Antony reached him the man began groping with his hand in a rabbit burrow. After putting his hand down as far as his shoulder would let him, the man brought forth out of the rabbit-hole another bottle. This bottle he handed to Antony Dine. He then burrowed again. Antony felt that he must have come upon an earth goblin who kept a cellar amongst the rabbits.

Antony Dine drank. His new friend became talkative.

"You don't know I, do 'ee?" he said.

Antony shook his head.

"I be Dairyman Warry I be, an' fond o' they maidens—an' me 'oman she don't know where me beer do bide."

The drinker by the wayside leaned closer to Antony.

"Wone glass for supper bain't all I do get wold 'oman—vor I do know where beer be."

Antony helped Mr. Warry to stand upon his legs; he was still talking.

"Thik road-man Pike, 'e don't know nothink, 'e don't, do 'ee 'ear I? There be a new maiden come to village, a new maiden vor I to prankie wi'."

Mr. Warry crept through the hedge and tried to climb into his cart. Antony helped him up. When once in his cart he whispered mysteriously, "Don't 'ee now tell thik road-mender, but I mean to take she in 'ay loft up wold broken ladder come Sunday." The horse and cart began to move slowly along the road.

Mr. Warry leaned over the cart and looked back.

"Where be thee a-going to?" he called.

Antony's reply was lost in the rumbling of the wheels. Antony walked on laughing; he had never laughed before in his life. He had seen a new kind of creature, a queer, fantastic being who hid bottles in rabbit-holes and drank them by starlight. How different to the town, how unlike anything he had seen before.

Mr. Dine began to think of man as a merry, careless country being, drunken, happy and free, who talked of maidens and road-menders and who left work wisely alone. The stars themselves winked and looked down kindly at such a life. The folly of such doings clearly amused the immortals. A sprawling drunkard crowing like a corn-fed cock was plainly one of their jests.

Antony watched the stars winking; he too liked to think of man as being only that. He had seen the other side, the working side; he now wished to see the play. "Where was this merry delver after earthly bottles going to," he wondered. Antony half wished that he had climbed into the cart beside him and taken the same course that he was going. It must, this course, have led him on between green star-lit hills, arriving at last at some cottage habitation beside a tall tree.

Antony Dine walked on.

He went by one or two villages. Lights were shining in the windows, and the freshness outside made the human dwellings appear all the more inviting.

A car passed with flaring, shining lights. Antony stood and watched the thing flash by, and after it was gone he drew solace from the intenser darkness.

CHAPTER XIII
GREEN GRASS

AFTER having passed along the great Wessex road for some ten miles, Antony Dine turned up a narrow lane between high, chalky banks. It seemed natural to him to turn out of the road at this particular point; he felt as though he were being guided by an unseen hand.

Passing along this little lane, the townsman soon found himself in the midst of a village through which ran a little brook.

Antony Dine lay down upon the grass.

Vega and Arcturus shone brightly upon him from above.

Antony lay upon the soft grass of the place like an entranced being. He looked up at the stars, who in their turn gazed at him with a shining that understood, as though he were the only man upon the earth that concerned them. Antony smiled into the water; he saw the stars there too.

More than one little child came near to him and looked inquisitively as if he was a new creature upon earth.

Antony listened to the brook that ran merrily over the little stones, making the music that has been loved in all ages by the greatest poets.

Antony had felt himself to be for so long the battle-ground of great forces; he was now something different, something that was not a mere battle-ground, something that was more like a moving figure in a picture.

His was a conversion not uncommon in religious by-paths, a conversion that frees the soul from bitter warfare and places it in security and peace.

Antony touched the grass to be sure that it was not a roll of green cloth; he took up a stone out of the brook, and was glad when he knew that it was not beeswax. The music of the running brook soothed him, the very gentleness in its running expressed a power that was more than any power of labour upon the earth.

Presently the form of a man came along the pathway with a dog. The form—so like a picture shadow—came near, waited and passed by, looked cautiously round again, called the dog to heel and slowly vanished.

Antony might have been in Mars, so different was the look of his surroundings to what he had been used to. His burdens being fallen, he really began to be amused by life. In so dreadful a thing as love he had found no peace, neither had he found peace in labour, but now he found not peace alone but amusement. He could laugh now that he was outside the prison walls.

Other shadow figures passed, looked curiously at him, stopped still, muttered a word or two and went by.

Antony was more than ever amused; he was the unknown to these good people, something that had dropped into their lives from afar, something that filled their minds with the usual sense of wonder that they bore to any unprobed mystery.

Antony listened, voices came from a half-broken wall that was near; it was almost as though the stones

were speaking, the voices were so earthy and dream-like.

"Thik big star do shine like Farmer's lantern over hill. Why even the poor dog be a-looking at thik star."

"True, true, me dog do know when they stars do shine."

"There be a man lying outside of Pound."

"Yes, I do thinkie 'twas a man."

"Some poor man who never knew there weren't no inn at Enmore."

"Poor peaceful man; he came here no doubt thinking to have a drink and a bed, same as some of we mid when we go to Heaven, and only to find the wold place all shut up and darkened."

"No, no, neighbour; I do think the stranger be come to Enmore to seek out some young woman that 'e mid 'ave loved in former times."

"Thee don't know nothing, thee don't, Mr. Warry; what man of sense would ever want to be tormented with they silly girl folk. When young they be crying babies, when grown up they be scolding wold 'omen, and they don't know nothing no time, they don't."

"Me dog do know."

"Poor Farmer Hart be worried."

"So 'e be, so 'e be; they do say that losing the wold red cow do make 'e mournful."

"So 'tis said."

The dream-like conversation droned on. Over the low hills to eastward three new stars had appeared.

Antony Dine slept.

CHAPTER XIV

FREE OF THE POUND

THE stranger outside the Pound had slept for two full hours when Mr. Matterface spoke the word.

"Time," said Mr. Matterface. The landlord motioned with a courtly wave of his hand—as of old he used to do—his friends towards the door of the Enmore Pound.

Outside the Pound the men stopped beside the sleeping form of Antony Dine.

"Poor humble man," said Mr. Warry feelingly. "'Tis sad for 'e there bain't no young female for 'e to cuddle on wormy grass."

"Best for 'e there bain't," came the quick reply of the stone-breaker, "for all the plagues of lice and flies that I've heard read out of Bible be as nothing to they 'omen folk at night-time. They 'omen be real plagues, they be."

"Me dog do know 'is own barrel," said the shepherd thoughtfully, "but thik poor sleeping man don't know nothing."

"'E bain't in a snare, be 'e, poor man?" remarked Mr. Chipp, thinking of many a rabbit that he had seen lying on the grass caught by the neck.

"'Tis my opinion, neighbours," said Mr. Matterface, after the countrymen had watched Antony Dine for some minutes, "'tis my opinion that we had best carry this sleeping man into inn-yard before policeman do come."

Suiting his action to his words, the evicted landlord

of the Enmore Inn placed his strong arms under the shoulders of Antony Dine and, with the help of the remaining good friends and gossips, bore the still sleeping townsman to the most sheltered corner of the Enmore Pound and laid him gently upon the grass.

Antony Dine slept on. . . .

At Enmore the late summer lives long. It grows old and is somewhat battered and torn, and its skirts rudely pulled, and yet it lives on. Rarely indeed does the Enmore summer give up the ghost until December is reached.

Colour follows colour in the country as flower follows flower. The last November knapweed nearly meets the first winter white violet.

The grey winter, even when it does come, sleeps as though it remembers, and many a daisy bright as a star peeps out of its sleeping bosom. Rural seasons pass slowly and merge into one another, and the mild autumn night that brooded around the village gave no unreasonable chill to Antony Dine. He slept late, and when he awakened a lark was singing. A bumble-bee had ventured into the Pound and had discovered a clover blossom. Antony watched the bee at its morning feast. The bee slowly buzzed through the gateway at the Pound; Antony rose and followed.

The brook was running over its little stones, caring neither for the bee nor for the man; beyond the brook Antony could see a path winding up the plough-land and leading into a turnip field where sheep were feeding.

Antony followed this path; he still lived in the vision

of a new world. He looked back at his past as though it were but a curious dream—a dream in which he sat at a tailor's board all day long. The dream seemed now past and over, and even the little girl who had moved in it was faded away.

Antony Dine reached the sheep; the shepherd was sitting upon the steps of his hut. The hut door was invitingly open.

Without a word, as though it were the most natural thing for him to do, Antony sat on the steps by the shepherd's side.

Mr. Poose pointed with his pipe at the dog.

"Thik dog do know," said Mr. Poose. "Thik dog be wise, 'e be."

Antony Dine looked at the dog with interest. The beast was a yellow collie with a sharp nose like a fox.

"Had thee's breakfast?"

Mr. Poose winked at Antony.

"I was going to ask you to buy me some food," replied Antony Dine, looking at the far valley where the autumn mists still hung in shroud-like folds.

"Be thee poor or rich?"

"Rich," said Antony, speaking to the distance. Taking out the notes from his pocket, he showed them to Mr. Poose. "Rich," said Antony.

The far hills uttered the same word; the distant heath, the sweet wind that came from the sea, spoke the word too.

"That be money," said Mr. Poose, and added : "You mean to bide here then?"

"Yes, here."

"It do rain into Pound sometimes; 'tain't every night that be fine."

Mr. Poose became thoughtful. He lit his pipe, looked at the dog and slowly shook his head. Jock, the dog, rose up, approached his master and looked into the hut.

"Thik dog do tell we what to do," said Mr. Poose. "Thik dog do know more than 'is master, 'e do. 'Thee'd best bide in hut,' dog do say, 'for nights be getting cold now.'"

"But your master, the farmer?" said Antony.

"Oh, never mind 'e," remarked Mr. Poose with a chuckle. "'Tis all the same to farmer so long as sheep be fed, and 'tis all the same to farmer's sisters so long as church do stand and parson do preach. They wold 'omen never stray out thik road; they do go where parson do go, they do."

The dog came to Antony, licked his hand and laid down at his feet.

Mr. Poose watched the dog.

"'Tain't every one that be free of the Enmore Pound," the shepherd said after watching the dog for some minutes. "Poor Parson Earley, 'e did try 'is best to stop road-mender talking—and wasn't it thik very dog that led I into Pound and so saved Master Matterface from drowning of 'imself in brook? Free of Enmore thee be, stranger, and 'tain't right for thee to stay without a roof over thee's head. And as to renties, why one of they slips of paper will do for I, and I'll take another—if it'll please thee to let me 'ave en, to buy food for thee's wone self."

Having thus spoken and having received from

Antony Dine two of the pound notes, Mr. Poose slowly made his way through the sheep-fold and so down the field towards the few houses that lay near to the village Pound.

Antony Dine was left alone. The sun warmed him graciously.

There was no machine for him to turn ; there was no girl child to fill his mind with a strange brooding. Hours could follow one another at their ease, tormented by no sharp-elbowed old woman whose mind was entirely filled with the prospect of buying another house.

Antony Dine looked into the hut ; it was to be his home. At the back of the hut there was a board covered with sheepskin ; that would be his bed. There was also a stove with a chimney, and an old broken chair. Antony Dine looked contentedly at his home.

" Thee's breakfast, and please what name be thee called ? "

" Mr. Dine, Mr. Dine," said Antony, and took the food from the small boy who had come up so silently.

The child departed.

Antony looked around him as he ate. He saw the cool green of the pasture, and the warm brown colour of the ploughed lands ; he saw the ever-changing look of the skies. He wondered how he could have borne so long, wedded to an eternity of toil, and yet the very cleverness of his fingers seemed to be rebuking him deep down in his heart for having left his labour.

He rubbed his eyes. " He must forget all that,

he must forget all that," he thought. "He was born a new man and all the long day was become his own."

Antony Dine forgot Hester.

CHAPTER XV
A CHANGED REFORMER

MR. EARLEY was modest and moral; he was also methodical. He arranged his day into portions, and he hoped that he never left undone anything that he should do.

Mr. Earley thought that he knew the country people. His friend, Mr. Haysom, always told him that he knew the country people, and he believed that he did. He had come to regard the country people as rather lazy and idle, and as what he used to call "heavy-headed." He saw them all as having no ideas, no inspiration; he felt that they were always more than half dead. He had hoped to awaken them; he had tried to awaken them.

When, through Mr. Earley's means, the Enmore Inn had been closed, that gentleman expected a storm of reproach to be heaped upon his head. He hoped that the people would break the Rectory windows, carry away the front gate, or at least set their children at him in the village. He was surprised and somewhat ashamed when nothing happened. The village, to all intents and purposes, remaining exactly the same.

One night Mr. Earley dreamt that Mr. Matterface was drowning him in a bath of beer, but this dream was indeed the only reply that was sent him to denote the feelings of the villagers,

Mr. Earley had—he felt—settled his life once and for all, after he had passed through the sad loss of the death of his wife. He had followed certain rules in "Law's Call"—a book that should be held in awe by all good Christians, because it assisted in the conversion of Dr. Johnson to the true Faith.

And so time went on.

Each day Mr. Earley's face became graver and graver. He saw what he fancied was wantonness and folly going on all around him. He hoped that the sullen temper of the people would break out into open revolt one day and so clear the air. The old women went to church as usual and the men stayed away.

Once Mr. Earley had, and he thought skilfully, introduced religion into a conversation that he had with Mr. Poose beside the Enmore green. But alas, Mr. Poose had at once changed the subject from the ways of God to the ways of his dog.

According to the plan of his day arranged under the advice of the pious Hall, one half-hour was spent by Mr. Earley in digging in his garden. He worked strenuously in the mire and the sod, hoping to do good to the garden, but sometimes he would look up to the heavens to see if any clouds were coming towards him.

One day, when looking up—his spade seemed to have clung to the earth more than ever that afternoon —Mr. Earley chanced to spy the new school-teacher crossing the dairy meads—going, as she naturally would do, to Mr. Warry's house, where she lodged. Mr. Earley, allowing his spade to remain in the mire, stood still and watched the girl. His mind, since his wife's death, often seemed curiously inclined to see queer things. He now fancied he saw before him the bars of the prison that he had made for himself. Outside the prison was the girl; inside was himself, Mr. Earley.

He dropped, as it were, all at once into a new conception of his life; it astonished him how strongly he was bound to the mire of his garden and to his village labours. Slowly his soul became flooded with sunlight, the prison bars faded, and he could, if he chose, simply let his spade drop and walk out to the girl.

She still loitered in the field. Mr. Earley devoured her, and half the field too, in his eagerness of mind. Although Mr. Earley knew very well that it was only Miss Hester Dominy returning from school, his whole outlook had become transformed.

Though it was November, the afternoon was wonderful; there was colour in the sky and there was still colour in the earth, and, wonder of wonders, the astonishing news flashed again through Mr. Earley's mind, there was still a girl.

Mr. Earley was fifty years old; he had arranged the hours of each day like the squares of a chess-board, that he must step into at the proper time. He knew that by that time he should have stepped out of the digging square, and stepped into the square that should have been old bed-ridden Betsy and a Bible.

He had missed Betsy, and, for all he knew to the contrary, he might be checkmated by the King of kings on account of his failure. What if old Betsy chanced to die at that moment?

A bell rang at the Rectory.

How long Hester must have loitered in the meadow as though she knew she was being watched!

Mr. Earley had jumped the Betsy square. He knew he must have, because the ringing of the bell showed that some one had called, and he had of course set apart a proper time in the afternoon to receive visitors. The girl had gone too, and Mr. Earley had, for the last quarter of an hour, been only looking at the meadow.

Mr. Earley now spent more time than ever in digging in his garden. There was no resisting the sunlight when it had once broken into his prison.

The breakdown in his usual life was complete.

Mr. Earley tried to do his duty, but Miss Hester Dominy was more than a duty: she was become an inspiration.

Mr. Earley laboured hard, but at a new labour. He made a bridge across the brook at the farther end of his garden—the bridge led into the dairy fields.

Mr. Earley began to lead a new life; he began to fetch his own butter and milk.

CHAPTER XVI

THE BELLS CALL HESTER

UNDERNEATH the ordinary outward appearances of life there are other appearances—this we all know very well.

A town girl with gold brown hair and a true girl's contour goes into the country to teach the infants in a little village school. The girl leaves behind her in the town a pestering old woman, who talks for ever about rats and the springs to false teeth. She also leaves behind her an ill-assorted set of children who, every Sunday, sat upon forms at the back of an ugly church, because there was no room for them beside the rich people who paid for their seats. So far so good.

But the girl also leaves behind her a stool, whereon sitting she has often watched a grey-headed tailor working a machine. This too is a good riddance— this watching an old man—so one would think, having regard to the outward appearance of things. Take a view, however, of the inward appearance and we see another matter.

The inward appearance in this town girl is a troubled sea of waves and tides, tides and waves that form deep whirlpools. They tear down wisdom, these tides ; they torment innocence ; they burst holy vessels ; they cast innocent thoughts to the dogs.

When the under appearance is at work, there is discontentment above.

Enmore did not please Hester as much as she had hoped it would. She even began to fancy that there must have been something of interest even in her mother's drooping cheeks and the pork and cabbage and talk about rats and false teeth.

Hester Dominy missed the bells ; she missed the children begotten of the by-lane ; she missed the sound of her own feet upon the pavement ; she missed the sound of the tailor's machine. The inner appearance told her only too plainly that she missed all these things. She walked lightly ; she spoke happily ; but her heart was always sinking like a stone into her past.

L

Hester taught the Enmore infants under the eye of Mrs. Heath, the head mistress, and in full accordance with the laws and customs of the school.

As she taught the children she heard in her heart the bells of St. Luke's.

Hester was unhappy.

Mr. Warry would talk about the weather or else of his pigs; and indeed it was small blame to Hester that she failed to understand that the dairyman was making love to her.

And such a love-making! The whole matter of which was nightly told to the good people of the Pound.

One Saturday, and the meeting seemed to be quite an event in Hester's dull routine, she met the elder Miss Hart out walking. Ever since she had been at Enmore Hester had watched these old women with interest. There was something about them that reminded her of herself; she seemed bound to the earth as they were by one sound. They too moved by habit by the unchanging voice of one bell. This bell was their brother, the farmer. The old women went to church; Hester had done likewise. They carried two pocket-handkerchiefs because there was always white damp on their prayer-books that had to be dusted away.

Hester used to watch their shadows. Whenever she took her eyes from her book she looked towards the wall on her left hand. The wall was clammy and cold like the sides of a grave, and upon the wall were the dim shadows of the old women, and the shadows held dim prayer-books in their hands. The bells of St. Luke's had taught Hester the way to look at the world.

Behind the Miss Harts there sat Mrs. Poose, behind Mrs. Poose there sat Mrs. Pike in an old black cloak, and behind Mrs. Pike was old Mother Matterface. Hester Dominy saw the shadows. She saw the shadows even when the sun did not shine.

Hester had not to ask twice before Mr. Warry expressed himself in reference to these shadows.

"They follow thik parson about," said Mr. Warry. "An' they do know how to work too—they do work, same as she do." Mr. Warry pointed to his wife. "They do work."

Mr. Warry looked at Hester ; he was, in the language of Enmore Pound, inviting her to go to Stonebridge fair.

"Yes, miss, they wold 'omen know how to work." He was inviting her to go for a walk the next Sunday. "They know how to make butter." He was asking her to creep into the hay-barn when no one was looking.

The ready ears of the Pound heard it all.

But to return.

Hester overtook Miss Hart in the lane that led to Shelton. Grace Hart had said "Good afternoon," and so Hester had spoken too.

"I thought to meet Mr. Earley," Miss Hart said. "I wished to speak to him about the working-party."

"Mr. Earley went home another way," Hester replied. "I saw him cross the dairy meadow."

"Oh dear," said Miss Hart mournfully, "oh dear !" The old woman looked at the Shelton hills with tired eyes, and then she trembled as though a cold wind had stricken her. " I be cold," she said, " I be cold. Sister says I be always cold."

Hester was touched. She was looking into the inner appearance of a human life ; she heard the sound of St. Luke's bells there too ; they brought up phantom children to weep and weep on the back forms.

Hester walked slowly across the dairy field to Mr. Warry's cottage. Mr. Warry was standing outside with a lantern, looking at his pigs.

" Good evening, miss ; nights be dark now," was all Mr. Warry could say.

Later in the evening Mr. Warry pronounced decidedly that " he'd been wi' thik pretty maid in wold cartshed for two hours a-cuddling."

CHAPTER XVII
RATTY

MR. WARRY remarked one evening that there were ten little pigs born, and the news being of interest to Mrs. Warry, the two good people departed with a lantern, leaving Hester alone. Hester thought this moment would be the proper one for reading a letter that she had found at the post-office that afternoon from her mother.

RIDGEWAY STREET,
EVELEIGH.

DEAREST HESTER,—

The large brown saucepan with the long handle be broke. 'Tis the rat that did do it and Mr. Haysom.

I were thinking of Mr. Haysom and his teeth when something ugly ran under the kitchen table. the saucepan be broke. I said to Mrs. Dine the saucepan be broke and all Mrs. Dine did say were I've bought another house, Mrs. Dominy. now tell me dear do Mr. Earley talk right, for I do know what will make he talk right if he don't—springs. Mind Hester when you see him coming down the country lane you stoop down low and pick a flower. He won't say nothing then but the flower will do it or else the stooping. there are always flowers in the country Mr. Earley must love a flower. 'tis best you keep a servant when once you be a clergyman's wife.

The wind be strong blowing in town. yesterday the wind blew my second best bonnet sideways when I were out shopping and I stayed for a moment by Mr. Pardy's big window to tie it up and Mr. Haysom come along. ' the children miss your daughter, Mrs. Dominy ' he said. Only he didn't speak it very plain. ' And Ratty,' I think he did say Ratty, ' threw a bad nut on Sunday across the pews, the nut hit Mrs. Pardy. the price of pork and cabbage be gone up, please mind the stooping for the flower when he do ask you to marry him don't answer at first, you best only stoop and pick another flower. I be forced to use the old saucepan that you burnt Christmas, the lace curtain be tore in bedroom.

Your loving Mother
GRACE DOMINY.

P.S. Mr. Dine be gone from home to London to buy houses.

Hester Dominy read the letter twice, and the little pigs still holding out of doors the goodman and his lady, Hester, having found Mrs. Warry's pen, and taking some note-paper of her own, she wrote an answer as follows :

ENMORE.

MY DEAR MOTHER,—

Never mind about the saucepan, mother; I will send you the money for a new one.

It's very sweet here and quiet, but the hedges are rather dark-coloured, and the sea is quite a long way off. There are seagulls sometimes.

Don't be so silly, mother, about Mr. Earley. He will never marry again I'm sure, and of course his teeth are quite good. I try to be happy here ; the country is all up and down and there's a field path and a stile. I love the stile. I put my legs over and then I sit on the top and listen for the school bell to ring. I jump down and run when I hear it ringing.

Mother, don't be silly, it couldn't have been Ratty who threw the nut ; there is no girl called Ratty in the Sunday school at St. Luke's. Nancy might have done it, though. I sometimes used to hear crack, crack, by my side in church. That was when Nancy trod on them. But she didn't always tread on them ; sometimes she cracked them with her teeth and spat out the shells. I wonder if my chair is still in the same place in the church, and I do hope no one has taken my hymn-book.

The roads here have big stones in them and large heaps of dirt by the sides, and Mr. Warry always knows when it's going to rain.

I liked it here at first.

You have to walk up and down the ridges in these fields; it's rather tiring—it's like going up and down green waves.   Mr. Earley often digs in his garden. There are two old women who make shadows in the church.

I hope I shall come home one day.   Do the bells still ring the same ?   There's only one bell here, and the sound of that gets mixed up with the wind.

The head teacher has such thin hair; she says she goes to St. Luke's sometimes.   Do our sofa look as if I ever have sat upon it, mother ?   I wonder when Mr. Dine will come home.

Your loving
HESTER.

The letter was safely closed when Mr. Warry's voice was heard outside complaining to the yard gate-post that one of the little pigs had been eaten by its mother.

CHAPTER XVIII

ALWAYS THE SAME

MR. ROBERT HART, the chief farmer of Enmore, was a quiet and homely bachelor. He was a man of peace.   He moved slowly and his conversations never reached very far; his words remained indeed always at home.   The niceties of life he left alone because he liked comfort.

When Mr. Hart was displeased with the earth or with its fruits he frowned a little.   If anything went wrong on the farm he would but walk slower, be still more peacefully inclined, and might even—if the mishap were serious—stand silent for half an hour beside his own garden gate.

Mr. Hart divided the affairs of the world into two halves—that which concerned him on the one side and that which did not concern him on the other. He made his half the standard of virtue, of excellence, of everything in fact that he intended himself to be. All that concerned him he took quietly, sensibly and wisely ; beyond his own concerns he regarded nothing.

Every man in the world surrounds himself with his own colour. Around Mr. Hart there was ever a fixed and grey gloom—the kind of gloom that grows up in a man when everything that is his becomes and remains always the same.

In Mr. Hart's case there was no altering this fatal sameness in events. His bank balance, the result of his care and prudence, would—even if lesser matters went wrong—bring all equal.

He was used to hearing the slow steps of his maiden sisters, regarding them in the same manner as Mr. Oldbuck of Monkbarns would have done, as mere womankind. He expected their feet to move gloomily, as Mr. Poose's tongue did when the shepherd spoke about the shortage of turnips.

Mr. Hart's life had become near as sad and dull as any of the immortals to whom good and evil are one and the same thing. Every event that came in the daily round had its fellow with him in some other daily round of like measure.

There was always an even balance in his days and always an even balance in his years. The years were short, but the days dawdled on, no one faster nor slower than any other. The farmer knew the ways of the seasons; he considered the times. The seasons were always what he expected them to be; they were always the same. Mr. Hart saw the seasons exactly as they were in the pictures of his almanac. An old brown roof snow-covered for January; a child with hair blowing and running hoop for March; an apple tree in blossom for May; a June hay-wagon; harvest horses drinking from a pond in August; and a fallen tree being cut into fuel for October. It was indeed nearly the same thing to Mr. Hart whether he turned over the months of the year or whether he turned over the pages of his almanac.

The same recurring day always came to Mr. Hart when the hay-carts rolled with exactly the same sound, or else when the same silly crowd of fluttering gnats hovered in the same mild September evening. The farm matters moved always with the same recurring simplicity of trend. One had only to see country matters follow one another in a simple sequence of events to prove all things to be the same. The cows, the horses, the pigs, the sheep, the shepherd—all took turns to try Mr. Hart's patience. But none of the ordinary accidents of a farmer's life ever succeeded in affecting the mild and temperate habits of this good man.

Mr. Hart knew very well the kind of cow—the one with the white face—that would fall into the brook, and had to be dragged out with a rope round its neck under the supreme direction of Mr. Poose the shepherd. Mr. Hart knew the sort of year that brought the swine fever to Enmore. He expected thunder in June, and always looked for doleful clouds in that month that portended a heavy fall upon his newly cut hay.

But whatever came to Enmore, good or ill, Mr. Hart's affairs were always the same. The swine fever could not ruin him any more than a dead cow or a heavy fall of rain could ruin him. "Why?" —and this "why?" of Mr. Hart's was the highest flight that his imagination ever soared to in the direction of the unknowable.

Indeed Mr. Hart did sometimes have the hardihood to wonder, "Why was he always so careful not to be ruined?" He could never be rich—he was quite sure about that. The sameness was too much about him; there were always the grey winds of Enmore blowing. Always the same grey winds—no colour, no colour.

Once or twice in his lifetime the careful farmer had felt inclined to break out of his prison, but the thought of his sisters always prevented him from acting in any way rashly. There were always wrapped up in the woof of his destiny poor aged Grace and poor careful Susan.

Poor Grace, she had stepped indeed in the path of nonentity, and time moves slowly and silently with such a one.

The 19th of November found Mr. Hart expectant and prepared for dull and gloomy weather. In his almanac there was a picture of two horses with drooping heads standing with their backs to a wall. Mr. Hart rose from his desk where he had been writing; he went into the passage and took his overcoat from a nail where it always hung. He could never remember his overcoat looking or being any different or hanging in any other place. His overcoat was as grey and as gloomy as the weather.

Mr. Hart put his coat on ; Grace came out of the kitchen to help him, poor Grace ! Grace said something about a cup of tea. She always asked her brother to have cups of tea at odd times, but he would never even listen to what she said.

Susan Hart was upstairs dusting the bedrooms ; the farmer could hear her feet wearily crossing the passage from one room to another.

Mr. Hart slowly shut his front door and, passing through the little garden, he turned towards the farm stables.

As the farmer walked thitherwards he thought of the six-acre field that he intended to have ploughed. He knew quite well how this field looked without taking the trouble to journey to it. The field must needs be very wet, but of course it could be ploughed. All farm work expressed itself to Mr. Hart in the surface terms of the land—too wet or too dry, too hard or too heavy. And yet, even though there were these troubles, the fields were always ploughed, always sown, always reaped. One only had to wait a little. Mr. Hart had never known the wet state of a field to last for ever, or the hard clods of a dry summer always to remain hard ; no evil or good state of the soil lasted for long.

In the country all events are anticipated. The carter was no doubt expecting to see Mr. Hart that afternoon and expecting him to say exactly what he would say. The farmer of course would talk about ploughing when ploughing-time came—everything was expected at Enmore.

Mr. Hart found the carter in the stable. The carter was the kind of man who is neither good nor bad—a man who simply lived to be the tail end of a plough. Mr. Hart gave this man the usual orders about the next day, in answer to which the man smilingly bent down and lifted up one of the horse's legs that he was grooming.

Mr. Hart examined the foot of the horse—an iron nail had run into it and the place festered. Mr. Hart expected an accident like this to happen, simply because nothing of the kind had happened for so long.

The horse doctor had sent in his bill at the usual time and Mr. Hart had paid it. There were always times when the horse doctor came to the farm ; Mr. Hart expected his visits.

CHAPTER XIX
FARMER HART SEES A GIRL

LEAVING the stables, Mr. Hart passed along a stone path splashed with dull dung stains that led into the cow-shed.

This cow-shed was long and low, and in the wall there were round holes to let in the light and air. Robert Hart had come into the cow-shed to see how much dung there was, and to ascertain if the dung needed moving on to the heap in the field.

Mr. Hart had been to this covered shed many times. He examined the dung and decided that after the field for spring wheat was ploughed, he would have the dung carted. He had decided the same matter a great many times before.

The damp gloom of February hung over the low cow-house. Mr. Hart looked at the dull wet yard—on one side the yard was covered for the protection of the dung, on the other it was open to the rain.

Mr. Hart thought that he had been watching for ever and ever the rain dripping into the wet portion of the cow-yard. It was certainly not the first time that he had seen the same wet day, the sodden side of the yard and the dull, blackened walls of the shed.

Walking across the yard and entering the cow-stalls, Mr. Hart looked through one of the holes that let in the air. He had done this same thing often before; it was nothing new to him to look out upon his own meadow.

The farmer knew what he would see; a field of green grass—his own field, one or two pigs with their noses in the soft grass, an old dry cow, and the grey church tower. He knew only too well the homely curve of the footpath that went through his field, through the field beyond and led up to the dairyman's cottage.

Mr. Hart had sometimes seen the dairyman's wife, Mrs. Warry, a short, red-faced creature, shuffle that way, perhaps going to the mothers' meeting at the Rectory. Whenever he saw Mrs. Warry, she always impressed him with the same heavy dreariness as the field.

Sadly the gloom of a dull February day pressed upon

Mr. Hart as he looked through the round window, but this time he did not move away as quickly as he had been wont to do upon other occasions.

In the footpath he saw a girl walking.

Robert Hart watched the girl. At first he simply looked at her as if she were like the cow, like the pigs, like the church tower even if it could have moved. After a moment or two he watched the moving figure very attentively.

Of course the farmer knew who the girl was—his sisters always mentioned the name of anyone who came new into the village. New girls sometimes came into the village; they came and went, and he never took any notice of them.

The girls were always the same to Mr. Hart—they never made the least difference to his life. He saw them in church, but what of that—all the womenfolk came to church in Enmore. Mr. Hart did not even talk about them as girls; he was wont to say " young women," and he thought of them always as " young women."

And now, oddly enough, he found himself looking, excitedly almost, through a round hole in his cow-house wall, and looking at a girl !

It was true that this was not the first occasion that this girl had been seen by him, and he knew her as " the young woman who taught the infants."

As Mr. Hart watched the school-teacher, he felt that she was a different sort of creature to anything that he had seen before. What he saw now was not in the least like the young woman that he had before known her to be.

The difference was intensely apparent to Mr. Hart. A young woman never walked like that, but a girl could, and that was how the new world came into being—a girl could !

Was it the way she moved that brought the girl-hood so suddenly out of her to meet Mr. Hart ?

When she was gone the farmer turned to watch the cows enter the shed, each gentle beast going to its accustomed stall. After seeing the cows tied up he spoke to the cowman about the lame cow—there was always the lame cow, he noticed the one as it came in. Mr. Hart looked attentively at the cow, and agreed with the cowman as to what had better be done to cure the lameness.

Mr. Hart left the cow-house ; he looked at the wet side of the shed. The rain was still dripping into the dung puddle, but this time the farmer was not thinking of the dung.

CHAPTER XX

SWEET CONTENT

ANTONY DINE lived as a shepherd in Enmore. Every day he sent Mr. Poose's child to the village to buy bread. He fed in simple manner, and fancied that, as his money went so slowly, it must needs last for ever.

All Enmore people love a mystery. A stranger lived in the shepherd's hut and that led to questions.

Even Miss Grace Hart had something to say ; Miss Grace more than half believed that the man she saw one day in the field was a ghost. She said so to her sister, and all Miss Susan said was "that she hoped the ducks' eggs would not get stolen."

No subject of conversation had ever arisen in the Enmore Pound of more interest than Mr. Poose's stranger ; the good shepherd was asked about him every time the friends met.

"Thik man be poor though 'e be rich," remarked Shepherd Poose ; and he sometimes said, "Thik man be rich though 'e be poor." Whichever way the words went they expressed an interesting state of mind in the stranger.

Meanwhile Antony Dine lived as a free spirit ; his soul expanded like a plant in a warm soil. His old life he saw far behind as one sees the land when the ship sails seawards. He was never tired of watching the sheep feeding and the little birds in the trees. He walked for hours upon the heath and loitered in the low meadow and in the wood.

He lived in sweet content; he moved in quiet thought.

Antony forgot the dull surroundings of Ridgeway Street ; he forgot the machine, the beeswax ; he forgot the woman with the grease spots who was his wife. Antony Dine but lived and breathed. All things that he saw or touched pleased him, even the winter mists pleased him. Every drop of rain, every gust of wind expressed a freedom that he had never known before.

What had he been of old ? He knew now— merely a drudge, a slave of the eternal master, labour. His soul had been famished ; it was now filled with all the winds of the downs, with all the vast spaces between the worlds. He had lived like a mole ; he stood now upon the crust of the earth and saw the gods.

All things Antony saw as though they had been pictures hung upon the walls of time. Shepherd Poose moved, a pastoral figure amongst the flocks. There seemed to be no true labour—only slow movement. The carter walked behind his team and sang his morning song. Antony would see the man's lantern when he went to the stables, a moving star in the low farmstead.

He would watch the old women going to the well; he would watch them moving together, their heads wagging, their tongues clattering more than their pails.

It was all so different, so different to the labour that he knew. He could never have believed that these people who moved as in pictures worked. They never toiled, how could they—and look at the same time so picturesque?

The sweet things they touched—the hay, the yellow wheat straw, the plough handles so humanized as to know their masters. How could the word "toil" have a place in such matters?

Upon windy nights Antony Dine would lie in the shepherd's hut and think of the wonderful life, breathed upon by the very breath of God, that he was leading. What mattered now to him the little girl who used to sit upon a stool and watch him at work? What mattered now if he had loved her?

There was, however, one thing that Antony could not prevent happening—the slow diminishing of his store of money. It would not last for ever, however careful he was, this small sum. Once, as he lay awake,

M

he thought of selling one of his houses.   But the deeds were in his wife's keeping, and what St. George dare take anything from that dragon of a woman ?   Antony Dine smiled and slept, lulled by the winds from the sea.

CHAPTER XXI
LOVE AND A GHOST

MR. MATTERFACE turned in his chair, or more truly he stretched out one foot into the nettles and moved his body from one side of the stone seat to the other.

Mr. Chipp coughed, the rabbit-catcher was twisting a piece of copper wire, he hoped one day or other to catch a fox.   Mr. Poose sat between Mr. Warry and Mr. Pike and looked at his dog.

" Thik dog do know I," Mr. Poose thoughtfully remarked.

Jock, the dog, wagged his tail.

" What be it that do drive they poor farmer's 'omen after parson ? " inquired the rabbit-catcher in a hushed whisper, fearing no doubt that Mr. Earley was standing outside the Pound.

" I can answer thee's question, rabbit-catcher," said Mr. Warry in the same low tone.   " 'Tis love that do do thik little job."

Mr. Pike sniffed, and moved his head this way and that as a bull would who saw a red flag waving.

" What were thik word thee did use, dairyman ? " Mr. Pike inquired in a tone by no means so gentle as the others had used.   " 'Twasn't cow was it, nor pig-hog, nor cock nor hen ? " Mr. Pike looked around as though it were possible that some one had heard the word more plainly than he had done. " Mr. Warry do know so many words, 'e do—'twasn't love, was it, thee did utter ? "

" Yes 'twere, an' I bain't ashamed to own it, for word be writ in Bible plain enough ; I did hear parson name en only last Sunday," said Mr. Warry.

" Don't you now "—Mr. Pike shook his head— " don't you now mention they 'omen in such a quiet place as Enmore Pound ; 'tisn't fit that thik harmless dog should hear 'ee."

" No, no, road-mender," remarked Mr. Matterface, slowly filling his pipe. " No, no, women bain't so bad, neither. There were wold Kate that would often take a glass when inn were opened, and I won't never hear a word said against me wold customers. 'Tis my belief, neighbours, that Enmore village be witched since Parson Earley have closed inn. 'Tis no wonder they wold women do run after parson when there be a living ghost in fields. How be thik dead man up at yours, shepherd ? "

" 'Tisn't dead that he be. 'Tis a quiet man that do help I to set fold. 'Tis only they wold 'omen that do think 'e be a spirit. And true 'tis they do say that black spirits walk about this green earth like crows on corn-fields."

" True, true," said Mr. Matterface. " Enmore be different than ever 'twere in wolden days. There be they poor simple wold 'omen, farmer's sisters, a-going to church and mothers' meetings as happy as young birds and coming home again scornful and sad.

"'Tis love," said Mr. Warry, "that do do it."

"And some do say," continued Mr. Matterface, "that parson do cast his eyes at thik young party who do bide at dairyman's and who dairyman do talk of. And that bain't all the worst of it neither, for 'tis said that farmer 'is wone self do walk queer-like."

"Landlord do say truth," said Mr. Chipp, for Mr. Matterface had paused in his story for lack of breath, "for I did see en crooked up again' 'is own gate in a brown study, as 'tis called. An' sure," said I, "thik poor farmer be in a snare."

"Yes, thee do say it," chimed in the road-mender. "Snare be the word for they 'omen, and the younger they be the worser they be. 'Tis strange to I how men, who should be as wise as thik dog, should go after they silly creatures. Poor people that men be to be sure, and now 'tis farmer that be catched."

"Don't 'ee talk so, Mr. Pike, for I ask thee all one question. What better thing be there in world than a young maid in she's Sunday clothes?"

"Well, well," said Mr. Poose, "I do believe me dog be as good—and trouble do come to Enmore same as Pike do say through the 'omen."

"Yes, 'tis the Lord's will it should be so," remarked Mr. Matterface with a shake of his head, "and there be they two old aged 'omen looking up towards Rectory all day long, and poor farmer do stand up like post by 'is wone gate, and Parson Earley do follow thik young teacher under willow trees where brook do run. Yes, yes, 'tis a funny word thik 'love' that Mr. Warry do know so well."

Having had the last word that was ever his right

to have, Mr. Matterface called out "Time" in his usual manner and the friends of the Pound moved like shadows from the place of their meeting towards their respective homes.

CHAPTER XXII
OLD FEET

THE feet shuffled on in the mud of Enmore—the tired, aged, shapeless, human feet, the feet of old women.

"If there be no God," I can hear you say, reader, "who can give heed to them—no one else will, not man surely?"

You are wrong for once, clever as you are; you are wrong for once, for man as he should be and as he is at Enmore does hear.   For the true artist, the peasant artist, lives at Enmore.   Yes, lives at Enmore, and reads not the fantastic artistry of the modern story, nor yet the wordy wisdom of the schooled pen, but reads instead the human writings writ in the mud, by the terrible one who stoops to write in the crust of the earth.

But, oh dreariness incarnate ! the feet still move. They are coming from the direction of the church, and pass slowly along between the hedges that shadow the road.

It was the sort of sound, the sort of motion that was wont to occupy the thoughts of Matterface and his companions in many a Pound conversation. Indeed all the merry tales of Mr. Warry's pranks with the maidens were inclined to be dismissed with

a shrug of the shoulders and passed easily by when
the sound was named.   The good folk knew shrewdly
enough that the glamour of wantonness was too uni-
versal in its habits to give them what they needed in
their talk.

And so their remarks would often leave the poor
dairyman behind—unless honest Pike interrupted—
and go to poor Betsy even, who lay bedridden within
a yard or two of her own thatch.   Bedridden, a word
in season, my masters.   Was there ever such a word,
to take in and consider ?   For the manifestations of
poor Betsy's condition recur often in the world, but
are very much in the eye and interest of Enmore,
more indeed than are pretty Nancy and Robin in a
summer lane.

They know about it all these Pound companions ;
they see how soon the game is lost in the meadows.
But in the steps of the old women, who look for light
and find it not, there is a deeper meaning to carry to
the bottom.   Summer beauty may reach far, but the
mud of Enmore reaches farther.   Dainty steps touch
dainty things, but it is the gloom and the mud that
is touched by human feet that tell the true tale.

But 'tisn't only the road-menders who see the drift
of the jest.   I would have you notice those heaps of
mud by the side of the road, dragged there by Mr. Pike,
who was—and one would hardly have thought it—
always made merry by this occupation.

The human feet shuffle on, the feet of the two old
women who are walking in the road.   A thin, dreary
rain that wets the mud and moistens the heaps of
dirt by the road-sides, and falls, drip, drip, from the

trees—tells tales of the summer, does it ?   No, I hardly think so!

The clothes of the two women are of a drab colour, and match very prettily the heaps of mud by the roadside.   It is said that in the vast space of ether there are dead worlds that move like black ghosts in the firmament, untouched by the power of creation, touched only by space itself.   Of such dead matter are our old women who walk in the road.   But are they really dead ?   Near to these dark human worlds of ours another world has come dangerously near—too near—a world that may set alight these dark universes.

But they walk still in dead earnest, they walk in the middle of the road, their feet shuffle.   Are they the last human creatures making the last human sound ?

They now begin to speak to one another in sad, dreary tones.

"What can he see in her ? "   It was the elder Miss Hart who spoke.   "What can he see in her ? " Grace Hart sighed.

The two sisters, their shapeless feet still heavy in the mud, move on.

Susan's lips move too, but she utters no word.

"What can he see in her ? " Grace says again. "She is young, of course, but her shape, her body ; have you noticed how clumsy her back is and her neck ?   No doubt she is always looking at him, though she does sit so far back in the church."

The season is Lent.

An evening service has just been held.   The Miss Harts have been to church together ; they are now returning to their home.

"What can he see in her?"

Susan muttered "Nothing!" but her sister paid no heed.

"It's all because she's so young, only a young girl; that's what she is, only a young girl. . . . There must be something in a young girl that attracts, something that he feels, something that he cannot get rid of. He looks at her in church, even when he preaches he is looking at her—but what is she to be looked at? He might look at us, we love him, but he only looks at her, only at her. Oh, how dangerous she is, how dangerous!"

Danger, danger, danger in the vast spaces, a piercing scream, a dreadful cry, is even heard high in the firmament. Danger to dark worlds. A Nova may flare up anywhere, no heart is too cold, no world too dead. In a moment there is a star of the first magnitude, but soon it dies slowly down into nothingness again.

"Have you noticed her eyes?"—the feet lift slowly out of the mud—"they are so moist, so large; one could almost drink from her eyes. I have watched her with her large eyes; she is a snake, a serpent. Oh! yes, I have watched her—she would melt altogether if he did touch her, and then, of course, he would touch her more than ever——"

"More than ever," murmured Susan.

"Oh! I know her tricks." The elder sister went on with her complaining. "I know how she behaves. She is only too ready to catch flies like the sun-dew. She is hard and cruel; these children can claw when they want to."

"No one will ever love us," Susan Hart said drearily.

" No one, no one," Grace muttered, almost fiercely.
" He likes to have her a little way off—he might
have had her in his house if he had wanted to ; she
was only a servant to her own mother before she came
into the school. He lets her lodge at the dairy
because he likes to take her home through the fields,
he thinks some one ought to go with her—he said
all that to me once—because of the soldiers, and she
knows all about the soldiers."

" Oh, yes, she knows," whispered Susan.

" What can he see in her ? "

" Oh, they talk about the stars, don't they ? "

" Yes, I once heard them talking about the stars."

" Could either of us walk like she does by his side ?
We might have tried to, but he would not have looked
the same. Oh dear no ! "

" It was only last night that I saw him pointing
with his stick at the stars."

" What do the stars concern us ? "

" They were looking so intently up at the sky, and
I heard her say : ' What is the name of that star ? ' "

" She did not really want to know "—the two
voices were now speaking in turns—" What do the
stars concern her ? "

" Perhaps the soldiers were waiting too, and looking
at the stars, waiting for him to go."

" Do you know, sister, I often think that youth
is like a thief in the night—it steals from us."

" Yes, all children are evil, and now that we are
getting old we have nothing to be cruel about. We
cannot ask questions as she asks them ; we dare not
ask about a star even."

Miss Grace Hart opened the garden gate, and her sister passing through first, they both walked together up the path to the prim farmhouse.

There was a light in the window, and they saw the shadow of their brother upon the drawn blind.

Entering quietly, the sisters went slowly up the stairs to their own rooms to take off their cloaks. After doing so, they began to prepare the front room for supper.

The room was tidy, minutely tidy, and Mr. Hart was sitting at his desk looking over a few bills that had come by the afternoon post. Beside the bills was his cheque-book

CHAPTER XXIII
A PLAN FOR THE MORROW

LOOKING down from the Enmore hills Antony Dine saw the whole world as fair and fruitful. It rippled on, the village life, like the brook over the stones. The murmur reached Antony and he blessed the murmur. Not for one moment would he have believed that anyone living in such a gracious way, and moving amongst all the sweet things of life, could be anything else than peaceful and happy. A happy night's sleep was to him an untold blessing ; to move, to touch the hurdles, to carry hay to the flock that had so many happy lambs, was to Antony an exquisite pastime after his former toils.

How astonished would Antony Dine have been had he peeped into the old farmhouse that lay so primly under the hills and listened to the talk of the two old women who lived there.

The Miss Harts were whispering together as they dusted the rooms.

" Mr. Earley has gone that way for years on Good Friday ; he always used to go that way with his wife ; he used to even walk down the steep path sometimes."

The two old women whispered together. As they whispered their cheeks flushed, and each of them would look in a startled way now and again at the window, as though they suspected some one to be looking in.

" Of course he would never ask Hester to go with him," said Grace.

" What does she do on Good Friday ? " Susan asked.

" Oh, of course, she goes down to pick primroses near the great road ; she is sure to go there, all the village go there on Good Friday."

They whispered together again, and glanced at the door as though they expected some one to knock.

Antony Dine was watching a wonderful pink colour that the sunlight had given to the barn roof.

" How happy those must be who are born under such colour, and move in surroundings so suitable to man." Antony looked into the fields ; a man was bending down upon the hill-side ; he moved a little and bent again : it was the rabbit-catcher. The sun shone on his spade that he used to dig out the rabbits. The man stood solitary, a picture in himself, a being as old as the world.

Antony thought of the people of the town who are jumbled together like maggots on a sheep's back.

He began to plan an excursion for the next day :

he intended to walk to all the spots that he loved best in Enmore, to the wood, to the heath, to the wide fair meadows. He would lie for hours in a grassy spot that he knew, where there was an oak-tree whose roots formed a mossy couch.

He longed for the new day to come. He would be busy with Mr. Poose all that afternoon—for even the shepherd wished to go a little journey on the morrow and wished to be forward with his tasks.

Antony Dine began to move the hurdles in order to set the new fold ; he looked about him at the green fields, where all seemed peace and contentment.

CHAPTER XXIV
MRS. PARDY'S DEVOTIONS

UPON the breakfast table next to his plate Mr. Earley found one morning a letter from Mr. Haysom.

He read it at once.

ST. LUKE'S VICARAGE,
EVELEIGH.

DEAR EARLEY,—

I wish you would write to me more often.

There are so many Jannes and Jambres here in this town, men of corrupt minds.

Only last Sunday, as I was crossing the road to enter St. Luke's, rude girls in a crowded motor came by and threw a broken black bottle at me.

I hope it is not wicked of me, but I shall be thankful to God when I have finished my course,

There is something wrong, my friend, with the world that we live in. There are false accusers, there are the uncharitable.

Mrs. Pardy, our churchwarden's wife, wants the school-children to sit even farther back than they do now during the services. She complained to me that a girl named Nancy hit her face with a large stone during the second hymn. (I think it must have been a small nut.) She says the children could hear me, quite well enough for them, if they were right back against the wall. It's hard to serve God and Mrs. Pardy.

I wish to treat this wife of an elder as a father should, but it is very difficult. I would much rather be a father to all the children that Hester taught. I do indeed always try to put the children in a right mind to obey the magistrate : Mr. Pardy is a magistrate. But do the wives of the magistrates always show the meek and holy virtue of forgiveness ?

My left hand is bound up in linen cloths ; the broken bottle the girls threw at me cut all my fingers. I dare say I was a tempting mark for the bottle. I fear I must have been, and besides, it had to be thrown somewhere.

Earley, you must forgive me saying so, I have not had your advice for so long, but I fear the Church is not to us what it used to be. The love of it is so much lost in the error of fashionable Godliness. The children throw stones (or nuts) ; the town goes its own ways ; the Church goes hers.

I hope I have not said too much. I do not want to be unjust to Mrs. Pardy—the nut striking her suddenly might really have hindered her devotions, poor lady—but I wish all the same that I could have the children in the front pews.

I hope I haven't tired you with all this talk.

Yours ever, my dear Earley,

RICHARD HAYSOM

A day or two after receiving his friend's letter, Mr. Earley wrote the following in reply :—

ENMORE VICARAGE.

MY DEAR HAYSOM,—

I am a debtor to you. I should have written before. The holy time of Easter is near, but I feel unprepared for its blessings.

We all have our trials, Haysom. But at this moment I think it is wonderful to be alive.

No, Haysom, you must not let the children be put farther back, no, not even if they do throw nuts and hit Mrs. Pardy. I wonder if that little Nancy is a very wicked girl?

Do we clergy know enough about sin, I wonder? In order to help others, I mean.

This morning, when I looked out of my window, all the sky was filled with a soft burning light. The morning was almost wicked in its beauty, almost wicked.

Do you think there can be anything wonderful in the beauty of wickedness? Is it better than mere nothingness? We are rather stagnant here in Enmore, you know.

When I pray beside old Betsy, I often wonder what

she is thinking of.   Alas, I fear our very garments
carry false pride in them sometimes.   What if Betsy
only thinks how nice it is to have a gentleman praying for her.   Would she let me pray for her if I
were a ragged tramp—do tramps ever pray ?

Haysom, I hope the young woman you recommended to us is happy here.   I want all Enmore to
be happy.

I wished when the inn was closed that the people
would come to church and learn to be happy.   I hope
I am doing good here at Enmore.   Oh, Haysom, I
often wonder whether I have done right, and still
more whether I am going to do right.

I cannot forget that wonderful wicked look in the
sky.   Forgive my nonsense, this spring weather is a
little tiring, I think.

Ever yours,
ALBERT JOHN EARLEY.

CHAPTER XXV

CONVERSATION

THE Rev. Richard Haysom had always advised
his friend, Mr. Earley, to be friendly to all
his people, to do good to all men, and to talk in modern
fashion.

" In these days we must follow the times," Mr.
Haysom used to say, " and although we, no doubt,
do waste a great deal of our time, one can never
tell what good may not come of a quiet conversation."

With his life's work falling—as he feared—all to

pieces, Mr. Earley would try when occasion offered
to at least follow in little matters, if he failed in the
big ones, the advice of his friend.

And so this 2nd of April, the day before Good Friday, when Mr. Earley, as chance, or else his destiny,
would have it, found himself standing just inside the
village school door near to Mrs. Heath, the head-
teacher, he found himself obliged—thinking of his
friend—to talk to her.

As a fit subject of conversation Hester would not
do for the moment in hand.   For one reason Hester
was also in the schoolroom putting away the registers,
and for another, Mrs. Heath might not be best pleased
with the turn affairs were taking in the clergyman's
mind.

Searching about for a proper subject Mr. Earley
rushed upon H. G. Wells.

"Yes, yes, a clever writer," the mistress remarked,
and nodded her thin head.   Mrs. Heath's lined face
looked more than ever shallow and pinched, as though
all the cramped and pinched minds of her pupils had
indented their teacher's head with their stupidity.
Mrs. Heath was standing with her wearied face almost
touching the whitewashed wall that was dulled by
time into being nearly the same colour as the skin of
the teacher.

Mr. Earley forgot his friend's counsel.   He longed
to beat the poor woman's head against the wall that
she so much resembled, and then to enter the schoolroom and throw himself upon Hester and stifle her
with kisses.   As he talked about Mr. Wells, Mrs.
Heath nodded her head again.   A narrow strip of

dirty white hair curled round her left ear as she nodded.

Presently, after praising Mr. Wells, she began to speak of the Church services and of the bishops. For the first time in his life Mr. Earley hated the bishops and the Church services.

Hester was now come into the porch, and was standing near to the bell rope. She was also standing so near to Mr. Earley that he could almost feel her breath.

Mrs. Heath was saying—Mr. Wells having led up to something grander than himself—that she intended to go to Eveleigh next day in order to attend the service that was held at St. Luke's.

Mr. Earley saw the service, he also saw Hester.

For several hours on Good Friday old women were wont to kneel down at St. Luke's while the sullen and prolonged service continued, one curate after another taking his turn and then flying away from the church, nearly as thankful as Satan when let loose from Heaven.

Mr. Earley saw Hester. She was looking out of the doorway ; she was bored and utterly tired of the country. Her look of boredom excited Mr. Earley the more ; she looked as though any sin in her state of mind would be agreeable.

"What are you going to do to-morrow ? " Mr. Earley asked timidly of Hester.

"Oh, I suppose I shall go and pick primroses," Hester replied ; "all the people about here like to pick primroses on Good Friday."

Mr. Earley wished himself a tiger, so that he might spring upon and devour every bit of her.

N

CHAPTER XXVI

FARMER HART AND A GIRL

FARMER HART was gone out into his field to see to a cow that had calved.

He knew it would. A cow generally calved in his field—and usually it was a red cow—in the spring of the year.

Farmer Hart expected this to happen, only this calf was born nearer to the parson's hedge, that was the only difference in the case.

It was a young red cow this time that had the calf. The bull had jumped the hedge—yes, he remembered that—and now here was this young calf under the hedge. That was how life went on.

Mr. Hart had seen from his own house door the shining red body of the calf, and near to the calf was its mother lying down. He walked slowly up to the cow; the meek creature lay resting and taking no notice of its calf.

"What a lovely little calf!"

A girl had been walking across the field at the same time as the farmer; she had followed him to where the calf was lying, and then she had spoken.

After the day that he had peeped through the cow-house window and seen the girl, Mr. Hart had been a different man. The times had changed; indeed, his whole outlook had altered. He now saw the motion and movement of young women as something worth looking at. He had been carried along all the years of his life towards this pretty hope—towards a girl! Since the day when he had first peeped at her, there was always in his mind the picture of a light figure crossing a field.

Through long dismal years it had come to this at last. How slowly, craftily, the years had drawn him on—to this.

At first in his tradesman's soul it was wrapped up—this fine pretty hope—like a mummy, so he hardly knew what the thing really was. But there were signs of the years dancing, of the seasons dancing, within him.

In all this extremity of new wonder, Mr. Hart kept his cool usual countenance, while to his sisters he was gloomily the same.

"What a lovely little calf!"

Farmer Hart looked round.

All the years of his life, all the sameness assumed one shape—a girl's. Mr. Hart hardly knew what he was or who he was, and yet he seemed to be the same. Something had been—an explosive he thought—working up in him, and now it was likely to burst.

It was perfectly natural that Hester should be returning to her lodgings on this Thursday. As the school had broken up for the holidays—only three days—she had been rather later than usual. She was now returning to Mr. Warry's for tea.

Mr. Hart helped the calf upon its legs. Hester looked on ; she noticed how gently the farmer handled the calf.

Mr. Hart looked timidly at Hester, he wished to speak.

This new wish—to speak to a girl—was the first outward sign of the change in his life, and his voice, when it came—he hardly himself knew the sound of it—was so different to his usual tones.

"It's a big calf for such a young cow," remarked the farmer as he dragged the calf to the cow's head for the mother to lick.

"The beast seems fond of its calf." Hester spoke carelessly.

The calf, the field, the old women at home, all the sameness of the farmer's life departed from him. He only felt the presence of the girl who stood near to him.

"How will you spend to-morrow?" the farmer asked.

Hester did not reply for a moment; she might have gone home to Eveleigh on Good Friday, but there were ghosts in Enmore, and the ghosts were more alive than the St. Luke's bells. More than once she had seen a shadow in the sheep field, a shadow that was not Mr. Poose. Hester intended to solve the mystery of this shadow before she returned to the town.

There had been rumours, even Mr. Warry had said something, that in the Pound he had enlarged into a visit to the bar-room at Shelton with a girl—it had really been a word about a ghost.

And then there was Miss Hart too, who was always seeing strange men about now that she was always thinking of one man so much.

Hester Dominy looked upwards, a flock of white gulls were flying towards the cliffs. Hester watched the birds.

"I want to go to the sea," she said. "I have never been to the sea all the time I have lived at Enmore."

"My sisters pick primroses on Good Friday," Mr. Hart said thoughtfully.   "But you are going to the sea."

"Yes, I want to find the steep path that leads down to the beach."

"Oh, you will find it easily, easily," the farmer said.

The cow had risen and was feeding near, and Mr. Hart began to guide the calf towards the farm, the cow lowed and followed.

The farmer turned and watched Hester—she was colour, wonderful colour, all the colours of the rainbow. She was more than that even to the harmless simple man : she was music, celestial music ; all her being touched divine notes of harmony.

Hester stooped down to pick a cowslip ; she too turned and smiled, and the sun shone upon her, all about her there was a warm shining glow.

CHAPTER XXVII
A FALSE SCENT

THE day was Good Friday. The Miss Harts told their brother that they were going to pick primroses. It happened to be the first real lie that they had ever told, and they blushed as they told it.

"Of course, he would not understand if we did explain our plan to him," Grace said. "How could he understand ? He always goes on in the same old way. How can he know anything about a woman's thoughts ? "

Farmer Hart was sitting at his desk turning over

the leaves of his pass-books.   He appeared lost in his
accounts, but he looked up as his sisters went through
the gate and watched them go ; he even rubbed his
chin as he watched.   He fancied that they shut the
garden-gate more noisily than usual.

Mr. Hart closed his pass-book ; his hand trembled
as he closed it.

The Miss Harts had gone through the gate as
though they were really going to pick primroses.   They
went a little way down the lane and then turned into
a meadow and took exactly the opposite direction.
After walking along the path that passed at the back
of the village blacksmith's shop, they began to climb
the upland downs that led to the sea.

They walked hurriedly, nervously, as though they
were followed by all their past years that flouted the
final hope of their lives.

When at last they reached the cliff, the sisters breathed
deeply as though encouraged.

A sweet free air was blowing, the scent of the gorse
bloom warmed by the spring sun came to them like
fairy favours.   They did not speak to one another,
they felt too ashamed ; they felt too ashamed almost
to move, but at last they began to walk slowly on the
short dry turf.   Reaching the cliff they looked down
the narrow path that led to the sea.   To them it
appeared as a mere cut in a precipice that went down
for ever.

"Mr. Earley always comes this way on Good Friday," Grace Hart said, trembling.   "Oh, if we were
only down there he would be sure to see us, and we
can't wait about here like the birds."

A young rabbit scampered down the path : the way seemed quite easy for the rabbit.

A seagull swooped down and settled upon the sands. Miss Hart sighed ; the going down had been so easy for the seagull.

Grace Hart put one foot into the path, but quickly drew it back again.

" Is there no other way for us to get down ? " Susan asked sadly.

" Yes, dear, there is another way if we have time." Miss Grace considered. " Yes, there is time.   Mr. Earley never starts out at once after his lunch ; he waits a little and rests."

The two women—older than they wished themselves, alas! and more slow—began to hurry as best they could along the cliff. They walked stoopingly, without speaking to one another ; they walked in a strained stiff manner, as though their whole happiness depended upon their getting to the sands in time to be seen there.

Reaching the sands at last, a sad doubt came into their minds.

" Will he come ? " Grace Hart asked aloud.

" Oh yes, he always comes this way on Good Friday "—Susan Hart was sure of it—" so why should he not come to-day ? "

They were walking towards the widest reach of the sand, to where they knew anyone passing along the cliff would be sure to see them.

" Why should he not come to-day ? " Susan said again a little pettishly.

" Because of her."

"Oh, she has gone to pick primroses.   He would never go there to-day, he could never follow her, because the children would laugh at him."

"Would Mr. Earley mind what the children say ? "

"Oh yes, he would mind what they said."

They had now reached the stretch of yellow sands, the nearest way to which was the steep path.

"If he came he would help us to climb up ; he likes to help."   Grace Hart looked at the steep path with fear and trembling : it did not appear to be quite so dangerous from below.

They watched the cliff.   In the distance there was a figure slowly walking ; the figure stopped sometimes and looked towards the sea.   It was a man.

"It must be, it must be Mr. Earley," they both said with one voice.

They watched the figure intently.   He moved slowly, and now and again looked back.   He seemed to be expecting some one to meet him.

He was nearer now, nearer, and the sisters, knowing that they were seen, crossed to where the steep path began to climb.   The old women were excited and happy.   He was watching them, they were sure of it ; he would, they knew, never let them climb that steep path alone ; he would see the distress they were in, he would be sure to help.

They trembled as though they had suddenly caught fire.   They were not dead stars any more, they had blazed up into a glorious Nova.   He must help them, he must love them, they knew it.   "He would hold their hands,"—oh, how their aged thoughts ran riot ! —"he would hold them close if they tottered."

They struggled up the path, they clutched at the chalk ; their hands were bleeding, but they never noticed the blood.   They were half-way up the path; he would come down to them, he must come down.

The path turned slightly, and they saw the man: it was not Mr. Earley, it was—and the sisters could hardly believe their own eyes—it was Mr. Robert Hart, their brother.   Oh, cruel Fate ! what a dastard stroke to deal to aged love !

They went on slowly climbing, there was nothing else left for them to do ; their hands and feet would not let them fall, they clung like black bats to the side of the cliff.

Mr. Robert Hart descended slowly to help them. . . .

CHAPTER XXVIII
THE SAME THING AGAIN

NEAR to the farm Mr. Hart left his sisters and turned into his dairy meadows.   He had walked a few yards behind them all the way from the cliff.

The Miss Harts had never looked round at him once; all the way home their thoughts had hurried back to their past life, as though it were—all the old simple way of it—their only refuge.

They never even looked to see, as they turned from the cliff, whether the priest had come after all.   Their hopes were stricken dead by this one shaft of Fate.   A ghost, like the man who walked in the sheepfold, their hope had become ; as a ghost they must pass it by now, always pass it by.

Their failure brought them home again to the home

that they knew best. They now thought of Mr. Earley only as a kind gentleman whom they would be always ready to help in his village labours. The old women slunk home like beaten dogs to their kennel. They had been dragged back by their own weary years; they must go into the narrow pit again that is, after all, only a kind of preparation for a narrower. Very soon they would be again patting the butter, pat, pat, pat, and the churn would wearily rumble round. And then, of course, a dirty child comes to the door with a penny for some skim milk.

They would be in Church again the next Sunday and the next; there would always be the next Sunday until the end.

The nearer the farm the slower the two old women walked. They walked limply, dejectedly; the gleam of glory was gone, they were now eternally themselves.

But slowly, too, there crept back into their hearts their old order to comfort them.

"Perhaps we had better use the new table-cloth to-night for tea," Grace said. "It will be nice to see something new, and we might try to make a new covering for the arm-chair."

These homely plans rose up like ancient servants to comfort them. They had been driven out of the courts of love by the weight of their years, and now they returned as true old maids would return to the little pieces of furniture for comfort.

"To-morrow we will clean the silver," Grace said.

"And the back-kitchen ought to be whitewashed," Susan added.

"Yes, and we must ask Robert about the new chair."

The two old maids' thoughts, like soft feathery moths, were fluttering about in the darkened rooms amongst the varnished sticks. They had tried the sunshine for a moment, but for a moth the brightest sunshine is the deepest gloom.

CHAPTER XXIX
HIMSELF AGAIN

WHEN Robert Hart turned from his sisters and entered his own field, he was dimly conscious that a light had gone out in his heart.

He walked about the field, and as he walked he kept asking himself:

"What had he been doing? What had he been thinking of? What was it all about? Why had he gone up to the cliff?"

How did he know? It was enough for him that the sameness met him in his own field.

He was the same again, the field was the same? Why had he ever been different?

Perhaps it was the ghost that his sisters had talked so much about. Mr. Poose had a friend—the farmer knew—who helped the shepherd sometimes. Mr. Hart never troubled himself about strangers. He was out in his own field looking for another calf—yes, perhaps?

The farmer stood still and watched his sisters entering the garden-gate with a basket. The old women were walking softly, demurely; Mr. Hart had once seen two old grey cats walking in exactly the same way.

Where had he been, too, meanwhile? Into wild seas of foaming colour, into no safe places—and, after all, an utter sameness in life is the best haven of security. After all, he had only to step ashore in order to be saved.

Ever since he had watched—oh, "a young woman," from the cow-house—he had been swimming in the wildest seas. How unnecessary that seemed now, when life could be so quiet, when he could simply walk round the farm as he had always been used to do, and perhaps lean over a gate and look at the rooks in grey weather.

As the farmer entered his own garden he was thinking of his bank-balance.

He was looking at the worst side of the question to see if he could possibly be ruined. No, how could he ever be ruined? The swine-fever had made no difference, and the last bad harvest had made no difference. How could this wild walk of his after a young woman make any difference?

Mr. Hart quietly entered his own door and went into the parlour. The first thing he did was to open his writing-desk and take out his pass-book and compare the figures with the old returned cheques. As usual at that time of the year, there was the correct balance ready for the rent.

Mr. Hart could hear his sisters talking about a ghost. As they talked they moved about like grey old cats and set the table. But the ghost seemed to silence them, for they talked of nothing more that evening.

CHAPTER XXX
THE LOST PRIMROSE

ON this eventful Good Friday, Mr. Earley was walking with a quick step.   He had finished his lunch early and was hurrying towards the primrose copse in a gay mood.   His way led over a little hill, and then he would go down to where the main-road crawled like a white snake in the green valley.

Within Mr. Earley's ken there were little figures that scampered ; the figures wore coloured frocks.

" They must be the children that always go out to pick primroses on Good Friday," Mr. Earley thought.

The priest wished to be with Hester ; he intended to pluck her as though she were a pretty primrose on this blessed Good Friday.

The idea of picking her—a girl—as though she were a primrose, pleased Mr. Earley.   His walk was joyful ; he knew the birds were twittering gaily, he understood now, he knew what the birds meant by their singing.

There was no doubt in Mr. Earley's mind as to where Hester was : she had said herself that she was going to pick primroses, and of course she would be there.

He knew—for he was wiser even than his friend, Mr. Haysom—that there were many hidden places in those primrose copses.

" No, she would never have said she would be there if she did not mean to be."   He was quite glad now that he saw Hester so very clearly as his one sin. " Every man must sin once," he thought, " once."

And, after all, the little good deeds that he did in the

village had driven him to it. Mr. Earley had now reached the top of the hill and looked down into the valley.

Little strips of colour were running here and there under the hill. Hester was, no doubt, already in the copse picking her first primrose.

Mr. Earley had never picked primroses before. To pick primroses with Hester ! What God could wish to take away such joy ? There was no need to hurry ; why should he hurry ? There was only a rather late evensong to go home to.

" They might even go into the dairy meadows and find some cowslips."

Of course, there would be the remorse—afterwards —but that even would be better than the dread apathy that he so loathed.

Mr. Earley swung his stick as he went down the hill; he even leaped upon the bank on one side of the lane and sang a verse of a vulgar song taken from the soldiers. The yellow sunshine met him, he was conscious for the first time in his life how much he loved the scent of the wind. Though he was not actually near to her yet, Mr. Earley felt her near; he felt her as a part of himself even. He could have shouted for joy.

" How cramped and disgusting," he thought, " is the virtue that expels love."

Mr. Earley had now reached the great road ; he heard the merry laughter of children in the primrose copse—he knew she was there.

By the side of the great road—Roman in its beginnings—there is a wide grassy place that stretches away towards the heath. Mr. Earley chanced to look that way and saw the figure of a man walking. This was by no means a strange thing to see on Good Friday, but walking after the man, a few hundred yards away from him, there was a girl. Mr. Earley knew the girl—she was Hester.

Who hath ever turned aside from the safe and beaten track, so well known, to wander amongst rose-bushes that have thorns—and tries to pluck one perchance—will know only too well the sudden ebb of Mr. Earley's emotion. Hasten to the beaten track, quick, quick, while there be time. What do roses matter? 'Tis all illusion. Back to the commonplace, back to the dull routine, back to the sermon, back to the gloom!

His eyes had been shut, of course, till that moment; all lovers' eyes are shut. But now, here was it all so open—Hester so plain to see—all of her. Of course, she must mean to meet that man on the Heath. But what was Hester? Oh, quite gone, utterly lost was that short mad view of her.

Of course he had come for a walk—so natural a thing to do—on Good Friday. Even a preacher of the Gospel must sometimes go for walks in the roads, for after all the roads are free.

Mr. Earley turned and began walking up the hill again. He never looked back. Hester might follow the man whithersoever she pleased, the children could laugh on now—he never looked back.

Mr. Earley began to think of his evening service.

He followed up this pious line of thought with the coal club; he hoped the members would each have a ton and a half of coal by Christmas if they paid all the summer. He must look over the names again to see how many belonged.

As he went down the little hill into the village, he wondered whether he was well enough off to have the Church organ tuned. He would give up smoking, " Yes, that would pay it." He would also ask the Miss Harts to collect in the village—they were so ready to help.

Near to the village Mr. Earley met an old woman who was gathering sticks. Mr. Earley stood with bent head and talked for half an hour to the old woman.

When he left the old woman he began to make plans. He would open all the missionary boxes that very evening, and stick new labels on each box ; they had been collected, these village boxes, some days ago— and now he would open them.

On the Tuesday next there was to be a prayer-meeting in the schoolroom ; he must think of a suitable subject for prayer—the primroses, perhaps ?

Such thoughts, like old homely cows, browsed about in his mind, but instead of eating the plain grass they were eating the flowers.

Mr. Earley slowly entered his gate, and going indoors and into his study, he took up his pen in order to make a few notes about the evening sermon.

The servant knocked at the door gently, as though she half expected to find her master praying. It was Mr. Earley's tea : the usual teapot, the usual plate and cup, the usual cake and bread and butter.

The creatures who ate in his mind raised their heads, as though they sought for more flowers, but they saw none.

Mr. Earley looked at his fingers as he cut the cake. They were fingers made to open little boxes of money and to hold prayer-books.

Mr. Earley saw his life—until the end. There would be all the good advice he would give to his friend Mr. Haysom, about the services, and what else ? Oh, those little wooden boxes of money, and the prayer-books he would have to hold—until the end. His old flatfooted way had come into him to live with him, relieved only as it might be with a talk sometimes with Mr. Haysom, but it would stay now, and Mr. Earley knew it, until the end.

Mr. Earley rose wearily from his chair. Though he had cut the cake he had eaten none of it. The last church bell was ringing, the five minutes' bell. He knew its tolling sound ; he wished it was for himself that it tolled.

In the church he read the lesson where the Bible opened, without chosing a passage, and as he read a voice seemed to speak to him saying : " From darkness unto darkness is the way of man."

And the words out of the book proved the voice to be true : " Woe unto you that desire the day of the Lord ! To what end is it for you ? The day of the Lord is darkness, and not light."

CHAPTER XXXI
NATURE THE HEALER

THE same Good Friday had a certain importance for Antony Dine, because he had reached his last shilling. The day was also important to Hester

Dominy, because of her final revolt against Enmore. It was important too to the men of the Pound because during the evening of Good Friday Mr. Warry was wont to entertain them with some more than usually tasty stories. It might have been the springtime, perhaps, that would inspire Mr. Warry, the spring-time that brought out the old women with their sun-bonnets on, so that even Mr. Poose did not know his own mother when he met her in the road.

Antony Dine and his last shilling had met and were looking at one another.

Up to that moment, from the time he had left his own doorway, Antony had been living as though in the wonderful lunar plain called the Sea of Serenity. He had learned to know by sight, if not by name, all the winter creatures who lived in Enmore. His ears had grown accustomed to the sounds of the elements. He enjoyed the splash upon the hut roof of the heavy down-pouring of the night rains. He had breasted the winds upon the hills until he was beaten almost to his knees by their violence. He had trodden the March ice in the woodland pond ; he had watched the snipe rise where the brook ran icebound in the low meadows. He had risen as it were from a doleful eternity of labour, from the mad longings of a stifled love, into a clean world of cold rain storms, of simple sheep, and wide free lands.

Antony had fled away free, and now here was his last shilling. Would it call him back ?—he feared it might. But what of that ; had he not one more day to spend as he chose ?

The kindly earth had indeed nursed him in the

lap of her joys.   The moan of the wind had entered
his dreams and blessed him.   And now spring had
come, and Good Friday, and his last shilling.   He
had one day more.   Antony Dine left the hut ; he
went down to the brook and washed, splashing his
hair and face in the cool water.   The larch-tree was
in bud, the chestnut-tree was in leaf.   The divine
spring had come.   He thought he would go from
one part to another of the scenes that had brought
him so much gladness.

He ate some breakfast, that his usual attendant, Mr.
Poose's little boy—a firm believer in ghosts—had
brought to him in exchange for his last shilling, and
then started for his walk.

He first climbed the downs, going by a footpath
that led up beside a thorn-hedge that was breaking
into leaf.   He reached the downs, the sun had warmed
the grass, and Antony lay down and smelt the earth.
Oh, how good it was, the rich earthy smell, how full
of the power of life, how full of the scent of the
gods !   He looked far away, down, down, down,
across the heath.   He would go there, where the
green knobs of the bracken were pressing out of
the soft sandy earth, so sweet a covering for their
winter sleep.

The sun was above him now ; as he descended from
the downs his shadow was not so directly before him.
He passed on and on, God's fairies, spring fairies, were
in his path.   There was laughter, and as he turned
once the form of a girl moved behind him.   It was
all good to see : Nature supreme ; labour drowned
in everlasting beauty ; action consumed in divine

thought ; the flames of loveliness rising everywhere, burning all the malice of the world.

Antony softly entered the wood. He climbed up into a chestnut-tree ; the green leaves hid him from the ground. He lay there amid the branches and forgot himself, forgot the world, and lived, lived in those moments as in eternity, surrounded by the spring beauty of the fresh green leaves.

CHAPTER XXXII

HESTER FOLLOWS A GHOST

WHEN Hester Dominy awoke on Good Friday she heard the bell of Enmore. It reminded her of those other bells that she used to know so well.

She did not like Mr. Earley ; she did not like " the stupid farmer," as she called Mr. Hart. There was more life, she fancied, in one little slip of a St. Luke's Sunday child—with all its nasty ways—than in all the Enmore infants. Hester was shrewdly aware, too, that in all village life there is a kind of goblin humour that spares none, a humour that grins at every human being as though he or she were a sort of peep-show for the Fates to mock at. The false teeth of the town, the smell of pork and cabbage, nay, the very town rats, did not seem to Hester's mind to be so evilly inclined as the humour that lived in the country.

As she dressed—hardly troubling to look into the glass—she wondered who the ghost-like presence really was that haunted the sheep-folds. Her mother had told her that Antony Dine had left Eveleigh, and had gone—so rumour had it—to buy houses in London. Hester had passed over this item of news, and, girl-like, she expected her friend to be at his machine if ever she returned to her native city. She never thought for a moment that the ghost of the sheep-fold was Antony Dine. And yet it was the mystery of this figure, that was wont to stand at eve against the skyline, that gave Hester—and she knew not why it was—the only thrill of pleasure that she had known at Enmore. This moving figure upon the hills and the church shadows were the only marks of interest that Hester had found. They uttered notes, those shadows—heavy dreary notes, like the bells of St. Luke's. And the figure of the man awakened that same curious home feeling that she had when the school-children born of the bells vanished in the street. She had sought in Enmore for something that vanished, and she found it in the shadows and the ghost. To flee back again to her old ways, to let the town, to let the bells, to let the rat, the smells even of the cabbage sink into a sameness that would become again as it had wont to be—a picture of shadows, a picture of ghosts, until, and such was Hester's desire, the dream of life should thicken, become stationary, become as a painting upon the walls of time, causing her, the bells, the vanishing children, and even the ferrymen to touch a kind of frozen immortality.

During this Good Friday breakfast Mr. Warry spoke respectfully to Hester about the weather, and expressed his opinion that it was going to be warm.

After helping Mrs. Warry in clearing away the plates, Hester took up her hat and went out. From the fields she could see the upland down; a figure moved there. Hester trembled. It was the shadow-figure—the ghost.

Hester climbed the downs. Midday came and went; she saw no one.

She climbed a tumulus and looked across the valley. The same form that she had seen upon the downs moved over the fields towards the heath and the wood. She would know the figure anywhere, though it were but a speck of dark dust upon the earth. Hester followed; she crossed the brook, the village lane, the grass fields again; she reached the great field that bordered the heath. The man must have loitered somewhere, for he was nearer now. The main-road ran beside this field, and Hester noticed that Mr. Earley was watching her from a gate-way.

Hester hurried on, and turned into the woods. She had seen the man, the ghost, go in under the trees. She walked through the wood, searching everywhere, but could find nothing; the whole wood was silent, the man had vanished.

On her way home to Enmore Hester met Mr. Pike at work on the roadside. The road-mender made her a pretty compliment, and she stood and talked to him. Mr. Pike was so loath to release her that he went on talking in a kindly manner—his voice getting louder and louder—as she moved farther, and even then he watched her until she turned a corner.

Beside the ghost and the shadows upon the church wall, Mr. Pike was, she thought, the most sensible being she had seen at Enmore.

Mr. Earley was "oh, so dull!" He would do nothing but talk about his friend Mr. Haysom, about the stars and about sermons. She could never think of Mr. Earley as being anything save what he was; she could never think of him vanishing.

As to Mr. Warry, he never spoke about anything except the weather and his pigs.

As she walked on after leaving Mr. Pike, Hester longed more than ever to be home again, to sit upon the tailor's stool and to listen to the machine.

Even her thoughts there—strange love thoughts—had become like ghosts, that flitted here and there in that stuffy room like dusty feathers. She liked it to be like this, she loved the ghost of love better than reality. The bells of St. Luke's called her, the bells whose sounds vanished—vanished in the high tower.

And what did Mr. Hart want to look at her for. He was the kind of man to be always the same, the kind of man that would never vanish. And what a look his was; it might have been a cow making eyes. Enmore smelt of cows, smelt of pigs, smelt of mould; she could bear the smell no longer.

At tea Mr. Warry remarked that he thought the sun had gone down rather red, but he hoped the next day would be fine.

Hester decided to send a note to Mr. Earley to say she could stay there no longer, and that her mother wished her to return home.

Mr. Warry left the note at the Rectory on his way to the Pound.

CHAPTER XXXIII

WORK BEFORE PLEASURE

ANTONY DINE did not leave the shelter of his tree until late in the evening. Since he had spent his last shilling upon his breakfast he had eaten nothing. Hunger, that driver of harnessed and bitted men, had begun to lash. Antony felt the blows, and already began to look towards the Eveleigh road.

Had all his joy been, after all, illusion? Had eternal labour, as sure of its prey as death, sought him out even in the uttermost wilderness? Was it true that real happiness dwelt in the country? Did the simple people of the country find their lives such a daytime of pleasure? Seeing things in the light of his last shilling—that was gone—Antony Dine felt himself to be in a doubting mood.

He wished to make sure, he wished to sample his fear, and so he thought he would betake him to the Enmore Pound and listen to what was being said there.

Making the best of his way to that place of harmony, Antony crouched behind the crumbling wall in order to listen to the conversation that went on. Were these men also stricken with labour of the world as he had been stricken?

Antony Dine listened to the talk within.

It had touched, this talk, as usual, upon the master

of the farm, who had been noticed by Mr. Poose
walking about his garden as though he had regained
his old step again. Passing from the farmer to his
sisters and then to the parson of the parish, Mr.
Matterface started the well-known turn.

"'Tis most like," the ex-landlord remarked,
"Warry 'ave something to tell."

"He did use to tell we some'at in days gone by," Mr.
Chipp murmured.

Mr. Warry coughed. "Thee do all know thik
wold barn of farmer's," the dairyman said in his
mildest tone, as though he were either confessing to
a priest or else telling droll tales to Satan.

"Yes, we do know where thee do mean," came
the chorus.

"Well, neighbours, after I'd seen to pigs, and carried
they cheese up to loft, an' cleaned out stable, an' fed
the bull—an' 'e be nasty-tempered too sometimes.
An' after I'd cut out some hay from stack an' planted
a line or two of kidney 'taties, an' driven hens out of
garden, an' cleaned me tools, an' got me sticks for
the morning, I took she into thik wold barn, an' I
do know now that she be a girl."

"I don't doubt your word, dairyman," said Mr.
Matterface, "for 'tain't to be expected that the other
kind would go so far as wold barn wi' 'ee."

"'Tis fair truth what I do tell 'ee," Mr. Warry
remarked, looking round at his friends, "for at t'other
end of barn there be straw still lying about same as
'twere when we thatched barn for farmer."

"An' what did 'ee take an' do to thik maid in straw,
dairyman?" inquired Mr. Chipp, who always liked

the details of a story. " I don't suppose you touched she or tickled she same as flea mid do."

"He, he," replied Mr. Warry, laughing, " I do know all about they maidens, I do."

"You never snared she, I hope," said Mr. Chipp.

"What time were it that 'ee took maiden into barn?" Mr. Pike inquired, with a knowing wink.

"Truth to tell, neighbours," replied Mr. Warry, " I never noticed the time, but 'twere all done after I'd cleaned milk pails out, and fed they calves, and given a drink to sick cow in shed, an' set rat-trap in apple-loft, and lit stable lantern for to mend a bit of harness that were broke this morning; no, no, I can't mind exactly what time 'twere when I went out to thik wold barn. An' I do now mind it, thik maid were scared at a great white owl that did fly out on a sudden."

"Thee be the one to snare they maidens," said Mr. Chipp, laughing.

"Maidens!" echoed Mr. Pike angrily; "maidens! 'tis snakes they be, ugly snakes; Satan's self, they be, in human clothes. Maidens! they bain't no more maidens than me wold cat be a maid. Don't I know their lying sneaking way, don't I? There be poor parson stung wi' en, poor man that 'e be to run after thik school teacher. Look 'ee round, landlord, at thik pretty small village, Enmore, 'tis its name where we folk do bide. Tales be told, 'tis the 'omen; needles be left in chairs, 'tis they 'omen; pub be closed, 'tis they 'omen; rates be rose, 'tis they 'omen 'ave done it. Squalling children be born—they 'omen again. But there be one thing they 'omen will never do, an' that be to work. Look at thik, Landlord Matterface!"—Mr. Pike displayed a large rent in his coat—"I broke thik in paddock six months ago. Now 'tis me belief 'twere Satan 'is own self changed to a maiden that dairyman Warry took to wold barn, and sad though it be, Warry is damned safe for having ought to say to thik wold cooty."

"Thee be wrong for once, Pike," said the dairyman, not a little put out however by the suggestion, "for I do mind seeing a horse's shoe put up on wold barn, and so, road-mender, thee be a liar, though I do say it."

"'Tis they 'omen that be liars," said Mr. Pike, retreating a little towards the entrance of the Pound as though to shake off the evil imputation that Mr. Warry had flung upon him.

"Don't 'ee say too much against they 'omen," Mr. Matterface said soothingly, feeling it was high time to interfere. "And don't 'ee say too much in praise of they neither, Mr. Dairyman. They be mortal bodies, they 'omen be, mortal bodies, though made something different to we menfolk. And no doubt God do know what 'E did make they for. We folk be blind sometimes, so 'tis well that God do see plain what 'E be about. Dairyman be right and road-mender be right and so Time it be."

Having had the last word and given his verdict, Mr. Matterface rose up and slowly made his way out of the Pound.

Shepherd Poose stood waiting for a moment or two after the others were gone. He had felt himself left out of the conversation, and wished at least to give his opinion, even though there were no one to hear it.

"They 'omen be some'at good, some'at bad," he said, speaking slowly, "but 'tis a mortal pity they bain't born dogs."

Mr. Poose slowly wended his way home, followed by Jock, who kept close to his heels.

CHAPTER XXXIV
THE ONLY ESCAPE

OUTSIDE the Pound wall Antony Dine had been listening to the conversation that we have narrated. Round and about the dairyman's fancy tales he had felt there was the same recurrent eternity of labour that is man's portion upon earth. Mr. Warry's humour acted as a thin garment through which the dark body of labour could be plainly seen. Antony Dine sat up and crossed his legs in the old attitude that he knew so well.

The recurring toil of every-day labour, all that everlasting cleaning up of pig-sties, dung-lifting for ever and ever, appeared to Antony Dine as being an even worse torment than his own trade. Antony Dine's heart that had rushed out to meet the healthful glory of divine nature now sank like a stone. His right hand moved as though it held the handle of a machine, his left hand deftly moved invisible cloth : he was immersed in the old toils again.

Antony Dine began to walk slowly through the village, going the same road that he had come on that starlight night in early autumn.

This night was even more beautiful ; all Nature was
clothed in a new garment, new life was everywhere
beginning.

Antony Dine strode on.

An owl went by so near that it almost touched
him with its wings ; the bird hooted woefully in the
meadows and passed away.

Antony walked on ; the everlasting scourge was
behind him, it bit into his flesh and drove him
on.

The stars did not matter now, they shone in their
eternal beauty, but the labour of the world deadened
their happy shining.

Antony did not look at the stars, he thought of
his wife. No doubt she was even then sweeping the
stairs with her sharp elbows sticking out like dirty
bone ends. She must be talking about the houses.
But possessing houses made no difference to his labours.
It was in his blood, this everlasting idea ; like a bee he
would soon be drowned again in the sea of his own
sad fate.

But—and a wonderful breath of romance passed
by as though it were a still small voice in the night
—would she be there ? Oh no ! Oh no, she would
not be there. The stool would be empty—empty
for ever. It would be only the noise of the machine
now, only the noise of the machine—and his hand
moving—and then darkness, darkness.

Antony was hot and thirsty ; he now passed by
the hedge, over which was the rabbit warren that
Mr. Warry kept for a cellar.

Antony climbed the hedge, unearthed one of the

dairyman's bottles and drank greedily. The beer dulled more than ever the sense of his late happiness. It could never have been ; there was no such thing as happiness under the sun; there was only labour, labour. If the sun shone, it shone in vain ; if the winds blew, they blew to no purpose. It was all the same everywhere in the world ; even among the stars there was the same eternity of labour. All men were driven to it, driven to it. It was the ideal of all, the longed-for state, the heaven upon earth.

There were those poor men of the Enmore Pound. Antony Dine saw their lives now—lives grey, beaten by cold whipping rains, lives dung-sodden. Even Mr. Pike, who had to dig forty yards by the village road before he could earn his breakfast, did not he toil on and on, taking one side of the road and then the other, but ever on and on.

Labour eternal ! it moves, moves, moves, moves. Where is the escape ? There was nothing in the earth, after all, save only the everlasting reiteration of the same forces of labour.

Suddenly Antony Dine felt different. A wave of infinite hope passed through him. He felt a sudden pain too that seemed to grip and slay him, but he did not care. One way there was that could save him, and one way alone. The beauty of Nature, the cold upland airs could not be drowned and lost in the deepest seas.

The pain increased, but slowly faintness overcame the pain. Antony walked on, but was he walking ? —he hardly knew. No, he was standing beside a little girl sitting upon a stool. He lifted her up and held her to his heart. Ah ! his heart—the heart of an old man, a breaking heart !

And then came the stroke of Fate, the saving stroke. Antony reeled and fell.

CHAPTER XXXV
THEY MAIDENS

A T Eveleigh there was to be held the usual Saturday sheep-fair, and to the fair Mr. Poose was going, having obtained leave of his master to take a day's holiday.

Mr. Poose, who liked good company upon the road, was gaily sitting beside Mr. Warry in the open van, for the dairyman too had business at Eveleigh. Beside Mr. Poose sat Hester Dominy.

On the Good Friday evening, Hester had sent a hasty note to Mr. Earley, telling him that she had decided to give up the position of teacher in the Enmore school. She said she had grown tired of the country. Hester then arranged with Mrs. Warry that a place should be given to her and to her belongings in the van the next day.

When the dairyman heard of this plan he was by no means so pleased as any reader of our little story would expect him to be. Indeed, when he heard the news of Hester's going—he was lacing up his market boots at the time—he merely muttered in none too happy tones that the pigs would take up all the room.

The truth of the matter being that the good dairyman had invented certain little country tales about

Hester, tales that he hoped would make Mr. Poose and himself chuckle and cough as they went along. And there would have to be the heroine of all his little stories sitting at his very elbow. Mr. Warry felt himself to be most unlucky. And once his bad luck began, he feared it might continue even to the length of abstracting his last bottle from the rabbit holes that were his cellar.

After putting on his boots, Mr. Warry harnessed his horse and backed his van against the pigsties. Meanwhile Mr. Poose had come up dressed in his best, and was ready to lift the net when the dairyman placed the pigs in the cart. The shepherd made no comment upon the situation until Mr. Warry remarked in a tone that showed his discontent :

" Thik road-man, 'e do know someat."

" Very like," Mr. Poose replied, " but 'e bain't nothing to me dog."

This simple reply did not go very far to ease Mr. Warry's trouble, and when one of the little pigs gave an unnecessary kick and entangled its leg in Mr. Warry's waistcoat, that worthy came out with the astonishing words : " Well then ! damn all they b—— maidens, I do say."

Mr. Poose, so taken aback by this extraordinary utterance, dropped the net just as Mr. Warry dropped the pig, which misadventure led to a chase of half an hour before the beast was caught.

During the drive to Eveleigh Hester Dominy felt annoyed because the cart went so slowly ; there was something sullen and disconcerting in the look upon Mr. Warry's face, so she did not even trouble herself to ask him to drive faster.

But on the whole Hester was happy. She would soon hear the bells; she would soon become a part of the dust and the dirt in Antony Dine's work-room; and she would soon see her mother's drooping cheeks and listen to her eternal talk about the rat and false teeth.

When the party reached the rabbit warren, Mr. Warry stopped the horse, descended from the cart and crept through the hedge; the Enmore shepherd followed. Proceeding from one rabbit hole to another, Mr. Warry thrust his hand in. He found nothing, even a bottle that he had placed there a week or more ago had been taken.

" What 'ave 'ee been looking for, dairyman ? " asked Mr. Poose, who was an interested watcher.

" Rabbits," replied Mr. Warry.

At the next bend of the road they saw lying under them beside the blue sea the town of Eveleigh.

Before descending the hill, the horse stopped of its own accord. Up from the valley, across the blue bay of water, over Jordan Hill, there came the sound of bells tolling.

" A funeral," thought Hester. " The bells of St. Luke's."

CHAPTER XXXVI
HE'S DEAD

MR. WARRY put Hester down beside the town clock, excusing himself from taking her any farther by saying that the pig-market was no suitable place for a young maiden, and that it were best for her to go to her home by another way. The dairyman added that he would bring her box round to her home in the afternoon.

Hester's heart grew lighter as she walked upon the well-known pavement, and even when she opened her mother's door in Ridgeway Street, she was pleased with the odour of burnt cabbage that greeted her.

Inside the kitchen she found her mother sitting by the table with a duster in her hand and the silver teapot upon her lap.

"You didn't get 'im, then?" were her mother's first words.

"Who, mother?"

"Why, Mr. Earley of course."

"No, mother, I've left Enmore. I am going to teach the St. Luke's children again; I'm tired of the country."

"I suppose Mr. Earley be the same as Mr. Haysom; he won't 'ave springs to 'is teeth. Well, I dare say you were right to refuse 'im, for what good is a man with his front teeth falling out. Mr. Earley can't afford springs, and Mr. Haysom can't afford springs; that's what's the matter. And I did offer to show Mr. Haysom 'ow easy they were: you 'ave only to take out the top and bottom at the same time."

"Oh, I know, mother," said Hester, smiling. "And the rat," she asked. "Antony Dine's rat?"

"That rat be the trial of my life," Mrs. Dominy moaned. "He comes over from next door now and runs up by the side of the wall. That rat's as large

as a rabbit, and it's because Mrs. Dine 'as bought the
next door that the rat lives there."

" Mrs. Dine's bought the next-door house, then ? "

" Yes, and she says she'll 'ave ours next year. Since
Antony's lived away she's saved more than ever."

Hester sat by the table ; there was pork and cabbage
for dinner.

The scent of the room, of the dinner, carried her
back to her childhood.   How many times after eating
such a dinner with that smell hanging about the house
had she run off to Antony Dine, often being greeted
with an angry " What be doing here ? " from the
sharp-visaged Mrs. Dine when she crossed her path
in the passage or on the stairs.

After eating a little, Hester Dominy sat upon the
faded sofa and allowed all the queer, fluffy home
feelings to gather about her—feelings that she knew
well enough were more to her than the whole world
and all its glories.   These same feelings had led again
to the tailor's work-room.   The poor work-worn
man was turning the machine ; she sat upon the stool
as of old.   Hester sighed a child's sigh.   She longed
to go to him and to listen to the machine, the everlasting
machine.

Hester went to a side-table that was covered with
a greasy green cloth ; she knew the very grease spots
upon it.   She wrote a short note to the Vicar of St.
Luke's, telling him that she had left Enmore and
would, if he wished it, take up her old duties as Sunday-
school teacher at St. Luke's.

As soon as Hester had written her letter, there
was a knock at the house door.

Hester had often heard the knock ; it went through her as a happy knocking, a home knocking. She had heard no sound so pleasing in all Enmore.

" It must be Mr. Warry with her box." She knew so well the pleasant suspense, the wonder. No, she had told Mr. Warry that he could send her box by a market porter—and the man had brought it already.

"Who could it be ? " All her childish inquisitiveness rose up in her.

Presently her mother appeared in the doorway ; her fat white cheeks hung almost over her neck.

" He's dead," Mrs. Dominy said excitedly.

"What, the rat ? " asked Hester.

"No, no, not the rat, not the rat, but Antony Dine."

CHAPTER XXXVII
SPRING AGAIN

MR. THOMAS, the oldest ferryman of all, discovered one day that the sun was shining.

After making this exciting discovery, Mr. Thomas knocked out the ashes of his pipe below the cannonball and walked slowly along beside the iron railings that guarded the quay.

Mr. Thomas knew every knob, every crack in the stones that lay between the wall and his boat. He looked over the rail as though he wished to discover something. He saw his boat ; it had water in it, but it still floated upon the surface of the quay. Mr. Thomas leaned over the railings and spat into the water. The spring had come.

Mrs. Thomas began that same morning to take the rags out of the crevices in the windows. She opened one window a little and looked out.

A girl passed in a white blouse ; Mrs. Thomas called out something nasty at the girl and shut the window again.

The spring had come to the town of Eveleigh.

Mr. Haysom was thinking about his sermon ; he was wondering if he could ever persuade the wives of the churchwardens to allow the school-children to sit higher up in the church. He turned the subject over and over in his mind, and at last he decided to ask his friend Mr. Earley again what he had better do, and so he left it there.

The bells of St. Luke's were ringing, but only the old women and Hester Dominy listened to them. And after they had rung for a while the old women moved slowly towards the church door. The Sunday-school children were already in their places upon the forms. The choir boys marched singing to their seats, and the service began.

In front of Hester were the backs of human creatures, mostly women ; all these people were moving along .the haunted road called " living." And yet they sat there in all the ugliness of St. Luke's.

These black prayer-books were now open. The odour of the church was as the odour of old women's garments.

Hester Dominy looked round at the children. One child had run a pin into the leg of the child who sat next to her. The face of the pricked child turned purple with rage. Hester looked sternly at the children.

Hester opened her prayer-book; the small print looked odd. What was it all about, the little black book with its small print? Prayers and hymns. Would Mr. Earley have known or the Miss Harts, or the shadows on the Enmore church wall; she wished she had asked those shadows.

After the service Hester marched with the children for a certain distance and then she left them. She saw the children vanish. Where had they all gone to? Hester did not know.

Hester Dominy walked slowly home.

Mrs. Dominy was nursing the teapot; she asked Hester whether Mr. Haysom had spoken to her. Hester said that he hadn't.

" He should 'ave springs to 'is teeth," Mrs. Dominy said. " You can't marry a man without springs."

Hester sat down wearily; the heavy scent of the cabbage hung about her.

" And the rat's been running along the wall again, the ugly thing."

In the afternoon Hester went to Mrs. Dine's.

There was a curious smell in Mrs. Dine's house, a smell a little like soaked cabbage and yet a little different.

Mrs. Dine was dressed in black, but the white bones of her sharp elbows could be seen even through her dress.

Mrs. Dine explained to Hester that she had not wished to " dirt a bed " and so she had had him laid upon the tailor's board. He was now in his coffin.

Hester Dominy went up to the well-known work-room of her friend.

She sat as usual upon the stool, pieces of cloth were strewn about ; some one had upset the bag of bits that she had numbered so carefully. All else was the same.

Beside the coffin was the machine and the scissors, the beeswax and the thread, the stove and the iron.

Hester allowed her head to sink into her hands ; she was seeing things. She saw before her a little grey old man working a machine.

The grey old man would sometimes look at her, with those little dark eyes of his, so curiously.

But he had wished her to go ; he had told her to go. He had sent her out into the sunlight. But was there any sunlight ?

Surely not.

ABRAHAM MEN

TO
STEPHEN TOMLIN

JODOCUS DAMKODERIUS, a lawyer of Bruges, (praxi rerum criminal 3. 112) hath some notable examples of such counterfeit cranks; and every village almost will yeeld abundant testimonies amongst us; we have dummerers, Abraham men, &c.

CHAPTER I

" DO you know, John Dunell, that they stones bain't real stones ? "

Without replying to his friend's remark John Dunell led the horse and cart away from the discarded heap. After doing so he slowly walked back to the stones and watched George Pring of Little Dodder spreading them in the road.

Large rooks flew by over the road very slowly as though they had overheard George Pring say something and wondered what he meant by it.

The rooks flew away to Angel Hill and settled around the one dead tree. They wished, no doubt, by their gestures, to communicate a fine piece of wisdom to one another, for they settled in circles round the tree and nodded their heads as though they were talking in parables.

"You be thinking some'at," Dunell said in a peaceful tone.

George Pring paused in his work and leant wearily over his shovel. The two men regarded the stones in silence with a blank stare.

"'Tis funny that stones be stones."

Brooding over his own remark George Pring raked a clay pipe out of his pocket and, after knocking the bowl of the pipe gently against the handle of his

228

shovel, he dropped it again into his pocket, where the pipe escaped once more into its old hiding-place in the lining of Mr. Pring's coat.

Meanwhile John Dunell looked distrustfully at the stones that were so carefully spread. George Pring had awakened distrust in his mind about these common things. He tried to free himself.

"Leastways," he said, "they stones bain't loaves of bread, an' 'tis near time for I to go to dinner."

This grand view of the stones not being bread made Mr. Pring more interested than ever in his own doubts about them. He moved his hand down very slowly until he touched a stone. Taking the stone up he looked attentively at it, as though he were trying to find out what it really was. He then placed the stone back again in the road.

"Stones be stones," he said.

The imagination of George Pring had settled again into the mud of the road.

After placing his fork in the cart, and very cautiously turning his horse round so as to avoid the ditch, John Dunell slowly moved away, the cart-wheels crunching the stones.

George Pring watched the departure until the cart went out of sight around a bend of the road.

His solitary state set the road-mender moving. He contemplated the bank, and taking from a rush basket a piece of bread and cheese, he began to eat. Realizing after some moments that he might as well be seated on the bank instead of looking at it, George accomplished this feat, turning his face towards a stile that was near at hand and set in the opposite hedge.

There was a spring dimness abroad, as though a summer dove had flown by out of the winter's clouds, and had given a warm feathered feeling to the air by the movement of her wings.

Mr. Pring moved his eyes from the stile to the stones.

The road-mender was a little man, with an elf-like look about him as though he dreamt queerly. He looked like a person who expects to hear a voice walking in the darkness. He had the gait of a creature who is always being surprised to see the marks of its own steps in the mud. There was a kind of distorted expectation in his look, that showed itself in the way he kept searching out his pipe, but never lighting it. George Pring had the appearance of a man who is for ever stooping before an expected sandstorm when the winds are still.

The road-mender turned to the stile again.

A robin perched upon the top rail. The bird held its head to one side as though it listened. Presently it flew away with a pert gesture. Its place was taken by a girl who swung merrily on the stile, moving her legs.

She was Rose Pring.

CHAPTER II

SEVENTEEN years before our story begins Mr. and Mrs. Pring had adopted Rose. She brought lovely baby toes, a dimple and the promise of £100.

Mr. Pring saw the money in the skies. Anything

that he touched in fancy had always, from his youth upwards, excited Mr. Pring.

One day when he was a little boy his father had told him that money was to be found in different parts of the earth's surface.

George had always looked.

He believed that a large brown rat had once been seen in the village with a golden tail.

When the baby Rose came into his house with a £100 floating somewhere between her dimple and her toes, he believed nearly as much in her as in the rat. When the baby turned into the money, Mr. Pring intended at once to commence the stocking of a small farm that he had set his heart upon.

A letter had come from a lawyer, saying—though to Mr. Pring this letter threw doubts over it all— that the £100 would be paid to Rose on her twenty-first birthday.

Apparently Rose had no relations, the advertisement merely called her a " baby in search of a good home."

Mrs. Betsy Pring always knew her home to be a good one, because she could iron a tablecloth to perfection and make a pungent blood-pudding. With these certain reasons behind her she wrote with the back of a new pen an answer to the advertisement.

And so Rose came to Little Dodder.

The girl gave another little kick with her foot, came down from the stile and carried a can of tea to the road-mender.

After looking into the can and tasting the tea to see how sweet it was, Mr. Pring asked Rose how old she was that morning.

"Oh, you silly!" replied Rose. "Why, you gave me a present to-day your own self, you know I'm eighteen——"

Mr. Pring looked up vaguely into the February skies.

"If a maid be eighteen to-day," he asked a large cloud shaped like a bear, "how wold will she be in three year?"

"Oh, my money, that's what you're thinking of —of course I shall get it then. Mrs. Topp talks of nothing else down in village, and as to Dark Eliza——" Rose tossed her head, her dark hair caught a glint of gold from a sunbeam that crept out from under the belly of the beast in the sky. In her hurry to carry out the tea Rose had left her hat behind.

Rose lay back into the hedge and sighed, her breathing showed her sex. She tightened herself on purpose and then let her breath go. Her bosoms became little soft mounds in the grass. She kicked out a foot and looked up at the hedge. As she looked her eyes became a violet colour. Rose smiled.

"Thee's money were truth once." Mr. Pring took the can away from his mouth and looked at the girl. "Be thee's money true now?"

"Oh, if my money wasn't real, I wouldn't be real."

George Pring was not convinced.

"I've never seen thik money," he said.

"Oh, you know lawyer Bedford said I should have it, and Squire Kennard he believes in it too."

Mr. Pring had not followed her reasons—he was still looking at his own questions. And as though

to try to prove the problem that confused his mind,
George Pring moved his hand towards the girl's foot
until he touched it. The fact that the girl's foot
was real did not appear to convince him about the case
in hand.

Mr. Pring wished for further proof; he moved
his stained, twisted fingers all over the girl's body,
feeling her in different places.

Rose laughed.

"I know I'm quite fat," she said, "but you mustn't
think I'm Monday."—Monday was the pig.

"Thee be a real maiden, bain't 'ee?" George
Pring fumbled with her skirt.

"Why here be Carter Dunell coming," Rose called
out, "and mind, mother says you mustn't be late
home for tea because she has something nice."

Mr. Pring blinked, shut his eyes, and blinked
again; he believed that he might find the £100
waiting for him on a spread tablecloth, fried like a
blood-pudding.

Rose jumped up; she shook out her skirt like a
bird. She ran across the road, climbed the stile, and
was gone.

Mr. Pring had watched the last of her and then he
began slowly to rub his left side, as though he were
hurt. As he rubbed the pain seemed to grow worse.
Mr. Pring stood up groaning, as though really worried
by some hidden trouble.

Upon Angel Hill Squire Kennard's sheep were
feeding greedily. They had dispersed the rooks that
were now flying in circles above the tree forming
black wheels. Mr. Pring looked discontentedly at

the rooks, as though they were lucky and could do things that he wanted to do.

"They blackbirds bain't hurt wi' nothink," he said aloud, and looked down mournfully at the stones. While he stared at the stones he slowly rubbed his left hand up and down the handle of the spade that shone with much using.

Looking at the place where Rose had been resting, he said, " Maiden be real gone I s'pose—— An' I do mind me wone father did tell I of thik rat wi' 'is golden tail ; blessed if I wouldn't give thik golden rat if so be I might——"

Mr. Pring rubbed his side again—the pain must have been there. He began to move his spade slowly over the spread stones.

Near at hand there was a man coming leading a horse. Mr. Pring watched Dunell's cart-wheels ; the wheels uttered slow, ponderous notes.

CHAPTER III

LUKE BIRD gave up his post at Milverton in order to preach the Word.

For twenty years Luke had been employed in doing the accounts for the Standard Brewery.

Luke wore a dark moustache and decent grey trousers, which he turned up in imitation of a sidesman at St. John's. He was rather quick with his pen and could make eights very prettily. He would form an eight like this, and fancied the figure was more handsome than any Squire Kennard of Little Dodder could make when he ordered beer for his servants.

Luke Bird had grey eyes, a good nose and a weak chin. He was the usual man's size, for any ready-made trousers would fit him ; and he never had to try on a cap, for his head was just a man's. In the winter his chief entertainment was to watch the water running under the town bridge when the lamps were lit. And in the summer he would walk out into the fields and watch the cows feeding the other side of some strong railings, or else he would walk along the western road where the little trees grew. He never dared take Winnie to the pictures, because he was afraid of meeting a certain little girl, called Nancy, who once spat in his face when he watched her swinging on a tree. The thought of her spitting at him again as he walked with Winnie was more than he could bear.

Winnie lived in the house in Grove Road where Luke had his rooms ; she was always very kind to him and he never wished to hurt her feelings. She was the daughter of his landlady and had soft hair.

Luke never exactly knew why he did not marry Winnie. He hoped perhaps that there was something better waiting for him. . . . And so there was.

One morning Luke awoke when it was quite dark. Lying awake, he saw the world in a new way. Things were not as human eyes see them. The cooper who hammered wheels of iron round the Standard barrels might be different, if he wished to be. He received £3 15s. a week, but he might receive more than that if he wished : he might receive an immortal crown.

As he lay in his bed Luke Bird saw visions. He

looked away from the Standard accounts; he looked away from Winnie.

His parents had been dead for some years, but he saw them alive again in his vision, and he heard his mother telling him to rise up and to go out into the fields and to gather in the harvest.

Luke lit the candle, shivered and locked the door. Sometimes Winnie had crept into his bedroom during the dimness of dawn to wish him good morning. Her soft hair being always softer than ever and more unfolded at that early hour.

Luke dressed slowly; he gazed out of the window for a period of time that he could not count the minutes of; he then went down to breakfast.

Winnie, who had special reasons of her own for wishing to be kinder than ever that morning, had crept along the passage and tried the door, but finding it locked, she crept back into bed again, hid her soft hair under the clothes and cried herself to sleep.

At breakfast Mrs. Scard, Winnie's mother, brought in his tea.

At the proper time Luke went to his work. At twelve o'clock a gentleman came into the office of the brewery to pay for two eight-gallon casks of K.L. XXX. The gentleman was Squire Kennard of Little Dodder.

The squire wore a very large furry overcoat and joked about the rainy weather. He said that if God came to earth again—and this time he hoped He would come Himself—He would have to wear an overcoat and rubber boots. Luke regarded the office floor with a new interest; he gazed at a little black spot where some wine had been spilt—the spot became the stained soul of the unconverted squire.

Luke felt unhappy about the squire's state of mind. He should not have added the remark about the rubber boots to the clothes of God. The first part might have been used by a sincere man as a symbol. God clothed in an ancient furry garment as with a cloud —a thunder-cloud he thought the most likely to fit. But the rubber boots were altogether blasphemy. God didn't wear boots like a man ; He might wear two rocks on His feet to trample the sinners, but they wouldn't be in the least like boots. And had He even heard of rubber ? Luke thought not.

Luke Bird considered this remark of the squire's as a call to him to come to Little Dodder. He felt that squire Kennard must be a bad example to the simple villagers. He probably led them all to damnation with his talk about the rubber boots. If the squire could be so profane, he wondered what the clergyman would be. And then there were the people ; how they must be all toppling into the dismal ditches by the way because they had no shepherd.

Luke decided to go to Little Dodder that very moment. He informed the manager of the brewery of his altered position in heavenly and earthly affairs. The manager—Mr. Lambert—thought the man crazed, but he gave him his money and let him go, saying graciously that "the Standard Brewery would miss his eights."

The manager thought this was the best course to take with a man who wished to preach the Gospel. For by letting him go quietly he would no doubt save the reputation of an old-established firm and perhaps even save the money in the till where the cash for odd bottles of whisky was placed.

"One never knows," Mr. Damory Lambert thought to himself, "what might not happen in a case of this kind."

Luke Bird started out at two o'clock to walk to Little Dodder. He stopped by the third milestone, that was sheltered by an ash tree, and considered for a moment. He was thinking of Winnie's soft hair. For the next hundred yards he ran away from temptation. Being rather tired with his running, he walked more calmly until he came near to the village that he wished to dwell in.

Never had Luke been so excited. The little birds flew round him and the clouds danced like mad rabbits across the sky.

CHAPTER IV

WHEN he turned another bend of the road, Luke Bird saw a man working. The man was spreading stones. A cart that had just been emptied was moving slowly away.

To Luke's changed mind any human being that he saw now was wonderful. A man was more than a man : he was a body of magic, a mass of hungry feelings waiting for salvation. A man had only to be unloosed and set flying to become one with God. They might be but clods, these poor Dodder labourers, but waiting clods, clods from whence there would be heavenly sproutings of green if the Word were spoken.

And he had come to them to speak the Word.

Mr. Pring had seen the stranger approach, but went on with his work as though he had seen nothing.

When the stranger came quite near to him the road-mender leant upon his spade and inquired, as though he had been waiting for Luke all the morning :

"What do 'ee think, master, they stones mid be if they weren't stones?"

Luke was surprised and a little shocked at this simple question. Was this man taking words out of his own mouth? Luke Bird was silent.

"If thee don't know, I think I do know," remarked Mr. Pring. "If they stones bain't stones, they mid be golden pounds three years to come."

Luke had intended to speak about the stones, calling them bread, but he now merely looked on as the road-mender continued his work. The would-be preacher was not shaken in his purpose of doing good, but he was beginning to be aware that the thoughts that moved in a working man's mind were not quite what he expected them to be. A townsman's conception of such matters being that country labourers had nothing in their minds at all.

Luke regarded the fields; he wondered whether every one was like this road-mending labourer. He had never been to Little Dodder before.

The village was a little way down the road, and the Manor House looked square and proper and just a squire's. On one side of the road and almost in the middle of the village there was a grassy hill. On the top of hill there was a decayed stump of a weather-beaten tree.

"No doubt," thought Luke, "there would be a little brook running through the lower part of the village, and by the brook a mill—yes, there was a mill."

It was all very fit and proper—a good soil for work.

The squire's house was square and the squire a very wicked man who talked of God's rubber boots —the clergyman no better perhaps. All the souls under the green hill were waiting for a real preacher and now he had come.

The grassy hill, the fields, the stones of the road even would be trodden by the feet of the saved, the low village doorways would be entered by the regenerate. The running waters of the little brook would be watched over by the eyes of thankful women—thankful for God.

Besides all this view of Little Dodder, Luke also noticed the stile that Rose had climbed over. The stile must lead somewhere. Perhaps it called him to green meadows and a cottage—the green meadows would carry him there upon soft waves of grass.

It was a by-path that Luke Bird wanted so badly— a by-path that would lead him on just where it willed. Every path must lead to some sort of human home. He knew this one did. He longed to choose a cottage —shadowed by a great tree perhaps—from whence the light of his teaching could shine forth burning.

He would live simply, humbly, there ; he would do good deeds while he preached to the people the wisdom of the generations.

George Pring watched with no small annoyance the looks that the stranger directed towards the stile.

Pring spoke in a cunning, inquisitive manner.

" If thee wants Mr. Mowland, thik be the way."
Mr. Pring pointed out a muddy lane that dipped into
a muddy field and seemed to wind on interminably.

" I wish to know where the stile leads one to ? "
Luke asked.

" Squire Kennard do bide in thik house," the road-
mender said, holding out his arm in the direction of
the squire's residence.

Luke began to feel curiously ashamed.   He almost
wished that he had come to visit Mr. Mowland or
the squire.   Evidently the road-mender would have
a poor opinion of him if he attempted to go anywhere
else.   Did the road-mender know him as the young
man from the brewery, or did he think that he had
come to Dodder to buy hogs of Mr. Mowland down
the muddy lane, Luke wondered.

Mr. Pring watched the young man nervously, with
the troubled expression of a plover that would lead
a child away from its nest.

" It be a pity," the road-mender said, trying to cover
the stile with his wings ; " it be a pity that three years
bain't three days.   But I do suppose that days and
money be all wone to the Lord."

Luke turned away from the man and began to move
towards the stile.

" Hi," Mr. Pring called after him.   " Hi ! Parson
Colley don't live that road."

Luke stopped.   He wished to know a little more
about the clergyman—a lazy preacher perhaps, or else
a high churchman who would be angry with a true
evangelist.

"Where does Mr. Colley live?" he asked with his hand holding the top of the stile.

George Pring felt for his pipe. Dragging the hidden culprit at last from his pocket, he knocked the few remaining ashes out against the handle of the shovel —Mr. Pring wished to gain time.

"'Tis a good man Parson Colley were," he said dreamily. "No, no, there don't bide a party in Dodder that 'aven't been christened, married or else buried by thik good man. I do mind 'e well in this very road. Good Parson Colley were out walking wone rainy day and shading 'is knees with umbrella. The good man did speak to I. 'E did tell I that they wold Romans did walk by here times past. And that King George III were a good king to they Romans till a party called Bony came : 'tis a pity Parson Colley be dead."

"But the present clergyman," Luke inquired, "does he live far away?"

"Over Angel Hill, master; you mid go down by Foxholes and through Hatchard's gate by wold barn and into Shelton Road, an' by side of thik road, before you come to Farmer Boys' hill, you'll see Vicarage."

As though he had settled all the matter and finally defeated the purpose of the stranger to climb the stile, Mr. Pring bent to his work again. In his mind he saw the stranger after some hours' wandering ringing the Vicarage bell in the Shelton Road until the door was opened by a little maid-servant whom Mr. Pring had once seen going in at the gate.

Luke Bird was a little mystified by the plover-like manners of the road-mender, who seemed to be again so busy with his stones. But instead of taking the direction indicated by the man, he climbed over the tempting stile and saw before him a pleasant winding path that led through a green field towards a cottage.

Luke's hope revived. He saw a daisy growing by the side of the way; he stooped and picked the daisy, but at once let the flower fall. The daisy had reminded him of Winnie's soft hair.

CHAPTER V

MRS. DUNELL, the wife of Carter Dunell, the small-holder of Dodder, pushed the teapot and plates into the middle of the kitchen table, for by being more crowded they were less clamorous to be washed up. Mrs. Dunell looked reproachfully at the fire. The fire appeared less likely than ever to recover from a fit of dejection that it usually suffered from at that hour in the morning.

Mrs. Dunell walked out of her kitchen and, going into her front room, she moved aside the lace curtains and looked out of the window.

Mrs. Dunell had a merry twinkle in her eye; she was plump and old and her grey hair trickled down her neck whenever it saw a chance of escape from its two pins.

Mrs. Dunell's gaze out of the window was by no means directed towards the beauties of Nature. She had no use for these so-called beauties; she preferred getting on with the story of Adam and Eve. Mrs. Dunell had placed a marker in a certain Dodder page of this wonderful story book. She had left off where

Mrs. Bugg had fainted in her garden, choosing a new patch of nettles to fall into. That fall was but dull, and Mrs. Dunell wanted to get again to the exciting part about Rose and her money. It was always something to turn to, that subject; it was even better than Mrs. Waterson's quarrel; it was better than Joe Bradish's theft of a three-legged rabbit.

Mrs. Dunell moved the curtain a little more to one side. She saw Dark Eliza coming up the lane from the mill where her cottage was. Dark Eliza was walking cautiously in the muddy ditch. She walked as though she were afraid of being run over by an invisible wagon. Dark Eliza was coming to the shop.

Instinctively Mrs. Dunell turned her eyes the other way. She scratched her neck—a wisp of grey hair was teasing her. Mrs. Bugg had come into being by the well. No doubt Mrs. Bugg felt better; she had already filled her bucket. Susan Dunell was well aware that Mrs. Bugg always left her bucket by the well when she did her shopping.

Presently the large friendly figure of Betsy Pring came into sight. Betsy hurried as though she wished to catch a train. Her apron blew in the wind. She looked as though she hadn't a moment to spare because the train was signalled, and she had her ticket to take.

Betsy Pring was going to the shop.

Mrs. Dunell waddled about her front room like a duck on unsafe ice.

She rummaged in her mind, peeping into dusty places. At last she fancied that she wanted some washing powder. She had a dim sensation, that seemed

to come from her feet, that there was a packet somewhere in her house. But her uncertainty as to this
possession merely egged her on to want some more.

The plates were heaped up in the middle of the
kitchen table. They called to Susan, and Susan looked
at them. She placed them in an enamel bowl. The
fire had gone quite out and the water in the kettle
must be cold.

These two important facts were the starting-point
of Susan's adventures. She knew the book would
be open. With such a dull, staring failure in life as
her fire was, there could be only one thing to listen
to—the story.

Susan Dunell unfastened her cottage door and went
out into the road. There was nothing in the road;
there was not even a cat to look at. There was only
Angel Hill above and the rooks, and the rooks were
but birds who did not matter. The February mud
had more life in it than the rooks, because, though
the mud felt as cold as December, it splashed like
spring.

Mrs. Dunell gazed at the stony corner of Tuck's
mill, and thought she heard the voice of the miller
swearing at the water. She wondered why the miller
was swearing at the water that drove the mill.

Susan Dunell walked along the road to the village
shop.

Inside the shop there was a moist, sugary smell and
conversation. Some events must have fallen upon
the village from the moving clouds of the night.
These events were being recorded in the book.

Susan Dunell opened the shop door—the little bell

attached to the door rang. The sound of its ringing pleased Mrs. Dunell—the sound opened all listening corners. She shut the door softly, and the bell rang again as softly as she shut the door. Mrs. Topp was standing behind the counter. Her large eyes and pale cheek bones shone with a vivid interest. She might have been listening to the divine Jehovist reciting the poem of the Creation for the first time in the valley of the moon.

Upon the counter there was a bar of soap and a packet of sugar waiting to be popped into Dark Eliza's basket. The sugar and soap were resigned and timid ; they believed in God ; they were willing to remain where they were for ever.

" There be money in the world," Betsy Pring was saying when the little bell rang.

There was a moment's silence, and every one regarded the new-comer in a watching, back-hair manner.

" She did name money," whispered Dark Eliza timidly, as though to inform Mrs. Dunell what was in the wind.

" 'Tis Rose's money, no doubt, she be speaking of."

" Time do roll on," said Betsy Pring, " an' years they do curtsy away."

" Were thik about the years put down in Will ? " asked Mary Bugg in a meek tone.

" 'Twere best time were mentioned," muttered Dark Eliza, " in case any poor folks were run over by carts."

" Things do happen to all," Mrs. Topp remarked

sagely. " I do mind poor Maud Tucker of Hubert's Down—she were married and dead the same day."

" Sure 'tis, this world bain't a safe place for we to bide in," said Susan Dunell, scratching her neck.

Dark Eliza looked aside nervously ; she was conscious of her usual haunting fear creeping up beside her even in the safety of the shop. Her fear hopped around her like a black mouse, and, in order to escape, she pressed herself in the corner by the counter. She believed that a grey horse would run away from somewhere in the world and rush madly into the Dodder shop and run over her. Dark Eliza edged herself behind the wide, goodly presence of Betsy Pring.

Betsy Pring looked at the bell attached to the shop door ; she was anxious to change the subject. The idea that any doubt, however vague, could be touched in connexion with Rose's £100 troubled her. She felt the time for her news had come. For years the topic of Rose's money had been the certain thing to raise interest in Dodder. Betsy had never objected till now of the way it was talked of. So long as the £100 was a decent distance away all seemed safe and easy. But now that the year of consummation approached and there was wondering abroad as to whether time was mentioned in the Will, Betsy Pring was rendered more and more nervous by the doubt.

" Who would have thought it ? " said Betsy in a tone that showed that she at least had fresh news to tell. " Who would have expected this to happen ? "

" No one be run over, be they ? " Dark Eliza asked nervously.

Mrs. Topp was thinking of the stamped heads that she kept in the drawer.

" Be the King dead ? " inquired Mrs. Topp.

" 'Tis Squire Kennard maybe," remarked Susan Dunell, " that's been bitten by a black dog."

Betsy Pring waited for the expectant silence that she knew must come, and then she said gravely :

" When we do die we be all going to Heaven, save they folk that do go to Hell."

No one spoke. The gossips knew very well that this must be the beginning of some sort of important information.

" 'Twas when I were shaking cloth, him wi' the big darn, out of doorway—for Rose do tell I to because of they little bread crumbs—that I seed some one were coming."

Each listener formed and created the new-comer in her own mind.

Dark Eliza saw him as a black-bearded driver of a traction engine who smoked a clay pipe. She shivered with dread.

Susan Dunell saw a swart gipsy woman clothed with clothes pegs and surrounded by little dirty children with pert, inquisitive faces.

Mrs. Topp thought the visitor could be none other than the rate collector who was become post master and who had come into the village to inquire of her about a certain stamp that was lost.

" He did say," went on Betsy mysteriously—" so quiet-like—' I be Luke Bird and I want a lodging.' ' One pound a week,' I called out before I could catch me breath, ' and no coals.' I never were so taken off my feet, never! for the young man walked into house same as if 'twere his own. An' he did sit down to table and begin to write ink words in a book that he had in's pocket. You do all know me George, I do suppose?"

Dark Eliza nodded.

"George did walk in as usual at tea-time, but he never saw thik young man. An' George do see most things you know. 'E bain't blind as yet. George did eat they poor slices of bread tiger-like, and did look at Rose. An' after tea he went out into wood-shed and he did hammer they poor sticks. You do know"—Betsy Pring turned to Susan—"'twere they large logs that used to lie down by side of Tuck's mill. George did bring they home one at a time. An' when they were all gone, he did say to Tuck, 'They logs be missing out of ditch, do 'ee know, miller?'

"Mr. Bird spoke to George, naming God to him at tea-time. But he never seed God no more than he seed Luke Bird. 'Twere only miller's logs that he did mind."

"He might have seen Rose's money maybe," suggested Mrs. Dunell.

"He do often look at Rose without saying anything —and it maybe, though I bain't sure"—Mrs. Pring shook her head knowingly—"that he do see pounds in her lap—for he do look down-like when he do watch her.

"Supper-time came an' 'twere only a bit of cheese too—but Rose did bring it in grand-like, as though 'twere bacon. An', bless me, if thik young man didn't say grace to en as though 'twere killed meat.

" ''Tis to Hell thee be going,' he did say, looking at we."

" He never named carts nor horses, I hope," inquired Dark Eliza anxiously.

" No, no, but he said he wanted to save us, and had come to build a chapel to take we out of Hell by."

Betsy Pring stopped her story ; she had noticed that Mrs. Topp was shaking her head.

" They chapels won't do for Squire Kennard," remarked Mrs. Topp. " Squire don't want no wone to name God save 'is own self."

" No, that he don't," said Dark Eliza eagerly. " For only yesterday, when I did shout at 'e for driving so near to me toes, 'e did call back ' God damn and take you, Eliza, why don't 'e climb over hedge ? ' "

" That be only his manner of speaking," Mary Bugg ventured to say. " But 'e do talk of God more than most careful folk should."

" 'Tis a hard subject," Susan Dunell said consolingly, " an' 'tis me belief that they tombstones be the best talkers of en. I do mind poor Tom that do lie under one of they—' Gone to God,' 'tis said on stone—poor Tom ! An' 'twere only yesterday as I were walking up Angel Hill to see if thik dead bough be loosened ; I don't know how it were, but thik word that the squire did use came into my mind—out of dead tree I do think."

" 'Tis a funny word," Dark Eliza said fearfully— " 'tis a word that do creep along ground between folk's legs like a snake "

" 'Tis best forgot, save on they tombstones," Susan whispered.

Mrs. Topp gazed thoughtfully out of the window. There was a feeling somewhere that another person, other than Mrs. Topp, was moving about in the world —some one who could not be seen.

Mrs. Topp looked hastily at the two parcels on the counter. She was pleased to see they were still there. That some one might be in league with the robbers for all she knew.

Mrs. Topp moved her hands nervously and touched the parcels. Taking up the sugar and soap, Mrs. Topp placed them in Dark Eliza's basket, which that lady took into her hands. Mrs. Topp then gave a packet of starch to Mrs. Dunell and a box of matches to Mary Bugg, and leaving Betsy Pring to think of what she wanted, she retired into the back kitchen to continue her own morning's employment—that consisted in skinning and preparing a rabbit for her dinner.

CHAPTER VI

ONE morning in March Luke Bird awoke out of a happy dream.

His first waking thoughts were about Winnie. The wanton breathing of a spring morning inclined his heart to think of Winnie's soft hair. He almost felt as though he were leaning over Winnie and stroking her hair. She used to melt in the springtime like the snow in March, and then there was always the sweet moss underneath for him to touch.

R

All these delicate thoughts and remembrances, that came to Luke through the lattice window died down when he remembered his call.   His call rudely forced him away from Winnie's soft hair.   He felt the burden upon his back—the burden of his mission that must put to flight the wanton feelings that the spring morning had brought to him.

Instead of thinking of Winnie, he began to wonder what he had done to save others.   So far he had only talked with the odds and ends of people that he had met, and now he felt the time had come for him to preach.

It might be a long time before he could catch the people in the net of salvation—it might be years. Could he last out so long ?   His own savings in money would keep him, if he were very careful, for a score of years or more.   A dozen years ought to be enough, he felt, wherein to save many souls.   His money would not last for ever, and he did not feel inclined to use it in bulk even to build a chapel.   For suppose the people were not saved in time and the money gone—the four walls of a chapel would not help them then.

Luke decided that he must not build with his own money.   But if some one else would lend or, better still, give him £100, he would then add the chapel to his chances of success.

Meanwhile he must preach somewhere ; he must break fresh ground ; he must fight the mountain of Evil.

To create a cloud in his mind—a cross he called it— and to shut out if possible the sweet blue of the sky by some daring act, Luke Bird decided to go that very day to the squire.

After taking this important resolution, he relaxed a little and allowed himself to listen again to the lark singing. The lark sang to him about Rose. If the bird had known about Winnie, he would, no doubt, have sung about her. But the lark only knew Rose and her father.

George Pring was not, so far, a convert to Luke's ideas. Whenever Luke spoke to him about redemption the good road-mender would shuffle off to his wood-shed and beat the sticks. But Rose and Betsy would be left in the house.

The lark sang on. The song filled the heavens with sound; it became the one thing that lived.

Luke pretended to himself that he was thinking of a way to convert Mr. Pring, but he was really wondering if Rose ever danced at fairs.

The lark sang on.

The two women would listen to him so attentively when Mr. Pring was beating the sticks. They did their sewing so quietly—a contrast to the banging in the wood-shed—and were so interested in all that Luke told them about the sweet inward feelings and the need for belief.

Rose was not always quite so still as her mother; when she tried to thread her needle, she would move a little and lean forward, and then settle herself again with her legs placed a little differently. Luke was always compelled to own, when she made these movements, that she was a girl.

He remembered Winnie.

As a rule, after he had talked for some while, Mrs. Pring would get up to put the cat out of the room, and so the evening would end.

The lark sang on.

The bird was wickedly hinting that there might be soft moss to touch if the snow covering of Rose's soft girlhood did but melt.

The lark sang on.

By reason of its singing Luke was even brought to think that Winnie had only been a temptation, but that Rose was another matter in the universe, quite another matter. She would be the one, and a girl too—Luke trembled to think so—who would help so much in the grand plan of converting others. She could help him in so many ways. Indeed he had not been in Mrs. Pring's house for more than three minutes before Betsy had told him all about Rose's expectations. And once settled there, it was a matter of certainty that he should hear the same history twenty times every day. Even Rose herself had said a word or two about it.

The lark sang on.

It was singing high over the stile.

Luke often used to walk up and down the green path thinking over his plans, and Rose would sometimes come by and climb over the stile. Luke felt that his thoughts hurt him rather when Rose climbed over the stile when he was so near. He could not help thinking about her in a queer, uncomfortable way when she climbed over. She caught hold of him and sprinkled him with soft snowflakes that turned to moss flowers, even though he never watched her climbing.

One day Luke Bird had written upon the stile in large, black, staring letters : " He hath bent his bow and set me as a mark for the arrow." In the sublime innocence of his heart Luke Bird hoped that the complaint from Lamentations would ease his trouble. But alas ! the very next time that Rose came to climb the stile there was a white mist and a pink, unforgettable cloud that hid the letters, and a little laugh that drew him into the magic valleys of the unseen.

The lark sang on.

CHAPTER VII

LUKE BIRD groaned in spirit. He rose up from his bed and dressed.

He shut his mouth tight ; he was tormented by the blue of the sky and by the larks. He strove to cry out against beauty and loveliness. He longed to tear the glory of the golden day, as a beast might do with a hooked claw. He would stop the lark singing ; he would visit the squire who spoke of God's rubber boots.

After breakfast Luke set off. In the village lane, beside a small paddock, he encountered Mr. Dunell. John Dunell began to speak without looking round to see who was coming ; the presence of anyone was a sufficient cause for him to open his mouth. All men and all women were suitable listeners to John Dunell.

" They wold horses do know that spring be come."

Mr. Dunell was looking over the gate at his two

horses when he made this remark; the horses were biting contentedly at the sweetest grass.

" 'Tis like this wi' they horses," Mr. Dunell continued—" they do lie up in stable o' nights in winter time an' do dream of buttercups, and when the real spring do come they do think that all the world be gone crazed wi' flowers. No, no, preacher, don't 'e tell I nothing about Zachariah nor Timothy neither. I do know what you would say, and so do they horses. They poor beasts haven't lived so long without knowing what grass be made of."

Luke Bird had no word to say; it was impossible for him, after hearing Mr. Dunell's remarks, to say anything about salvation. So instead of beginning any Bible discourse he merely inquired the nearest way to Squire Kennard's. Mr. Dunnell turned slowly, nodded his head, and pointed to a field path. As Luke was walking away, John Dunell shouted after him :

" 'Tis a pity thik wold horse do have they sand cracks so bad—though George Pring do say ' Sand cracks bain't worser than side bones—but they bots be bad enough.' "

Luke hurried away; even in the fields he heard Dunell calling after him about the bots. Above the field where Luke walked there was Angel Hill. Upon the summit there was the one stunted tree that possessed but three boughs and those were rotting. Luke waited for a few moments because the hill had a queer way of looking down on passing people.

He knew, too, that the people of Little Dodder looked at the hill with a sort of awe that amounted to veneration. He had even found Dark Eliza upon her knees one evening near to the stone wall that crept like a lizard's tail round the bottom of the hill.

A dreadful thought came to Luke that the woman might be praying to the hill. He asked her sternly what she was doing there. She only said, however, almost in tears, that there was a wagon coming up the road and she had fled there to be safe.

Luke also remembered a silly tale that had got as far as Milverton—he had laughed about it with Winnie one day; it was only that if anyone spent the night upon Angel Hill at Little Dodder, he or she or, better still, both together would never have the headache again.

Betsy Pring had told him, too, that a real angel had been seen one summer evening on the top of the hill by young shepherd Cluett and poor Maud, who were amusing themselves—to the sorrow later of poor Maud—under the shadow of the dead tree. Both Maud and the shepherd said that the angel had watched them with a smile and had even offered, "because she looked so pretty" he said, to pluck out one or two bits of grass from Maud's hair.

"He was such a nice young man with wings," Maud whispered.

Luke knew, of course, that it must have been the Devil, because he has wings shaped like an angel's, though black ones.

Mr. Tuck at the mill had seen something, too, on that same day, so Betsy said.

It was Whit Sunday, and the miller said that the water in the brook turned black all of a sudden, but, as the rats had eaten a whole sack of corn the night before, they might, he thought, have turned the colour of the water.

"But, of course, it may have been the Devil," Luke thought.

Luke continued his way ; he thought he would brave the Devil and ask the squire's leave to preach the Gospel upon Angel Hill. He could at least preach there, standing by the tree, until he collected the money for a chapel. Yes, there was the hill above him ready and prepared, an open temple not made with hands. Upon the slopes of the hill, blown upon by the sweet spring winds, sheep were feeding.

Luke longed to surround himself with a listening flock and feed them, together with himself, with the sacrament of the Blessed Word.

Turning from the footpath into the main drive to the house, Luke hung his head a little. He was beginning to be nervous. Simple Dodder people had never paid bills at the Standard Brewery, but large gentlemen and squires were wont to come there, amongst whom used to be Squire Kennard with his wicked talk.

Luke Bird had come to Dodder like a simple virgin of the Lord. The peasant people were altogether new beings to him.

He had wandered into their ways and had found all their ways to be a new language—a language with words strange to his ear.

When Dunell talked about his horses, the man spoke of their very bots and side cracks as though they were the mystic part of a wonderful story—a story more wonderful than the utmost immortality of man could reach to. The people moved between magic hedges in cloud-haunted fields—all hours and days and winds were to them moving beasts and gods and sweet flowers. They heard the mighty movement of a song that underground heaved up in life and sank in darkness, that touched everything, that became all. For ever the times and the seasons beat, beat in undulating monotony upon those who dwelt below Angel Hill. The sun shone sometimes, and the autumn rains lashed slant-wise against the lattice windows. The curlew would cry in its flight over the hill. The lambs would bleat plaintively to their dams. The robin would pertly hop upon the stile. And the dread song would go on moving, eternal in its changes, below it all. . . . Squire Kennard was another matter. It was he indeed who had first called Luke to Dodder. But the squire had not called him to save himself but to save others. Luke began to fear that he might not have anything to say before such a man. Plain simple Gospel words might not sound proper in the presence of one whose cheques he had taken and whose eights he had copied. Everything, his own little failings even, might be brought up before such a man. The squire might read things in his heart; he might even begin to talk about Winnie. But was not that carrying his fears too far ? It was quite impossible that the squire of Dodder could have heard Winnie's soft footsteps, mouse-like, creeping along the passage while her cheeks were so rosy.

Winnie was quite out of the question, but there was Rose Pring.

Luke had never touched her hair ; he turned a little sad——he had always wanted to.

Luke had heard in the village that the squire was quite a poor man. " He had spent fortunes, but was now become poor," Mr. Dunell had said very grandly.

When he reached the house Luke did not expect to find a very large assortment of servants, but he wished, when he rang the bell, that there might be one to let him in. He stood meekly upon the top step for more than twenty minutes after ringing the bell. He did not like to ring the bell twice ; it was a rude thing to do, unless you were the rate collector.

At last an old woman opened the door. Her name was Mrs. Candy. Tom Candy was the squire's gardener——one of the unconverted because he drank. Mrs. Candy invited Luke to sit down in the hall while she went to call her master.

Before leaving the young man she remarked, looking up at the ceiling, where there were cobwebs : " Squire be full of blessed words this morning ; he weren't downstairs for five minutes before he began to speak of God and the Devil." Mrs. Candy untied her apron before she went into the study.

Luke Bird sat in the hall chair with the Kennard crest upon the back, like a post. He felt more than ever certain that he had merely called on business from the brewery, and that he had tied a knot in his handkerchief in order to remember to ask for the empties to be returned.

CHAPTER VIII

SQUIRE KENNARD was a merry gentleman who loved his jest. He connected every person he saw with some animal or other. He believed his housekeeper to be a wise kind of goose, and he saw the horse in Mr. Dunell. He fancied Dark Eliza to be a timid black cat with one eye, who could climb trees. And Mrs. Topp was an owl with a white beak. When a real owl hooted in the large elm by the drive gate, Mr. Kennard said, " There's Mrs. Topp selling the sugar." Only one person in the village the squire could fit into no likeness of an animal, and that was Rose Pring.

The squire was nothing daunted by his present poverty, incurred on account of a foolish speculation. Even though the estate was mortgaged, there was still a little money coming in.

Mr. Kennard was a widower without children. He was fifty years old and loved nothing better than a gramophone. Unfortunately his wife had never allowed him to possess one. He put her into his mind's cage as a porcupine, but said nothing.

When his wife was dead he found himself too poor to buy a gramophone. Being critical in matters of music, he could only think of possessing the best. It was one of his axioms in life—" That the best was good enough for him."

Whenever Squire Kennard went to the town he would stand and stare through the glass of the music shop. There was a wonderful gramophone there to be sold for 100 guineas. He thought he might

manage the odd shillings, but the pounds were
wanting. He thought the man in the shop was like
a stoat, and never dared to enter.

On the whole Luke Bird was received kindly at
the Hall. Squire Kennard was serious and polite, and
looked gravely at his guest. His gravity was caused
by his wondering whether Luke ought to have a tail.

Luke was quite pleased when the squire said :

" I fear you will not gain many converts in Little
Dodder, Mr. Bird—we are all too absent-minded for
religion. I might even say we are too unworldly ;
we have God so much in our minds that, if you will
excuse the expression, Mr. Bird, I fear we get a little
tired of Him."

Mr. Kennard smiled.

He saw the Almighty in a new way—he saw a
flea.

The squire now began to talk in a polite manner
about the new brewery chimney at Milverton.

" There used to be a tower like that and nearly as
high on Angel Hill," he said, " only Kennard, the fox,
pulled it down and planted the tree instead. The
Christian name of my ancestor who pulled down the
tower was Angel—I merely call him fox because he
looks like one in his portrait. That is why the hill
is called Angel Hill."

Luke Bird sighed, and meekly asked for permission
to preach upon the hill.

The squire gave him leave.

" But you won't disturb the sheep, I hope, Mr.
Bird," he said gravely. " I say this because the sheep
might find you a little strange at first—and suppose you

grew tired of preaching and began to sing hymns. Of course, as a landowner, I see no objection to hymns, but there is no knowing what Mr. Tuck of the mill might say if he heard them. I have heard him remark more than once that the noise of thunder disturbed the grinding. It is possible, Mr. Bird, that Mr. Tuck—he's a queer animal, you know—might consider that the sound of hymn-singing might make the brook go dry. Or, as a lesser evil than that, a hymn might make the miller thirsty.

"Be careful, Mr. Bird—be careful. You know the Little Dodder folk are very jealous of their God. He might dry up the waters. A long time has passed since the Flood. Time for thought, Mr. Bird. It might come into His mind to take the other line.

"And there are the sheep, Mr. Bird, they might disapprove of hymn-singing from the mouth of a—— I mean from you, Mr. Bird."

Squire Kennard took Luke to the door; he even walked with him a little way down the drive.

From the drive Mr. Pring's cottage was easy to see, and Rose was walking across the meadow with a basket on her arm.

"They say that young woman is to have a £100 on her twenty-first birthday," remarked the squire pleasantly.

Luke followed Rose with his eyes. Her small dark figure was a dainty thing amid the white dots of March daisies.

She was but a girl, but Luke saw her as a helpmate to him and the builder of a God's house.

The squire was thoughtful.

After shaking hands with Luke, he stood for a few minutes and watched Rose. When Luke was gone some fifty yards down the path, Mr. Kennard called after him :

"Try not to disturb the sheep, Mr. Bird," he said.

Luke watched the country-side as he walked—the Squire's warning, though only about the sheep, was ominous. Luke saw all the country filled with gins and queer desires. The gins were hidden in the grass; the desires crawled like serpents. He had expected all the country to be mere sods of earth upon which walked men and women formed of the sods.

The idea was simple and delightful, and Luke had believed it.

He knew, of course, that all manner of preachers had doubts and troubles to contend with. But after all it would be only the trouble of getting rather damp sticks to burn.

Even now, as he walked away from the squire's, he hoped to succeed. His thoughts burst upwards—they soared high. He felt that, if he really succeeded in converting the village, he would light a candle as big as—he could only think of the brewery chimney. That was horrible; he meant something else, but what ?

CHAPTER IX

NEAR to the village of Little Dodder there was a lonely valley. In this lonely valley there were diverse pits, where past generations of road-menders had dug out stones.

About half-way up this valley there was a man digging stones.

This man was George Pring.

Near by there was a heap of stones that he had shifted. His method being to dig the stones, sift them, and then to wheel them in a barrow to his heap. At night-time he would turn his barrow upside down over his fork and pick-axe, and, supposing these tools to be very well hidden and protected by the barrow, he would go home, contented.

The lonely valley near to Little Dodder was a place where things happened. Only very brave and experienced young women would go that way on a Sunday. The more modest and less initiated preferred Angel Hill.

Old William Mellor used to say that a strange, tall, black man, with a long tail sticking outside his Sunday coat, had been seen in this valley, and been met too, so Job Tory would have it, by Alfred Dreamer, who was looking for his lost ferret.

Poor Gertie Loverley had met something too, Susan Dunell used to say. Gertie was looking for mushrooms one September morning when the mists were about. She saw the evil thing moving like a frog in the bottom of the valley, in jumps.

Gertie dropped her mushrooms. Susan Dunell said that poor Gertie was always unfortunate; "She could never get her warts cured."

As George Pring worked, he looked from time to time towards the farther end of the valley where the lane was that led to the village. He was expecting Rose to bring his dinner,

George Pring appeared to be more thoughtful than usual. He picked thoughtfully at the stones. The lonely valley was as good a place for thought as for stones. George Pring wondered and wished—the lonely valley was good for that too.

George Pring needed inspiration; he looked around him in search for inspiration. He also needed encouragement, and he looked at an elder tree.

The elder tree was near to George Pring.

It manifested, under the eyes of George, fantastic, swelling roots.

The roots grew and rounded; they became female legs.

They even grew up into a body whose head was a large, rotting fungus.

George Pring found his inspiration in the root legs.

But they were not quite proper, these legs. George wished to give them a better body than the tree gave them, and he wished to clothe them.

George Pring turned uneasily to the stones. His arms worked, but not so strongly.

Ever since the arrival of Luke Bird, Mr. Pring had been in a state of unhappy uncertainty. He had always counted on one day possessing the £100 that would come to Rose when she was twenty-one. When she was quite a little girl she used often to say to him that when she grew up he might buy a cow or a camel with her money. Whenever Mr. Pring chanced to dream, there would always be the same wonderful creatures with huge backs and wide white faces that shone cold like the moon. These beasts would walk up and down the wide, empty furrows of Mr. Pring's mind until their loud lowings disturbed the alarum clock.

When this happened and honest George was fully awake, he was wont to wish that the large creatures had been a little smaller. He lay always for a few minutes in order to bring them down in stature to the size of a fat pig, and even then he would sometimes doze off again and see the new-created pig as a camel.

But here was Luke Bird come to Dodder and George Pring only dreamt of flint stones that moved about like driven leaves, until they formed a wall across the road in front of the county surveyor's.

Mr. Pring had heard some one say that young men carry off girls to marry them. He saw danger everywhere.

How could he tell that Rose would not vanish like his dream of the beasts?

Coming up the valley to his work that very day, a gust of wind had rolled a branch of dead furze by him. He had noted that piece of furze before and intended it for his fire. And now the wind had run away with his furze, and Luke Bird was worse than the wind.

George Pring paused in his work; he slowly rubbed his hand up and down the leg of his trousers. His thoughts were being blown to Rose by another wind. She should feed him with more than his dinner that day. The other wind blew hard and hot. George Pring looked about him with crafty eyes. All the village had become like a girl.

Even before he left the Dodder fields he had noticed a young red heifer following a bull across a meadow.

s

The bull was walking peacefully and feeding sometimes. The heifer followed with a troubled, uneasy
step.

When George Pring passed the lime-kiln that stood
at the entrance of the valley, he saw a hawk pounce
upon a little rabbit and carry it away. Mr. Pring
nodded his head when the hawk flew away. . . .

George tried to work, but the other wind weakened
his arm. Every now and then he would stop and look
at the elder tree. . . . Suddenly he saw a policeman
walking in the hinder part of his own mind.

He knew the man at once. He was the Shelton
policeman who came to Dodder upon a new bicycle
and always found fault with the roads. And now
he was walking up and down in the hinder part
of Mr. Pring's mind. Had the other wind brought
him there?

George Pring leant upon his pick and looked round
at the sides of the valley.

He could only behold stunted elder trees, patches
of furze, and rabbit burrows. He felt sure there were
doe rabbits in the burrows.

After his fancy of the policeman his thoughts had
become queerer still. Mr. Pring's ideas ran backwards
into the past. He was meeting Betsy upon Angel
Hill. Betsy, who worked at the mill, was climbing
the wall; she slipped down, showing her legs; she was
hot and excited.

All that had happened long ago, but the other wind
that blows from everywhere had brought it back again.
The legs in the elder tree looked more human than
ever.

The stones that lay about took a golden hue. He must seize Rose up like the hawk did the rabbit and then she would be sure to want to give him her money. Betsy had given him things. He saw their old cat lick up a saucer of milk. Yes, that was how it was done.

Rose had washed her hair in the back-kitchen on Sunday. Mr. Pring had shuffled by her to find a nail. A plank of wood was loose on his shed roof; he wanted to nail it down. There was a girl's neck and bare bosom and loose hair all about the back-kitchen table. Mr. Pring found the nail. He never knew he had watched her so closely until now. Rose was stooping to get the soap out of her eyes. The nail might have been on the floor or on the table. It was in his pocket all the time.

Strange, heavy things moved about George Pring— strange things were moving under him.

The things had great heads and moved in dank thunder clouds. He could feel their padded feet moving, though they walked upon soft, sodden straw.

The other wind blew.

The sides of the valley became curiously familiar —they drew near.

The other wind blew.

The body of the beast rolled about on the soft, sodden straw. George Pring felt its claws, they were holding the fur of a rabbit. The beast fed quietly like the bull. It stood chewing the cud.

The other wind blew the past away. It slipped from him.

Betsy on Angel Hill fluttered away like a moth from

a garment. There was nothing now near save the act he contemplated.

At the farther end of the valley near to the Dodder lane there had come into being a little black figure. The figure slowly became Rose, and sat down near to the heap of stones upon the soft grass.

George Pring hardly looked round at her at first. The creature that moved in him was trampling uneasily upon the soft straw.

The other wind blew upon the straw and it flamed.

In the rocky substance of his mind the man warmed his hands by the fire. A strong body was melting. George Pring moved greedily, as he had done years ago to touch a girl. He remembered the girl's boots stretched out.

And now he looked at Rose. . . . Mr. Pring did not speak ; he made a gesture that failed to show her the desires that possessed him.

Mr. Pring tried in another way to explain. He laid down his fork and pick-axe and covered them carefully over with the wheelbarrow. He did this to show to the people of England that that part of his work was over for the day.

George Pring walked stealthily to where Rose was resting and laid her down gently upon the grass as though he were putting her to bed. Rose understood. She turned white, and held his hand to prevent him from tearing her clothes. Mr. Pring softly patted her face. He wished to tell her not to mind what he did.

The other wind blew hotter than ever—George Pring had become the soft-footed beast. The fire burned the straw—it burned the padding on the feet and the feet danced. The fire burned to give light to the beast that clammered for the Sun of Being. . . .

An ugly struggle was beginning. The hawk tore the fur of the little rabbit.

But the hawk was disturbed in its eating; a grey crow flew by and George Pring let the girl go and looked up.

The person who had disturbed the crow was now only a few yards away. Mr. Pring looked inquisitively at the new-comer almost as though he hoped he had come to help eat the rabbit.

The new-comer was Luke Bird.

CHAPTER X

DAYS went by.
  Luke Bird had been round the village calling at the cottage doors.

When the doors were opened to him, he said gently and not without grace that there would be preaching on Angel Hill on the following Sabbath afternoon.

At Mrs. Bugg's cottage door he had added " that hymns might be sung too."

The one-tree hill was exactly opposite Mrs. Bugg's cottage, and Mrs. Bugg looked up to the hill as though she saw it for the first time.

" So thee be going to preach on top of thik tall hill, be thee ? " Mrs. Bugg remarked in a tone that showed her astonishment at the proposal. " 'Tis a place hill be, where sheep do bide."

" Will you come ? " asked Luke.

" I have heard that thik wold tree be dead."

" Come and hear me on Sunday ! "

" Where do thee wish I to come to ? "

" Come and hear the preaching," Luke said very seriously, "and bring your friends."

A hill and a tree had for the moment been manifested to the mind of Mrs. Bugg, but it faded rapidly and was gone.

Mrs. Bugg spoke slowly. " Churches be cold in winter-time, and I do mind the folk do say that seats be damp. They churches don't bring good luck to we poor folk. For when I did last walk over Shelton way Samuel Morey did die—'e had but woon leg but 'e did die. 'Twere woon of they days when rain-drops do fall, an' Mary Soul did say—she that do wash for miller—' Look 'ee up at thik little house, mother Bugg. They blinds be half down ; they won't pull no further, I s'pose—— 'Tis for poor Sam,' and so 'twere. No, no, sure 'tis church bain't the place for we poor folk wi' they damp seats."

Luke Bird turned away sadly. If the woman didn't believe in a hill that was exactly in front of her own doors, how could she believe in his message !

Luke Bird opened the shop door ; he began to speak, but was interrupted.

" They say swine fever be in London, and pigs bain't to be moved," Mrs. Topp remarked excitedly. " An' all they police have to wash their feet in Milton. Dunell do say that all the markets in the country will be shut, and the landlords be doing it. An' me maid Jane in London will starve."

After waiting for Mrs. Topp to become a little

quieter, Luke Bird ventured to remark that he hoped, God willing, to hold a short service the next Sunday upon Angel Hill.

Mrs. Topp was slowly dragged away from her fine vision of the swine fever in London to Luke's earthly affairs. She looked through the window doubtfully.

"'Tis a high hill," Mrs. Topp remarked without interest, and began to count her stamps.

The coming of the swine fever to London had made her suspect that the postmaster might come to Little Dodder.

Luke Bird gently closed the shop door. The sluggish mass that he was beginning to know a little about covered his hopes with a soft, moist garment. The women of Little Dodder, he feared, were worse than the men—they were more sodden in a dread being whose mass moved so slowly.

It was but a few days before that Luke had only just come in time to prevent a rape. A moment or two more and the harm would have been done. But even then the girl had gone home with her would-be ravisher as though nothing had happened. She had not even thanked her deliverer. Rose had gathered sticks on her way down the lonely valley and George Pring had tramped along as usual—he even found his pipe and tried to light it.

Luke continued his way round the village; the sun might shine, but his way was darkened. Every one he met had something to tell him that was far more important to them than ever his preaching could be, and before he had gone half round the village he felt that his following on the hill would be but small.

Everywhere he was met by strange fancies. Every one had something to say. Susan Dunell greeted Luke with a long story about her husband's grandfather who minded when the one-tree hill was ploughed by Farmer Jackson, who allowed his lambs to grow long tails and was buried in a brick grave at Shelton.

Luke said he hoped Mrs. Dunell would come to the preaching on Sunday, but Susan only looked out of her window and remarked gravely :

"It's a very wide hill."

Luke left the cottage with a heavy heart, but as he walked home he felt more hopeful ; the sun was shining and he hoped that at least a few faithful ones would collect together on the Sabbath, if only in answer to his many prayers.

CHAPTER XI

ON the Sunday afternoon Luke climbed Angel Hill in order to be ready at the appointed time. The sun was above, casting golden glances upon the green earth, and the warmed daisies were pleasant to walk upon.

Luke was glad that he had left the brewery ; the sun had never shone there. The Divine Word had once set the world a-burning, why should it not once more illumine the hearts of men ?

Luke felt, not unjustly, that his present calling was far higher than the mere making of an eight. Every man should follow, every man should climb Angel Hill, every man should climb to the Lord.

The poor people must come—the sun would guide them and the daisies would lead.

The poor people of Dodder had certainly said rather unexpected things. That was their folly, of course—their unreason. But there was something about them that was more than their folly. There was something they believed in.

When he spoke to any of them and they answered, he was dimly conscious that they were holding up a finger and pointing something out to him—something that he had not known before—something moist and dark and sluggish, that took the form in his mind of a wide marsh that had no border, that had no ending, of brooding, sluggish waters. Sometimes there were lights in the marsh, lights like stars.

Poor Luke was horribly conscious that whatever this thing might be—wide sluggish waters—they worshipped it.

Also—and the fear of this thought he could not escape from—they wanted him to worship it too. They dropped him always by the side of this dread thing in an odd, but none the less, sure way of getting him to stay there.

Whenever Luke Bird spoke to them of light and love, of God and salvation, they began to speak of Miller Tuck's supposed doings with Dark Eliza, or else of John Reeks, who swept the village chimneys and died of drink one day in December.

Luke Bird strode along. However odd his fears were the sun gave the lie to them. There could not be that pit of sluggish water and the sun—and yet there was the brewery chimney.

Something laughed. Was it the dead tree? No, the free winds that blew upon the hill, blew upon the dead tree too.

Luke kept his eyes upon the dead tree as he climbed. The dead trunk was one thing, the dead bough another: the bough appeared to end in a slender hand. Luke thought of Winnie. She was nestling against him, and her hand was stroking his face. This was terrible.

Luke felt certain that it was the Devil who had made the end of the dead bough look like Winnie's fingers. Would the Devil take him to that waste of waters and prevent his preaching?

"No," Luke cried out, "no"—to the daisies who did not understand him. He would preach for all that the Devil said or did. He would preach. It was better to be a preacher under a mocking dead tree than a clerk at the brewery who copied the eights of a squire who talked about God's rubber boots.

Luke walked on quietly. Near to the top of Angel Hill he was aware that sheep were feeding about the dead tree. When Luke approached the sheep they scampered away as though frightened. Luke wondered what he had done to frighten the sheep: he had only walked slowly up the hill, and the sheep had fled as though seized with a sudden madness of terror.

"Suppose the squire," thought Luke, "had seen his flocks running? Why, the man might think that the preacher had been hunting them with the Devil for his dog."

Luke Bird looked nervously at the sheep: they

had now collected all together, and, as though with one black head, they were watching him.

Luke opened his Bible and waited ; he knew the whole book nearly by heart, he had read it so often.

Leaning over one or two of the gates in the lane he saw men's faces who were looking up at him like the sheep. The faces were fixed to shadow-like bodies by the gates.

The time for the service was come. The only creatures that seemed to be aware that the time had come were the sheep ; they began to move with one accord towards the preacher, looking up at him with inquisitive glances. They thought he was a new kind of forked turnip imported from Germany.

One silly ewe, who was rather younger than the others, bounded to within three yards of Luke, then turned and scampered back bleating. The rest of the flock held up their black heads and sniffed.

Luke Bird raised his Bible. "Were the sheep," he wondered, "tempting him to some unknown sin ? " They were so human, and there was something certainly about the one that had come so near that reminded him of Winnie.

He raised the Bible again, but did not throw it. Some one laughed under the hill. Was it the Devil —or John Dunell ?

In his troubled state of mind Luke Bird began to sing :

> " It is not that my lot is low,
>   That bids this silent tear to flow ;
>   It is not grief that bids me moan,
>   It is that I am all alone."

His voice failed him, and he forgot the remaining verses of the hymn by Kirke White.   But the attempt settled the sheep, and they began to feed peacefully.

CHAPTER XII

SEEING that the sheep were now quiet, Luke began to preach in a timid voice as though to himself.

The afternoon weather had grown sweet and moist, the mists that hung over the brook beside Tuck's mill gave to that portion of Dodder the appearance of a wide lake.   Slowly the whole valley of the Dod became white and empty and the hill grew cold.

An unpleasant clammy something fed upon the preacher's words.   The hill was listening to Luke, not listening to what he said, but taking into itself his movements.   Luke also had the unpleasant knowledge that the hill was being diffused through his body, and that he was becoming a part of that something that in his heart he dreaded more than all else at Dodder.

The sheep were still feeding quietly, and there was something else feeding too more quietly than the sheep.

Luke Bird shut his eyes and preached on.

When Luke opened his eyes he was aware that he had another listener.

Rose Pring had climbed Angel Hill, for no better reason indeed than to make a faggot of the dead bough that she hoped had been torn off the tree by the night winds.

Rose had not thought about the sermon that was to be preached ; she did not like talking much of any kind, unless it were about her money or one other matter. But she had, being a hard-working girl, remembered that there was no wood to heat the copper for washing on the Monday. Rose knew that no one ever climbed Angel Hill except harmless lovers, who were turned to one another as a rule, and she hoped to drag the dead bough down the hill and hide it under the wall, to be fetched in the evening.

Finding Luke standing there and the bough still upon the tree, she was forced to relinquish her plan, consoling herself with the thought that it would have been very wicked to gather sticks upon the Sabbath.

Rose was a girl, and the idea of her £100 had always exalted her. She was beyond the others, she was a person with a golden star set in her forehead, she possessed an honour.

Believing in the pleasant spring grass that grew upon the hill, Rose sat down at the feet of the new shepherd.

Luke Bird stopped his preaching and looked down at her ; all he had in his mind at that moment were Winnie's white arms. Winnie's white arms were around his neck and he nestled into the waves of her soft hair. Winnie was none too pretty, but the visits she used to pay to him made her very beautiful.

Luke had been preaching about St. Paul. He now forgot this travelling snake-charmer and his thousand sinners, and sat beside Rose.

Her hand rested in the green grass like a babe asleep ; he took it up : Rose's hand told him many pretty stories.

Her lips had a babe-like look, too; he kissed them.

The kiss made him think of the chapel that he wished to build. One thing led to another; Luke began to think of Rose's £100. . . .

The sheep fed peacefully, and the thing that Luke had sometimes wotted of in those valleys sank out of sight. The presence had become gladsome.

Luke sighed. Rose was more wonderful than Winnie, the babes that danced in her eyes danced in a more lively manner. Rose might have slipped along the passage as coyly as Winnie had ever done it, and when the snow melted there would always be the girl underneath.

The green grass sang praises now, but to whom? The sermon was preached, the hymn sung, and the sheep were not frightened. Luke Bird began to think boldly.

There was no reason why Rose should not be his wife and help him with her money. Luke stroked her neck; there was the same soft down there that a dove has under its breast. He would feed the people in their pleasant valleys with heavenly manna.

Did some one laugh?

He would feed himself with Rose, he would drink Rose up as though she were a pool of cool water. The babies in her eyes would dance heavenwards; Winnie had always wanted him to help hers to dance— but then . . .

Luke thought he moved upon a long journey, but he merely kissed Rose.

The heavy mists that made the wide lake in the valley now rolled away. The sun beheld its own image, and Luke bethought him that his sermon had not been quite finished. He should have wound up with a parable. The human faces might have come again, and even peeped over the wall, which would have been nearer than the lane gates, if he had gone on a little longer. If they had done so, he might have known that they were interested even though they could not hear what he said. Anyhow, the haunted meadow near the mill where the deep grass grew might have listened, and there was the corner under the ash-tree where the kingcups grew.

At least his sermon had been for good, he thought. It had drawn up Rose to him out of the mist. Perhaps that was the meaning of all good sermons. They might all be meant as songs of welcome to beautiful girls. He had tried to make his a happy one, though other sermons were hard to stretch so far heavenwards.

A weasel ran out of the root of the dead tree. Rose screamed. Luke's last kiss might have frightened the weasel, or perhaps it was his earlier mention of the Last Day; anyhow, the little creature darted out and jumped about amongst the sheep.

Rose had jumped up when the weasel came out; she now shook her frock and laughed.

The sheep were rushing wildly this way and that, as though they fancied that the little weasel was a very large dragon. A little way behind the tree another figure was to be seen. This was George Pring, who certainly had not come there to listen to the sermon. But he was there all the same, and he appeared watching the sheep as though interested in their fears.

Rose ran laughing to him and said that she had been frightened by something that came out of the tree.

Mr. Pring looked at Luke Bird. The weasel was still running about. Rose descended the hill in company with her foster-father. They were both laughing.

Luke Bird gazed at the grass where the girl had been lying. The daisies that had been pressed were already raised up again and looked happy.

Wonderful flowers, what secrets they must tell to the worms !

Luke Bird tried to preach his parable. He found the Bible that had fallen into the grass, and opened it sadly at these words :

> *" And beheld among the simple ones,*
> *I discerned among the youths, a*
> *Young man void of understanding."*

Luke turned away from the dead tree and began to go down the hill towards the village.

CHAPTER XIII

UNDER certain conditions George Pring did not mind the rain. So long as the rain fell upon his back he did not care. If there were storms in the heavens George Pring always bent down towards the earth, and by so doing he never felt the rain. He knew from experience that if he walked or worked in this posture, the rain could never beat into his face. During the March rain-storms George Pring, according to his custom, turned his face to the ground and so was saved from annoyance.

George Pring was always listening as he worked ;

he knew the sounds that he made with his own spade so well that he was able to easily catch any other sound that came from afar.

Whether it was fancy or not, and Mr. Pring could never believe that anything he heard was fancy, there came from the village one morning as he worked the words " golden pounds."

Mr. Pring had no tobacco in his pocket. He placed the spade that he was using by the side of the other two spades that were already standing upright on the bank.

Mr. Pring looked at his three spades as though they were tools, new and divine, sent from God.

Mr. Pring nodded at the spades and proceeded to walk down the road into the village. Coming to the shop he pushed the door, that was not quite shut, open with his back, because he did not wish Mrs. Topp to know at once who this customer was.

Inside the shop Dark Eliza was leaning over the counter talking to Mrs. Topp about a horse-rake. This dreadful thing, she said, had taken up the whole of the Shelton road, so that she was forced to crawl on her hands and knees in the brook under the little stone bridge to avoid being raked.

Both the women looked at Mr. Pring as he turned and showed himself. Mr. Pring gently placed a shilling upon the counter. He hoped the shilling would tempt Mrs. Topp into speaking words. Mrs. Topp only gazed out of the window as though she were interested in the wild doings of a solitary rook that flew over Angel Hill.

The rook settled upon the dead tree.

T

Mrs. Topp smiled.

George Pring looked curiously at his own shilling and said :

"They preachers do know where folk's money do bide."

Dark Eliza nodded in confidence.

"They wilful preachers do look where they shouldn't for a maid's money."

George Pring took up three sticky pennies and an ounce of tobacco that had mysteriously taken the place of his shilling. He shook his head knowingly.

Dark Eliza began to wonder aloud about the evil ways of mankind in allowing horse-rakes to occupy the roads.

"'Tis a pity they angels be allowed," Mr. Pring grunted, "for 'tis on Angel Hill that he did do en."

Mrs. Topp smiled; preachers and angels were all the same to her.

On his way to the road again George Pring encountered Mrs. Dunell.

"Rose bain't no maid," he remarked, peering up into Susan's face with an insulting gesture.

Seeing Mary Bugg by her garden-gate, Susan Dunell called to her as she passed :

"They golden pounds be leaving Dodder."

CHAPTER XIV

GEORGE PRING straightened himself. He was working now under a high hedge that sheltered him from the rain.

A bicycle was coming by, and George indicated by

a wave of his hand that he wished to speak to the rider. The man who dismounted from the bicycle wore the blue garments and the stiff blue helmet of the law.

George Pring regarded the policeman for more than one moment in silence, and then he said sadly :

" I be afeared rain will wash they onions out of ground ; 'tain't the first lot I've planted, neither."

The policeman, whose name was Mr. Cobb, replied "That it was indeed a very wet morning."

Mr. Pring looked at his spade.

" If a maid do scream out on hill, what do thik mean ? " he asked.

The policeman did not know what it meant, but waited for more.

" The preacher did catch she and hold she—and ah, poor maid, that bain't none——"

Mr. Cobb was beginning to listen.

" And they sheep were frightened too. Me maid were only walking up hill after they yellow butter-cups."

Mr. Cobb didn't remark that the season was a little early for buttercups, he merely shook his head sagely ; buttercups were the same to him as dandelions or daisies.

" Be it murder," he asked, " or taking a name in vain, or else maybe 'twere an assult an' battery."

" 'Weren't none of they," said Mr. Pring, shaking his head, " but all same, 'twere done to poor Rose."

Mr. Cobb knew Rose ; he had spoken to her in a friendly way more than once by the stile, and one

Christmas-time he had nearly fallen off his bicycle in his efforts to see more of her than her shadow as she crossed a field.

He knew all about the £100 too, and was wont to fancy sometimes that such a lucky sum of money would help to furnish a snug villa in Springfield Road near the Milverton police station. Rose's dark eyes had a way of calling to him and their look suggested in his mind bedroom furniture.

Mr. Cobb became serious and took out his notebook.

"Let me see," he said. "You say, Pring, that on Sunday last an attempt at——"

"No, bain't murder," Mr. Pring interrupted, "'Twas thik kissing an' forcing, you know——"

"An attempt at outrage was made by—the name, please?"

"Bird be a name," Mr. Pring remarked cautiously, looking at his spade.

"An attempt at outrage was made by Bird upon the body of Rose Pring so called. And now, Mr. Pring," said Mr. Cobb gaily, as he put his notebook away, "do you fancy a warning or a summons?"

"Bird be a name," Mr. Pring muttered, as though he still wondered about the truth of his own statement. "An' he do bide quiet like in me wone house, and the only noise an' battery 'e do make be when 'e do read thik big book."

"What book?" asked Mr. Cobb, intent upon the evidence. "A wicked one perhaps with stories unfit for a girl to hear."

"'Tisn't I that do know much about en," said Mr.

Pring slyly. "'Tis a wicked book maybe or 'tain't a wicked book; 'tis the Bible 'e do read."

"Is there anything else you know against this young man's character?" said the policeman.

"Yes there be," replied George Pring doggedly. "Thik Bird did tell us—me womenfolk I do mean— that he hope we would all go to Heaven—before Christmas do come."

"That certainly sounds like a wished-for murder if not an actually attempted one," Mr. Cobb said sternly, and continuing as though he were at an inquest: "George Pring, I thank you for your information in the King's name; I will proceed at once to warn this man, and if he do one quarter of his wicked acts again, acts committed in Little Dodder, his kingdom come will be a prison."

The policeman shook his fist threateningly.

During this conversation the wind for purposes of its own had changed, and a cold splash of March rain lashed George Pring's cheek. The good man turned at once and began to dig in the other direction.

CHAPTER XV

BEFORE going to see Rose Pring, the policeman rode his bicycle to the village shop. After carefully placing his machine against the railings, he opened the shop-door and entered.

Betsy Pring and Mrs. Topp were in close conversation.

"There bain't no harm in preaching," Mrs. Topp was remarking, "an' I did stay an' watch 'e a-standing there by thik wold tree, an' they sheep did listen."

"What sort of sheep be they that do feed on hill?"
Betsy Pring inquired.

"All sheep be sheep," Mrs. Topp replied.

"But all'same to my mind," said Betsy, "'twere
a good thing that Rose did go up thik little green hill."

"There isn't anything else against this young
man, no larceny, I hope?" Mr. Cobb remarked,
joining modestly in the conversation.

Betsy considered the subject for a moment.

"'E do talk funny sometimes," she said, "an' one
night, when a big moon did wake I, 'e did cry out that
all they sheep did run from 'e save one small ewe."

"He didn't cry out anything else, did he, that
moonlight night?" asked the policeman with his
notebook again in his hand. "The squire hasn't
missed a sheep I don't suppose?"

"Thee best ask Rose about thik," replied Mrs.
Pring, laughing.

Mr. Cobb found Rose sweeping the front room.
Her sleeves were turned up and she smiled in a friendly
way when she invited him to enter. She said she was
not quite alone, for a young man who liked to help in
the work was chopping an oak bough in the woodshed.

The policeman requested Rose to narrate what
had happened on the hill. He said he had come to
warn Luke Bird against such rude conduct.

Rose blushed and replied that nothing had happened.

"We only watched the sheep," she said, "until a
naughty weasel ran out."

Mr. Cobb, being a modest man who did not like
to see a girl blush, left her in order to go to the wood-

shed. There he found Luke who was endeavouring with many little blows to break the wood.

Mr. Cobb watched the proceedings for a few moments, and then he said, looking sternly at the chopper that Luke had now laid down:

"I have come to warn you, young man, about a very serious matter."

Luke Bird raised his eyes to the roof; he could only remember the sheep. The squire must have informed against him. Or could it be Winnie? No, he felt sure it couldn't be Winnie. Then it must be the sheep.

Luke Bird said he was very sorry, but he hadn't meant to talk so loud.

"It wasn't that," said the policeman, "it was what you did. And, young man," he continued in a louder tone, "the next time anything happens like this you'll find yourself in trouble."

Leaving the woodshed the policeman hurriedly returned to Rose. He found the table was spread with a light repast in his honour. Rose had brushed her hair; she was sitting upon the sofa knitting.

Luke Bird left the shed: he had succeeded in chopping a few little pieces of stick; he picked these pieces up and piled them in a small heap in the corner. As he went by the front-room window, he peeped in.

Mr. Cobb was swallowing bread and butter; he was also looking kindly at Rose. His helmet was placed upon the table beside the teapot. Rose was looking with interest at the helmet.

Luke Bird crossed the meadow, climbed the stile and walked slowly down the road into the village;

he hoped he would meet some one to whom he might express the sorrow he felt for having frightened the squire's sheep.

The rain had stopped, there were bits of blue sky that peeped at him like a child who tries to smile between its tears. Luke wandered on sadly. He had really meant to raise the people of Dodder to a new life ; he had hoped to raise them up to the fine heights of song and praise. When he left Milverton to come to them, he expected to find them all thinking of the gross things of the earth, the mere getting and saving, the grinding and pecking, doing ill and not good, and so losing their immortal souls.

Unfortunately for Luke's expectations all these things seemed to be of even less importance to the people of Dodder than they were to him, and they also saw more clearly than he could ever do a certain something that moved in the valleys and lived through all nights and all days.

The people believed without any reason at all in this dark and dreadful something in the queerest fashion. Luke could not in the least understand their belief.

When he spoke to them of the God he knew, they merely referred him to the squire. And when he spoke Gospel truths to them in the roads, they merely asked him questions about bootlaces. One day, when he mentioned the Holy Ghost to Mr. Dunell, that gentleman, after considering for a moment or two, recommended to Luke Tom Tuckers' as being the best shop in Milverton for strong rabbit netting.

It was all so very confusing, Luke could make

nothing of it. Not one person in Dodder ever thought of a piece of wood as being a piece of wood. The days of their lives moved around them and peeped at them, but they never peeped at their days.

When old William Whiffer died, Luke had thought something might be done. He had gone to the house before the bearers were come, and he found all the family in dire consternation, not because their father was dead, but because the smoked ham ordered from Milverton had not come. It was a little sad that when Luke asked leave to say a prayer, Maud Whiffer should at once begin to dust the coffin, as much as to say that however much it went to 'dust to dust' by and by, there was no need for the matter to begin at home. And Maud Whiffer said that she didn't want to be thought dirty by the bearers.

" For thik Bugg," remarked Maud, " has his eyes everywhere."

Maud Whiffer looked down at her black skirt.

And yet, Luke thought, with all their outward conformity for things seen, there was under it all a real resignation that bowed low before the something more awful, the something more true, the something that is more living, the something to which men are but the shadowy fragments of a foolish dream.

Even after Maud had mildly demonstrated her opposition to the dusty law of death, all the room became silent, as though they felt the dread certainty, the only certainty, that pressed them one by one under the sod.

This state, that seemed, Luke thought, to go his way, was broken by little Nancy, who opened the door and presented a bunch of moon daisies to deck the coffin. Maud Whiffer took the moon daisies, looked at them scornfully and, when Nancy was gone, threw them out of the window into the back garden. The bearers coming in then, the funeral proceeded.

Luke was astonished too sometimes.

One starry night when he was going to the shop to buy some matches he met John Bugg. John Bugg was staring at the stars.

"'Tain't every chap that can make they little sparklers," John remarked, and shambled down the lane in pursuit of a shadow that might have been Dark Eliza.

Luke considered the town that he had left. In the town, amongst the respectable, there was nearly always gentility and good manners. Not the least of them, the clerk of the brewery had always tried to behave as a gentleman should, walking as he usually did on the Sundays either by way of the fields or else along the wide Stonebridge road set with little trees.

In the town small-sinning was a proper contrast to well-doing, well-doing that merely meant walking between the little trees. Town-sinning was so easy to preach against, and so very easy to wrap up in little pink ribbons by the town ladies.

In Dodder Luke had been unable to find out so far what sin was. The whole earth rolled on in Dodder; it had its sharp points that every now and again stabbed a man or a woman. Sometimes in its wanton rolling the great creature hurt men; sometimes they escaped—for the moment.

Everything that happened appeared to the people

of Dodder as a sort of experiment in moving things,
or else in letting things lie still in order to see if they
would ever move again.   The people saw all about
them something detached from themselves, something
that had the power of marking up the walls of their
days with curious pictures.

These pictures could always be talked about, they
were drawn for the purpose of conversation.   Big
or little, there was always some picture or other for
the Dodder wayfarers to speak of.

One day poor Herbert would happen to burst his
father's muzzle-loader, and blow away three of his
own fingers, by simply forgetting that he had already
loaded the gun three times before.   And so the sitting
partridge that. Herbert had crept into the miller's
field to kill escaped through the hedge.   It was a
May Sabbath and the partridge became very famous ;
it expressed the dangerous courage of a poacher, and
the bursting of the gun was as an eruption of Mount
Etna.   And so all things went on, and now and again
the murmur of a meaning voice touched the village,
creeping closer and closer, and becoming more sweetly
soft, until at last the thing crept clammy and cold under
the drooping eaves of a cottage and some one's life-
picture faded, became strangely distorted and was
gone.

In the matters of religion the Sabbath day at Dodder
would only put out a limp hand and stroke the lanes
and gravely tickle the people.

The Sabbath would convey to John Dunell the
desire to take a turn or two outside his own cottage
with his hard hat upon his head.   After doing this,

according to the usual custom of the Sunday, John would return indoors again and light his pipe; he would then go slowly into his own front room, having the look upon his face that he always wore in the presence of the stuffed owl, and would gaze for five minutes at an empty gilt frame that had once upon a time held the photo of a family group of a distant cousin. The photo, unfortunately, had fallen into the fire one Christmas-time long ago.

A Sunday sound would come softly to Mr. Pring and bid him look over the surrounding country with his eyes narrowed to see if anyone was coming before he dug a potato. The day would also be a sufficient reason for Rose to walk primly down a side lane that went past the squire's, and for Mrs. Topp to boil a bag-pudding in her parlour.

As to the real concrete life, the life that could be saved on a Sunday, there was none of it in Dodder. There was no historic sense of worship, there was no occasion to pray. What there was was all pure country magic.

Whenever Luke preached Christ, out of every Little Dodder cranny and cottage there came his own mimicked words back to him again. Nothing seemed to be of God, and yet all was of God. Magic casements opened to the light even in the very pigsties. Dodder was a quaint mixture of mud and Godhead.

Indeed, Luke Bird, simple-hearted as he was, was beginning to lose all sense of surprise. He was not even surprised now that the policeman should have found fault with him about the sheep, for he put the matter of the warning all down to them.

For aught he knew to the contrary, the sheep might be the gods of Dodder, or else they might be set on Angel Hill to guard some hidden maiden that the squire loved.

Luke Bird stopped beside the shop ; he had heard his own name mentioned. He was tired too, and he thought he might rest beside the shop-railing as anywhere else. He was utterly dejected and hung down his head, but he could not help hearing what was said inside.

"Thik young man that do bide at your house, 'e do talk," Mrs. Topp was saying.

"Yes 'e do," replied Betsy Pring, "'e do say all sorts of words."

"So do squire," Susan Dunell whispered mysteriously. "Dark Eliza do know what 'e do say."

"That I do," said Dark Eliza, pleased to be brought into the talk. "Squire did only say yesterday, when 'e saw I in mud—'What a damned dirty pickle thee be in, Eliza, God 'Is woneself wouldn't know thee."

"'Tis a world of wonder," Mrs. Topp remarked. "There's thik half-penny be a-taken off sugar, there's wold Colley be dead in workhouse, there's Rose Pring be lefted a £100, there's that young Bird that be after she—and there's Cobb the policeman,"—for Mr. Cobb was seen to be riding down the lane upon his bicycle.

"True, Mrs. Topp," said Dark Eliza, "this world be a queer place to live in. What with they carts and horses running over folk in roads, and they falling stars in sky, 'tain't a safe place to live in, this bain't."

"I do mind George Pring saying a long time ago

under they blue skies," remarked Betsy Pring, who
loved nothing better than her own family history,
"George did up an' say: 'Betsy, 'tain't worth our
while to wait any longer, we may as well take an'
do en; we've fiddled about together Saturday nights
and Sundays enough, I do think, an' so to church we
did go.'"

Mary Bugg rubbed her nose with her finger.
"They clocks do turn in day-time," she said, "an'
maybe Bugg do want 'is dinner. I did say to he only
yesterday—'I wish that the young preacher were
here in house and did see 'ee eat, 'twould be a fine
subject for 'is next sermon on a gluttony sinner.'"

"Poor young man, I be sorry for en," Dark Eliza
remarked mournfully. "''E don't mean no harm,
'e do only talk angry-like of thik black Bible 'e do
carry, and call we poor maidens 'is sisters. Maybe
God above won't notice 'e, for 'e do speak when
wind be blowing. An' now they do a-say that 'e
did walk after they woolly sheep."

"Ah!" Betsy Pring ventured, "I took an' told
Rose to be kind to 'e; you do never know what they
young learned men may do when they maidens bain't
kind. I do mind me George, ignorant though 'e be,
running wild-like into field where pigs were a-feeding,
and I did only tell 'e of something mother did mind
me of. Sure 'tis best to let they poor simple chaps
do what they be minded. 'Tisn't good for they to
roam the fields and the hedgerows, a-thinking of God
Almighty. Who's to know that 'e mightn't show
'isself woon of these days, and we don't want thik to
happen in Little Dodder, thee do know."

"Now lookee there out of window," Mrs. Topp observed. "There be Mrs. Dunell in lane."

"Sure 'tis she," said Mary Bugg. "Susan Dunell be a-going out in she's wold apron to cut they furze."

"So she be," said Betsy Pring. "The poor woman be watching they little clouds. Maybe 'er cat 'ave stolen thik rabbit that Dunell carried home breakfast-time under 'is coat. She do look troubled."

"So she do," said Mary Bugg.

"Susan be brave," murmured Dark Eliza. "She do stand in middle of road, she do ; she be going to cut they furze with a hook, I do think. She be now gone over stile and do climb Squire's Hill. She did look at they little clouds to see if 'twere going to rain to-day."

"No, no," Mrs. Topp said excitedly. "It do never rain when Susan Dunell be out. Susan Dunell do know what weather be a-doing ; she be out, Mrs. Dunell be, she be out sticking."

Luke Bird glanced at the window ; he was conscious of the faces of the women peering curiously out at him. He looked up at the hill and saw the figure of a woman that seemed still and yet was moving as in a tired dream over the hill. Luke watched the figure ; it climbed slowly over the hill, the hill of life, until it was gone.

Luke Bird moved away. "What did it all mean ? " he wondered. "What story did it all tell ? Were these country people real human beings, or were they mere shadow-pictures telling a sad tale ? " Luke did not know.

He walked slowly up the lane, entered the field

gate, and began to climb Angel Hill, and every now and again he looked up at the dead tree towards which he was journeying.

The hill was deserted; Susan Dunell had gone on to the other side and down into the next valley after her furze.

All about Luke there was gleaming sunshine, the grass breathed and was happy, the rain had given life and happiness to all green things. Luke walked up to the dead tree.

After waiting for a few moments very sorrowfully beside the tree, Luke Bird looked down the hill and saw Squire Kennard coming towards him. As he walked, the squire dug his stick into the grass. He appeared to do this merely for his own recreation, although the stick had an iron end that could root out weeds.

"I advise you, young man, to go back to Milverton," Mr. Kennard said in a cheerful tone when he reached Luke. "I have written to the brewery and they say they are quite willing to have you there at your old work; indeed, the manager remarked that your eights are very much missed. The country air has excited you, I fear," the squire said in a kinder tone. "I am sorry to say that people begin to talk about what you do here. The top of a hill isn't a very safe place to take a girl to, you know. It's all very well to fancy that this is a Mount Sinai, but Little Dodder is a funny place for fancies."

The squire moved away with a grave face, but every time he dug his stick into the grass he chuckled.

Luke Bird stretched up his hands over his head.

His hands touched the dead tree. He stood and wept. No, he would not give in without one more trial. He must make one more attempt.

He knelt down upon the grass. He would try once more. The very next day he would go about the village and preach of death to the people. That was a final word " Death "; they must, they would listen to that word. He stood up and thoughtfully leant against the tree. Below the hill a man's laugh was heard.

The sheep were coming.

CHAPTER XVI

GEORGE PRING was cleaning out a ditch by the roadside. John Dunell stood by and watched him as he worked. Every time George Pring put his spade into the ground he sighed.

" They girl folk do hurt a man," he said mournfully. "Thik Rose do hurt I."

John Dunell looked steadfastly into the muddy ditch.

" I were a quiet wedded man before she did come," moaned Mr. Pring. "But all they pounds be a lot of money; 'twould buy cows, money would, and maid do hurt I. I do mind maiden, I do; she were fluffy and small like a rabbit whose belly be white, and I did want she so till at last she did hurt I.

" I do dig out these roads most days, an' I've never know'd these roads to hurt I; they do bide still, these roads do, time I do dig they. I do suppose these be

U

real roads, but when I be digging, I do wonder what they be.

"'Twas in valley where the ghosts do bide that I did feel maiden flutter like a little chick in me hand. I must squeeze she till she do scream, I thought; I must glue she to me own self though I be but a poor wedded man.

"There were thik fancy money too that I did do it for; money do bite into I like a file, and maiden and money were both waiting for I, but 'tis pain we do get from they maids."

Mr. Pring looked up to the sky and nodded. He thought some one had spoken to him out of the clouds to confirm his sentiment. He nodded again.

At that moment a cloud formed itself in the sky in shape like a bull.

Mr. Pring gazed into the sky with an interested look. The clouds all became cows and bulls, and there were places of blue pasture in the sky. The sky showed him all the good things that he could have bought with Rose's money. Mr. Pring looked down into the road again; he shook his head sulkily, he thought the sky mocked him.

"Even in thik sky folk do talk about I," he said. "I be but a wold rag by roadside, and yet folk do talk. 'Tis all thik little maid. For eighteen years I've seen she's little hands upon table, and now she do hurt I."

Mr. Pring bent his head nearer to the earth.

He stood in the water at the bottom of the ditch and began to take out slowly with his spade large clods of dripping soil.

Mr. Dunell watched him with the happy interest of one who sees another work. That morning John Dunell had made up his mind to feed his cows along the Milverton Road. Before he began to watch George Pring he had noticed that by the roadside there was a gate left open. The gateway led into Squire Kennard's best pasture, and Mr. Dunell's two cows feeding quietly wandered in.

John Dunell had a sort of vision in his head that his two cows were eating spring daisies. The vision pleased him so well that he never looked round to see in whose pasture the cows were.

George Pring pressed his spade into the mud; his thoughts shuffled back to a day in the lonely valley.

"If preacher hadn't come I'd 'ave done it," he moaned, "but now she do still hurt I."

John Dunell became thoughtful; he wondered how he could help his friend.

"'Tis a truthful pity they maidens be made same as they be," he said slowly. "If they were made same as squire's rib-roller be made, 'twould be better for we."

Mr. Pring looked up.

"Our wold 'omen were maidens once," he said gloomily.

"I don't mind that mine ever were," Dunell remarked, looking into the vague past. "They days be over and done wi', gone they be, neighbour, gone they be."

"Preacher be coming," said Mr. Pring.

Mr. Dunell still looked into the ditch.

"'Tain't likely 'e do think thee be Rose."

" No, no, he mid be only going to talk to I for telling policeman that 'twere 'e that did lay Rose out on green grass."

George Pring bent to his work. The soft mud in the ditch yielded to him without a murmur. He worked hard, and in the muddy water his shadow worked too—a man with a spade.

John Dunell forgot the vision that was in his head and looked round so that he might see for himself the approaching figure of Luke Bird. He looked hard at Luke, but he could not prevent himself looking also into the squire's field where his cows were feeding.

The vision departed, sunning herself with a gay gesture and winking at Dunell. She carried away the gallons of milk that John had seen his cows yield. He was now forced to look at the rude reality of events.

" Bless an' damn they cows," he said, " blessed if they bain't eating."

Moving sulkily away Mr. Dunell proceeded to enter the squire's field in order to drive out his cows, leaving Luke, who had now arrived, standing beside the ditch.

Luke Bird stood silent for a few minutes ; he was considering how to begin his sermon about Death.

For a while George Pring continued to dig.

Looking up, however, after taking out an unusually large clod of mire that splashed black mud on the green bank, he said wearily :

" 'Tis a pity we bain't all dead an' dying an' rotting an' damned."

He flung this remark out at Luke in the same way that he tossed out the mud.

Luke felt that the man had covered him with black mud, he was betrayed, defeated, abashed. It was this idea of death and damnation that he had determined to carry like a burning torch through the village in his last journey of conversion. He had arisen early with this one thought in his mind for the spiritual conquest of Dodder. The people he had come to save should have at least this last chance of salvation. He would cry out death in their ears. and so win them to God. If he did not succeed in this last attempt he would be defeated indeed.

George Pring leant on his spade ; he spoke again :

"The only safe place be the grave," George said quietly. "The only safe place be the grave, I were telling John Dunell so, for the grave be a good religious end to every man's junketings. 'Twere best for we to be rotted in mud than to be hurt by they maids. 'Tisn't we that do do it, we don't want they maids, but they maids do want we. 'Tis worse than death, the pain they do make we feel. What good be living for we, 'tis a bad maid life be. Life do hurt same as they maids do hurt. Don'tee preach to I no more. God be like thik mud in ditch—silent. 'Tis best to be silent. . . . They little birds do sing, though 'tisn't because they do want to sing neither.

"Maiden be ever about me, an' thik silent one be ever about me too. I do mind well when Rose did move close up to I one winter's night when Dunell's pond were froze. She did put her arms round me neck and she did look at I. We were alone in house thik winter's night. I did sit in chair last evening, and were thinking of she. 'Do thee know there be wood to chop?' Betsy were saying. Yes, I did know it. I went out to woodshed, for I did know where rope were biding. 'Tain't no use living no more to be hurt, I did think, an' tied rope round me wone neck—'twere kinder than maiden rope were. I did try en, an' rope did break. . . ."

Luke Bird walked away, holding his hands to his ears.

He passed on down the street and entered the shop. Mrs. Topp was conversing with Dark Eliza. Luke stood beside the door and listened. He could not enter until Dark Eliza moved.

"I were walking in muddy ditch," Dark Eliza was saying, "when engine came along with squire's coal. I did hear en come near. An' then, blessed if I didn't step out of ditch right in's way. . . . All my lifetime I've been trying to save myself from they carts an' horses, an' now I be real tired. I thought I mid as well step out before thik engine. Yes, I've been afraid all my life of them carts, but when iron engine did come I did fancy I did hear some one call. I did run into my own fear."

"But you bain't crushed," said Mrs. Topp, looking cautiously at Dark Eliza, expecting, no doubt, to see her crushed into a pancake.

Dark Eliza shook herself.

"No, I suppose I bain't, but all'same I don't care now what do happen to I. Me fear be one wi' I now, we bain't two folks, we be one. They engine-men did say when they lifted I up, 'Thee be a funny wold maid to try an' kill thee's wone self. Engine must 'ave felt thee under en, for 'e did stop 'isself. Engine don't like to crunch a maid—'e bain't nor man—engine bain't.' 'Tisn't life that be much, 'tisn't death that be much," mused Dark Eliza. "I won't be afeared no more never again. . . ."

"I did hear they engine-men a-talking as they passed shop," Mrs. Topp said excitedly. "I heard one of them exclaim : ' Devil did put brake on sudden down Gallows Hill ; I hope 'e won't do same when we be steaming up to squire's.' ' Maybe,' engine-man said, ''e mid think there be another woman in road, 'e do like they dark women to live, Devil do.' ' My wife be dark,' the other man said sadly."

Dark Eliza nodded her head. She knew that she had made herself important in the firmament. Engine-drivers were talking about her.

Dark Eliza went away without fear and was contented. She passed Luke with a smile and walked away happily in the middle of the road. Mrs. Topp leaned over the counter and watched her go.

Luke Bird stood quietly in the shop. He had not come to buy anything, he merely watched Mrs. Topp. He was wondering whether it was not he, instead of the people of Dodder, who was being converted to a new gospel.

Mrs. Topp raised a little door in her counter and came through in order to water her window hyacinths.

"They flowers do die down every winter and rise up every spring," she said. "That be the way of flowers, an' these very ones I've promised to me own grave in churchyard. I do like a flower on a grave.

Rose Pring, she've offered to plant and water they flowers when I be gone."

Mrs. Topp looked out of the window towards Angel Hill.

"I do fancy that hill be growing," she said, "it do seem larger to I. An' when I do look at hill I do fancy that something else be growing out of earth, something that be green an' large like thik hill."

Mrs. Topp watered her flowers.

"The whole earth be a grave," she said, "a green grave mound that do grow up like thik hill, and on the mound flowers do grow."

Mrs. Topp left the window and went into her shop again. She began with a tired look to count her postal orders.

There was one postal order missing.

"You never saw Dark Eliza touch nothing, did you?" she asked Luke. "For 'tis most likely poor woman may have thought paper money weren't nothing. An' being near crushed she mid have picked up paper. But they postmasters do want to know where money do go, they be always wondering, they postmasters be. I do mind well when Mary Bugg did take two shillings from counter. ''Tis mine,' she did say, 'thik be, it be gone from me wold stocking under mattress, I do know dent in king's face, I do.' And she did take en."

Mrs. Topp spread out her hands on the counter.

"'Tis a pity there bain't no religion in Dodder folks," she said. "There were Joan Squibb that did have they dancing parties in her little house times gone by, an' one day her little maid Alice were found

wi' wold Stockly up under Angel Hill tree.   No one
did see they go up hill, only squire did happen to
walk round a-spudding.   Alice's stockings were tore.
'Tis a world for trouble.   Squire did turn Joan Squib
out of Carter's lane, and she were a good buyer of
salmon.   I do mind when Mr. Clapp's furniture did
come, 'twas the day when Shelton Church tower were
struck by lightning."

Mrs. Topp looked up at the window.

"Green hill be the same to-day and yesterday,"
she said.   "Green hill be the same, though all things
be moving somewhere I do suppose, but green hill be
the same."

CHAPTER XVII

LUKE BIRD turned away and ran from the shop
like a beaten dog.

No one had understood him, and every one had
taken the message of doom, that he had to give them,
out of his mouth.   Luke's thoughts went back in an
odd startled fashion to the beginning of his journey.

Before starting on his travels, he had opened the
county directory that was always at hand in the brewery
office.   He had looked up Dodder.   He had read
as follows :

"The soil is limy ; the subsoil is limestone.   The
chief crops are corn and meadow produce.

"The area is 1,222 acres.   The population in
1900 was 99."

And then he had read the names :

"Kennard, Robert, Esq., J.P.

" Pring, road-mender.

" Dunell, small holder.

" Topp, Maud ; the stores."

He knew them all now, and the soil was indeed limestone. Nothing he could ever do or say could change it ; it was so from the beginning, and it would be so until the end. . . .

Luke thought there was one chance left. Perhaps the squire might be changed by the magic word of death ; he might turn from his scoffing ways and repent of ever having mentioned God's rubber boots. Luke walked quickly up the Kennard drive. He felt he must win this last chance ; he would throw his bread upon the waters only this once.

Half-way up the drive he stopped and listened ; from Angel Hill there came the sound of a sheep's bell.

Luke hurried on. Some one was laughing at him, of that he felt sure, but who ? Was there a being born of this limestone, that moved in the pasture, that grew up in the daisies, that became a sheep's bell and laughed.

Luke ran.

He was not kept waiting long in the squire's hall. The housekeeper, with her apron half untied, conducted him to the study. The squire was sitting by his writing-table with a paper before him. He explained that the paper was his will, and he invited Luke and the housekeeper to witness it.

" You never know," the squire remarked gravely, " God will have His jests ; nothing in the world can stop His laughter. . . ."

After signing his name below the housekeeper's, Luke asked Mr. Kennard whether he had any orders for the Standard Brewery. . . .

Luke walked slowly down the drive; the sheep's bell was sounding, but he did not regard it.

As he passed the shop he heard some one say:

"Squire Kennard do meet Rose under hill, 'e do, an' they do cuddle together under stone wall."

Luke walked slowly on.

He came to a place in the Milverton road where a man had been working. There was a rush basket and bits of broken bread; near to the basket there was a girl's hair-ribbon.

Luke waited, he would have liked a last word with Rose. The stile was a little way off. He thought he could hear Betsy Pring calling her fowls. He felt all about him the home life of the simple family that he had lived with. They were always so close together.

Luke suddenly saw Mr. Tuck of the Mill and Dark Eliza close together too. Though Mr. Tuck was a prosperous farmer and Dark Eliza but a poor woman, they two seemed to be almost the same person. Luke saw as in a vision all the folks of Dodder stuck together with sticky mud. They were planted like maggots on the same piece of decaying earth flesh. A sodden picture they made of it, sodden and drab.

Luke Bird saw the green grass and the sheep upon the hill. He followed with his eyes the line of the budding hedge. A little way along the hedge there was the figure of a man peeping through between the thorns. This man was George Pring. Luke joined him. Luke peeped too. Under the dead tree that crowned the forehead of Angel Hill as with a bull's broken horn, there was movement and brown colour. After a short while the brown colour disentangled itself and became two separate forms. A man walked away from under the tree and began to descend, going in the direction of Dodder Hall. The other figure —a girl's—began to come down the hill towards the Milverton road.

George Pring chuckled to himself when the girl came near. She was Rose and she was laughing.

The man who had gone in the direction of the big house, now and again stuck a spud into the ground.

George Pring took up the hook wherewith he had been cutting the long grass by the roadside. He looked slyly at Luke.

"They maidens do take our pains upon them," he said quietly. "Hook be sharp and green grass do want en, that be the way of the world. Maiden won't hurt I no more now. 'Tis as good for we to see things done by the rich as to do them."

Rose blushed, and picking up her hair-ribbon she tied it in her hair.

"Hundred pounds be nothing to I now," George Pring said slowly, "for I bain't hurt now."

For a moment, for one moment, Luke was as a wise man having understanding.

He turned softly away and took the road to Milverton. As he walked he fancied that he had been reading a chapter in an odd kind of novel where a man steps into a picture and meets figures in grey clothes moving about amid green grass shining in the sun. And in the picture the hills grew into gentle shapes like the breasts of women.

Luke walked gladly, he longed for Winnie.

He left Dodder behind him as one leaves an old furniture-shop where the teapots talk too much and the gilt chairs tell stories of forlorn and forgotten days.

* * *

A month passed.

One morning Luke Bird awoke early; he heard a soft step in the passage.

The handle of his door was gently turned. Some one crept up to him and kissed his cheek. Luke opened his arms. Winnie had not forgotten him; she sighed happily.

After his work was over at the brewery, Luke walked out into the town. He was looking for a ring to give to Winnie.

Luke went by the music-shop ; Squire Kennard was listening to a gramophone playing.

As he passed, Squire Kennard spoke one word "Goat !"